Praise for Bella Ellis:

'Elegant, witty and compulsively readable – I think the
Brontë sisters would have been delighted'
ROSIE WALSH

'Brilliantly entertaining and original'
C.L. TAYLOR

'Evocative and utterly enchanting'
SARAH

'A gripping, t
ANGELA

'A splendi
GUARDIAN

'A gorgeous book – perfectly paced and completely
charming . . . an absolute treat from start to finish'
JANE CASEY

'Great Gothic fun'
RED

'Lashed with Gothic colour. Fun and inventive'
DAILY MAIL

'Brontë afficionados are sure to enjoy the accurate
characterization and context, the twists, turns and
Gothic touches of the plot, and the strong feminist
streak that manifests itself throughout'
TIMES LITERARY SUPPLEMENT

Also by Bella Ellis

The Vanished Bride
The Diabolical Bones
The Red Monarch

A *Gift*
OF POISON

BELLA ELLIS

HODDER

First published in Great Britain in 2023 by Hodder & Stoughton Limited
An Hachette UK company

This paperback edition published in 2024

1

Copyright © Bella Ellis 2023

A CIP catalogue record for this title is available from the British Library

B format ISBN 978 1 529 36347 0

Typeset in Plantin Light by Manipal Technologies Limited

Printed and bound in Great Britain by Clays Ltd, Elcograf S.p.A.

Hodder & Stoughton policy is to use papers that are natural, renewable
and recyclable products and made from wood grown in sustainable
forests. The logging and manufacturing processes are expected to
conform to the environmental regulations of the country of origin.

Hodder & Stoughton Limited
Carmelite House
50 Victoria Embankment
London EC4Y 0DZ

www.hodder.co.uk

Dedicated to Eunice Brown –
reader and friend, with love.

'Do you think I am an automaton? — a machine without feelings? and can bear to have my morsel of bread snatched from my lips, and my drop of living water dashed from my cup? Do you think, because I am poor, obscure, plain, and little, I am soulless and heartless? You think wrong! — I have as much soul as you — and full as much heart! And if God had gifted me with some beauty and much wealth, I should have made it as hard for you to leave me, as it is now for me to leave you. I am not talking to you now through the medium of custom, conventionalities, nor even of mortal flesh: it is my spirit that addresses your spirit; just as if both had passed through the grave, and we stood at God's feet, equal — as we are!'

Jane Eyre by Charlotte Brontë

Haworth, February 1853

If only it could be now, as it was then.

Villette was out in the world, and despite the pain and toil it had cost her to finish it, Charlotte was not glad.

Her instinct had always been to push on, no matter what. To rise and face the day and to work, despite what anguish the good Lord had reserved for her. This she had done for every torturous hour it had taken her to scratch one word after another, taking comfort in the idea that once it was finished, she would know some peace. And yet all she felt was a deep discomfort and the pervasive sense that somehow that book had changed things, and not for the better. That its creation had somehow shifted and altered friendships she had come to rely on, drawing them just out of her reach and leaving her alone once again.

George Smith and his family had abandoned her. Not so much that an outsider would notice, but just enough to leave a distinct chill where their welcoming warmth had once been. And Harriet Martineau's review had been fierce, cutting and cruel. She had dismissed *Villette*, saying she did not like the love in it, either the kind or degree of it, and its prevalence in the book, and the effect it has on the action of it. Charlotte could not help but feel betrayed by a woman she had thought of as a friend.

If her sisters had been at her side to commiserate or goad her out of her misery, she could have borne it better but, as it was, the comments festered in her breast like a wound. Perhaps Miss Martineau didn't believe that Charlotte could truly know anything of love, or what it might urge a person to do. Perhaps George . . .

Charlotte paused, forcing herself to confront what she already knew. That George had never thought of her as anything more than a profitable author to be flattered and placated. And that all that had passed between them was no more than a strategy to coax another novel from her broken heart. What a fool to ever have believed he might have cared for her! How could a man as young, vital and handsome as George ever love a small, deformed old woman like her? Oh, but it hurt though, to recognise that truth. It cut her to the bone.

That was why she wished so desperately for the alchemy she had once known, back in those last happy months when her family was complete. There was so much about that time that had seemed intolerable, then. Branwell inching himself ever further to the point of no return. Anne and Emily, their novels set for publication when hers was rejected at every turn.

Then *she* arrived and everything changed. Charlotte had sensed her even when she was very far away, nothing more than a hazy vision on a distant horizon. She had felt her approach, growing nearer with every heartbeat. Felt her materialise in the cold blue sky like a gathering storm, charging the air with static. There would be a phantom glimpse of her; always in the periphery, growing ever clearer and true. She was the herald that had ushered in Destiny.

She was Jane Eyre.

Jane, who raced and rushed out of Charlotte's brain and breast and onto the page in a flood of urgent creation that she had never known again. Amongst the turmoil and confusion, Jane had been at her side, a secret sister, walking amongst them as they crept through danger and skulduggery unlike any that they had ever encountered before as they searched for the truth behind the lies and illusion of the infamous Haworth poisoner.

Charlotte and Jane made and remade one another. Wrote and rewrote each other in turn. And though it could hardly be true, in the very eye of the strange and violent storm that had been the summer of 1847, it had felt to Charlotte as if they had also remade the world entire.

The agony was so intense that Abner Lowood could not think, nor speak or move. If he had ever been a man, now he was only pain. Great ragged strips of it seemed to be pulling him apart in waves of bloody torment. Fluid poured out of him, his body shuddering in convulsions that seemed intent on exorcising the very soul out of him. Desperate for any relief, he sought to press his shuddering bones against the cool dank flags of the dead house floor, as if he could find some solace in the dirt and death that coated them. Even lost to pain as he was, there was still a part of Lowood conscious and aware, that knew the pounding carnival music that went on and on ever louder was only his fever, playing him out of this life with one final cruel joke. There was enough of the tiny nub left of him to know that he would be burning in hell before this hour was out. That he would die here alone and there would not be a soul who would grieve him.

Barbara was near; he could sense her waiting for him. He thought he felt her rough, sharp laugh slice through him with its serrated grating edge. She'd laughed differently when he'd first met her, softly and musically, like a girl full of dreams and hope. He'd soon knocked that out of her, ensured he had bent her to his will until she became her own ghost.

It seemed fitting somehow that she had returned from the grave to claim him. The strange part was that even now, even here, the splinter of Lowood that remained did not feel one jot of remorse. He'd do it all again, given half the chance. He had been put on this earth to make misery, and he had been so very good at it.

'Mister?' Little Sally Wiggins stared dumbfounded at the sight of the boss, sprawled on the floor, face wildly contorted, limbs twisted as if they were about to be torn from his bony body. 'Mister, are you dead?'

'There's something wrong with Mister Lowood!' Sally called out of the door of the dead house, where she'd been sent to wash down the stone tables and floor. It was bad enough when it was empty, but when there were cold, grey corpses of the people she knew, it was worse. But the sight of the workhouse master, writhing in agony on the floor and frothing at the mouth like a rabid dog, was strangely mesmerising.

'Mr Lowood!' She shouted the hated man's name again and again until at last the nearby folk came over to see what the child was carrying on about. 'I reckon he's dead!'

'Looks like someone done for him like he did for his missus,' Edward Flack said as he came over, unmoved by the sight of the workhouse master on the floor. 'Go fetch Mrs Tolliver, Sally, and best send for the doctor too. Run now, girl!'

There was now a small circle of narrow, careworn faces peering down at the dying man.

'Pick him up, lads,' Flack said with a weary sigh. 'We'd better take him to his bed before he dies.'

'Oh, he won't die,' one of the men that hoisted Lowood's body up muttered bitterly. 'We'd never be so fortunate.'

6

Charlotte

July declared itself a cage. Thick leaden air seemed to imprison Charlotte so tightly within her body, she had to fight the urge to tear at her own skin.

Oppressive warmth pressed down upon them beneath the low cover of white clouds. The stifling weight of it filled every corner, saturating even the shadows with unremitting heat. Everything was disjointed and wrong; restless and listless. All she could think of was how wonderful it would be to run away. Racing out of the parsonage as fast as she could until the sweat ran down her back, and her hair fell loose of its pins. Running until she came upon Waters Meet, where she would plunge herself into the cool, fast-running brook, deeper and deeper until it bubbled over her head and her skirts billowed up around her ears.

Which would never do, of course. After all, she was not Emily. Besides, her dearest friend Ellen Nussey was due to arrive within the hour, and for Ellen everything must be perfect. Charlotte's beloved parsonage could not hold a candle to Brookroyd, Ellen's family home, but Charlotte was determined that everything should be just so, and had been bothering Tabby and Martha to that effect for the last week. It was essential that Nell's visit would pass pleasantly.

That the house should shine like a new pin and that every meal served should be delicious. That none of her siblings should disgrace her with their ideas, thoughts or habits, and that Nell should find her visit as gentle and as restful as could be. That would be her focus, Charlotte decided, her entire occupation from now until the moment Ellen departed. That would keep her from dwelling and sinking into the black well of gloom that called to her minute by minute from the very bottom of her heart.

Time to buck up, Aunt Branwell would have told her. Moping about never got the grate blacked. Buck up she must. Oh, but it was hard when everyone and everything seemed to conspire to make her miserable.

Emily and Anne were seated together on the sofa, their heads bowed together in a conversation that Charlotte knew was no concern of hers, and that made it all the more intolerable, for this was the first time in their lives that their fates had not been closely aligned with hers. Everything had changed when her sister's novels, *Agnes Grey* and *Wuthering Heights*, had been accepted for publication by Thomas Newby. Her own book, *The Professor*, had been rejected by everyone who had read it. Now Emily and Anne's stars were in the ascendant, and she was tethered to the land, no matter how much they all did their best to pretend otherwise.

Charlotte had tried to send the pair of them out this morning, telling them that they would be under her feet as final preparations were made for Ellen's visit. However, having recently become the most loving and dutiful sisters that one could possibly imagine, they had elected to stay and wait. Charlotte did her best not to show her regret at their decision.

It was just that if her sisters were not always within her sight, then she would not always have to endure the great care they were taking of her feelings. Somehow the tactful consideration of everything they did and said – all with the explicit purpose of avoiding causing her further pain – only deepened her humiliation. Their sweet sisterly solidarity only served to exacerbate the wound rather than salving it.

The shame of her failure was nearly unbearable. It would have been entirely so, if not for the encouraging words of one editor, a Mr George Smith, of Smith and Elder, who – like everyone else in London – had declined to publish *The Professor*, but who had told Charlotte her work had promise. This was the crumb of hope and dignity that Charlotte clung to while Anne and Emily made plans, checked and corrected proof pages and sent correspondence back and forth to their publishers, all under Papa's nose but without his knowledge. George Smith's words were the glowing ember that kept her belief that she had more to give the world barely alight.

There had been a few minutes in the dead of night when Charlotte had considered the possibility of giving up her hopes of being published. Of dedicating all her energies to nurturing and developing her sisters' talents instead. Naturally, she had realised at once that that would not be possible. She had to write, because she could not help it. She would batter herself bloody against the closed doors of the great publishing houses until one opened or she expired. There was no third path, no possibility of a mind quiet of ambition. Charlotte Brontë simply was not made that way.

'Tell us again what we are not to say to Ellen,' Emily asked, with uncharacteristic docility, pulling Charlotte out of her reverie.

'Try to avoid the subject of our brother as much as possible,' Charlotte told them. 'Nell knows of his troubles, but I would rather that she should not be confronted with such coarseness at close hand.'

'We will do our best,' Anne said.

'Though I am not sure that Branwell will do *his* best,' Emily said. 'He seems intent on only doing his worst these days. Perhaps, if we are lucky, he will not return home from his present *adventure* until after Ellen has departed, or at all.'

Anne shot Emily a reproachful look. Emily shrugged in response.

'And we should not mention our . . . *your* forthcoming publications,' Charlotte said with a brief smile. 'Ellen is familiar with our endeavours to support ourselves, but I fear she might find the idea of us – *you* – writing novels under the *noms de plume* of two gentlemen rather shocking.'

Anne and Emily nodded demurely in agreement. They really were intolerable.

'And we absolutely must not, under any circumstances, tell her of our detections,' Charlotte cautioned them. She hoped it would go without saying, but when it came to Emily Brontë, one was never quite sure. It was always best to be completely clear. 'Especially not London, no one must ever know that we were there.'

'I shall never speak of it,' Emily said, lowering her eyes.

'Nor, I,' Anne said. 'Or any of it. In truth I am rather glad that peculiar interlude in our lives seems to have come to a conclusion, as grateful as I am for how our detections have inspired and strengthened me. My mind craves a quiet life, just as we have enjoyed these last few months. God, writing, books and music: these are all a soul needs to lead a happy life.'

'Indeed,' Emily said. 'And dogs, I would add only dogs to your manifest, Anne. And cats and all animals really, and all of creation. And pockets.'

Charlotte too was very glad that there had been no further detections for the best part of a year. They had returned from London last summer, each profoundly changed by what they had witnessed there, and with an unspoken agreement between them never to speak of those few terrifying days spent amongst the thieves and murderers of Covent Garden again.

Sometimes Charlotte thought she would glimpse something in Emily, a passing shadow falling over her face, like a bird momentarily blotting out the sun. She was certain that Emily had stitched much of her pain and fury into her *Wuthering Heights*, for Charlotte had never read anything so full of rage and longing. Something so fierce with feeling that it frightened her more than a little. London had frightened them, and broken them too, at least for a short while. Their craving for adventure seemed to have been permanently sated. Though Charlotte couldn't help but miss it now, when the new horizons that her sisters were travelling towards did not include her.

Then came a thunderous knocking at the door.

'Ellen!' Anne leapt to her feet, allowing Charlotte to exit the dining room first, so that she might have the honour of greeting her friend first. However, it was not dear Ellen at the door, or at least Charlotte hoped not, for Tabby, their housekeeper, was doing her best to close the front door on the visitor's foot and using a tone that she usually only reserved for stray cats and beggars.

'Get away with you!' Tabby growled furiously, as she leaned into the door which was blocked by a filthy brown boot. 'Likes of you have no business at this door. There are young ladies here, and another soon to arrive. I'll not allow it, I shall not.' She turned around to see Keeper's head appear between Anne and Emily, as if he had just realised he might be lapsing in his duties as guard dog.

'Sic him boy, go now, sic him!'

Keeper's head vanished back behind Emily's skirt.

'Get away from this respectable house!' the older woman shouted once more and, with a gargantuan effort, closed the front door.

'Tabby, who is it that you turn away so roughly?' Anne admonished their beloved housekeeper gently. Tabby Ackroyd was more of a mother to them than their own poor dear mama; even so, there were times when she was a law unto her own. 'You know Papa would not want any in need to be spoken to so . . . oh.'

With a resounding bang, the door had been kicked open.

Anne's expression altered in an instant, the colour draining from her cheeks.

For as Tabby opened the door wide, she revealed a man so universally loathed, the devil himself might have received a better reception. Nevertheless, he resided within the boundaries of the parish, and had just as much right to petition the parson as any other resident of Haworth.

Charlotte steeled herself to deal with the matter as swiftly as possible. It would not do to have a suspected murderer on the doorstep when Ellen arrived. It would not do at all.

The fellow before them stood almost as tall as the door itself, his battered hat held tightly in his one intact hand, for where the other had once been there was now only a cloth-bound stump. He was reasonably well dressed, and though his clothes were threadbare, they were well made.

There were traces of a once handsome man still present, though every garment hung off his skeletal frame, as it might a scarecrow, and his face was as hollow as a death's head, his skin sallow and set with yellowing red-rimmed eyes, which were nevertheless alive with a particular intensity that was quite unsettling. In other circumstances Charlotte might have felt sorry for him, for he looked not a spit away from death himself. In this instance, though, just to look at him felt like something akin to bathing in the rivers of hell. For this was Abner Lowood, the infamous Haworth poisoner.

'You are not welcome here, sir,' Charlotte said shortly, drawing herself to her full height, and grateful to feel her sisters close in at her back. 'Leave at once before I am required to have you removed.'

'I am a man of this parish, like any other,' Lowood told her, his voice rasping and weak. 'I seek counsel from my parson.'

'You are not like any other man,' Emily said, her tone clipped with contempt. 'You stood accused of murdering your wife.'

'And was acquitted,' Mr Lowood told them. 'Found not guilty, that means.'

'And no one knows how you got away with it,' Anne said. 'The doctor who examined the body changes his mind entirely about the cause of death overnight? Witnesses who died or fled? All except for that poor foolish girl that you . . . Every soul in this parish and for a hundred miles around knows that you are a guilty man who cheated justice.'

'I was acquitted,' Lowood repeated. 'But I should have guessed that the Brontë women would not have much respect for English justice.'

'What do you mean by that remark, sir?' Emily asked. Charlotte realised she needed to gain control of this situation at once. Ellen would be appearing at the gate at any moment, and she could not have her sisters engaged in a furious argument with this man.

'I will see the Irish parson,' Lowood growled. 'I have a right to his counsel. I'm an innocent man who is punished daily for what I have *not* done! Hated in every direction I turn, defamed and reviled. I would that Mr Brontë should speak up for me, and set the people straight. I have a right to speak with him.'

'You do,' Charlotte said. 'But he is not here at present, so if you will return before dawn tomorrow, I shall arrange a meeting for you.'

'This beast has no rights at all,' Emily said, aghast. 'If life is so hard for you, sir, then leave Haworth. Go elsewhere and thank God that you have a life to lead, unlike your wife, and the countless children you dispatched.'

'I. Was. Acquitted,' Lowood repeated, his brows gathering over his burning eyes. 'And it was God who buried my children young, not me.'

'My father is not here,' Charlotte repeated just as firmly. 'If you wish to see him you must return tomorrow and I will—'

'I'll see you three then,' Lowood said, stopping Charlotte dead.

'I beg your pardon?' she asked him, her sense of unease deepening drastically as he leered at her with a familiarity that made her shudder.

'Oh, I am familiar with your good works, Miss Brontë,' Lowood said, with more than a hint of menace. 'I've heard tell of them, in pubs and back rooms round here. What you get up to when your pa ain't looking. Stories like you wouldn't believe. Good for you, I say. Why should a single woman worry about her reputation, or her pa's reputation when there are all sorts of shenanigans to get up to?'

'You get out of here, you hear me?' Tabby charged at full tilt, brandishing a broom she had fetched from the kitchen. 'Else I'll beat you into next week and finish what the hangman should have started. None round here would stop me!'

'Wait,' Charlotte barred Tabby with her hand, exchanging glances with her sisters.

'What can you possibly mean, sir?' she asked evenly.

'You help me, and I'll help you,' Lowood told her. 'I'll keep your secret for you, and make sure that any whispers heard around and about are soon snuffed out.'

'I don't know what you think you've heard, sir,' Charlotte began. 'We are but three old maids—'

'Don't give me that,' Lowood sneered at her. 'Don't you know you're famous round here? Amongst them that have no protection, and further afield too. You stand up for the weak, and the poor. The lost and innocent, that's what I heard. And I am the innocent.'

'If you think you can bully or blackmail us, sir, you are very much mistaken,' Anne told him. 'We will never be subordinated by a man—'

'You will return tomorrow an hour before dawn,' Charlotte told him. 'And you will go to the rear of the house, but not to the door. Wait in the lane.'

Then she closed the door in his face.

CHAPTER

THREE

Emily

'You cannot mean that we should do what that . . . that . . .' Anne
gestured at the closed front door, incoherent with rage. 'I will not
do it, Charlotte. I am not ashamed of the work we have done, and
I certainly will not be coerced into meeting with that man because
of it. Let him tell Papa, let him tell the village, and every town and
village beyond. Let him tell the whole world, for all I care!'

Emily said nothing, only crossing her arms and leaning hard
against the wall. She did not care for this sense of helplessness
at all; it was unfamiliar and unwelcome. Where had that beast
heard the 'tales' that he spoke of? It was true that from time to
time there had been whispers about them, especially after the
discovery of the Top Withens bones. But no more than that it was
they who had campaigned for the discovery of the poor soul's
name, and for a decent burial. All those who had been involved
in the Chester Grange business were far away now, and not a
soul, save themselves, knew about London. God knows, there
had been many midnight hours when Emily wished she could
forget it forever. This was intolerable and must be stopped,
for she could not bear the idea of grubby, nasty men such as
Lowood peering into her life and making it public.

'My dear, that is precisely why we cannot let the likes of
Abner Lowood determine your destiny, or Emily's,' Charlotte
said, taking both their hands. 'You may have no shame over

17

the good you have done, but do you believe that the rest of the world will see it the same way? That you, we, would not be judged as guilty of sins against womanhood and respectability because of the things we have done and seen? You would be shunned, Anne. Worse than that, you could be vilified, shamed.'

'Then let it be so,' Anne said, defiant. 'We shall tell Papa at once, the moment he returns home, and let the devil take Lowood's threats.'

'No.' Charlotte's denial was sharp and forceful. Frustrated tears sprang into Anne's eyes, but Emily did not come to her support. Though she wasn't sure how to protect themselves from Lowood, she knew that throwing caution to the wind could not be the answer.

'Listen to Charlotte,' Emily told Anne. 'She has sense in her head, so hear her out a moment. For a moment is surely all we have before Ellen is here and we will be obliged to make small talk and the chance to make a plan will be past.'

'Very well,' Anne said coolly, pulling her hand from Charlotte's. 'Tell me then, why do you say no, Charlotte?'

'For your books are about to be released into the world, Anne. You and Emily may soon be all that we have between us and destitution. I will not allow you to ruin your reputation while our lives are so precariously balanced above the very establishment of which Mr Lowood is master.'

'We would never end up in a workhouse,' Anne scoffed at the idea. 'Our friends would never allow it.'

'Perhaps not, but we could easily end up separated from one another, living out our days as governesses, or – worse – companions; alone and miserable,' Charlotte said. 'There is more to think about than simply what is right. There are your prospects, and Papa's health.'

'Charlotte, you cannot—' Anne began, but before she could say more there came another, lighter knock at the door.

'The hour is upon us, Ellen has arrived,' Emily said swiftly. 'There is nothing else we can do now but keep that meeting with Lowood, and find out more of his purpose. Do you agree, Anne?'

'I suppose I must,' Anne said unhappily.

'Then smile,' Emily told her, her hand on her shoulder. 'For our visitor is here.'

Despite all that had just passed, it was a pleasure to see how Charlotte's face lit up at the sight of Ellen. Emily was glad for her. The weeks since she and Anne had secured a contract with Thomas Newby had been hard on her sister, though she had dealt with it with her usual stoicism. Dear Charlotte deserved a little respite from her unhappiness and frustration, and now even *that* was tainted by this awful situation that had been thrust upon them. Still, it pleased Emily enormously to see Ellen too, so prettily dressed, as she always was, her soft features framed by her light brown curls. It was as though a little peace had arrived hidden in her skirts, released into the air with the effusive twirls and turns of the women's greetings.

'Nell!' Charlotte kissed Ellen's hands as she led her into the dining room. 'We had meant to be on the doorstep to greet you, but you have arrived and we are not ready. Please forgive us our country ways.'

'You know you need not stand on ceremony for me,' Ellen smiled as she kissed Anne, then Emily in turn. 'I am just glad to be inside; I cannot remember when it was last so hot and stifling. It is as if the wind has retired to the other side of the world. I do wish it would rain, just a little.'

'There's a storm brewing,' Emily told Ellen as she and Tabby hefted Ellen's trunk in between them. 'You can feel it thickening in the air. The longer it builds, the more magnificent it will be!'

'As long as I am safely indoors when it occurs,' Ellen said.

'Let me take your bonnet and shawl.' Anne relieved Ellen of her garments and handed them to Martha, their maid, who loitered in the doorway. Martha was John Brown the sexton's daughter, a good girl from a fine family, though, rather like Emily herself, she often had her head in the clouds.

'Will you ask Tabby to bring the tea things please, Martha?' Charlotte asked the girl. 'Poor Ellen must be weary and thirsty from the road. And something to eat too.' As if a spread fit for Queen Victoria herself, lavishly planned and painstakingly prepared, wasn't ready and waiting on the kitchen table.

Emily followed Martha into the kitchen, where Tabby put the finishing touches to her feast. At once Emily noticed the knot of worry sitting on her beloved housekeeper's forehead. Tabby knew a little more of their detections than most; she had helped them more than once. Yet it would not have been Tabby who would have spoken out of turn, Emily was sure of that. The dear woman was worried for them every day of her life, and would do all she could to protect them.

So, if not Tabby, who? How had Lowood discovered their secrets and what did he want from them? Emily hoped that he knew nothing, that he was posturing and chancing his luck in a bid for some financial reward. But this was the man who somehow turned the doctor who had determined the cause of death, the judge and the jury in his favour when evidence of his guilt was abundant and indelible. As she helped Martha bring the trays to the dining room, Emily mused on the unfamiliar weight that sat in the pit of her belly, and realised it was fear. Fear of what Lowood knew and what he might do to harm her family. And that made her all the more furious.

Still, there was nothing else to be done but sit and smile and pass the time with Ellen, as if they did not have a black-mailer's visit in their social diary. Charlotte prepared a plate of Tabby's finest delicacies for Ellen, and Anne poured the tea.

'You took so very long to come to Haworth,' Charlotte gently chided Ellen. 'I feel as if I have waited half my life for you to visit. Is society in Birstall so very fascinating that you cannot tear yourself away to visit your poor friends?'

'Not at all,' Ellen said with a smile. 'Would that it were! No, I have been obliged to attend to my brother Henry and his wife Emily of late. They have not made a success of their life in Hathersage and I had to help them pack up and depart overseas for a short while. It is both disagreeable and dull in the extreme, but I suppose necessary if I am to depend upon them for my income.' Ellen's bright eyes scanned their faces. 'So, tell me, what adventures have you been having while I have been mired in other people's domesticity?'

'None,' Emily said, rather too quickly. 'There is no life that is duller or more uneventful than ours, I'm afraid.'

Tabby swayed open the door with a swing of her hip and laid a freshly baked slab cake on the table with quite a thud.

'Is all well then?' she said, as she straightened her back, looking from Charlotte to Emily.

'Oh yes, we have all that we need,' Charlotte said, smiling as she perused the table. 'Thank you, dear Tabby.'

'No, I meant with the poisoner fellow, did you get rid all right?'

'The poisoner?' Ellen's eyes widened, her mouth parting slightly.

'Rat poisoner,' Emily added hastily. 'A rat poisoner came round hawking traps.'

'Not that we have rats, Ellen dear,' Charlotte said, horrified.

'No, he just came to see if we might need his services, and we sent him away,' Emily said. 'We have altogether too many cats to be much troubled with rats or mice. If only cats could be dispatched to finish off all vermin as effectively.'

'Whatever can you mean?' Ellen laughed. 'You Brontës with all your funny ways and little jokes. It can take a person a few days not to feel like quite the outsider, you know.'

'I apologise for Emily,' Charlotte said.

'And I apologise for Charlotte,' Emily retorted. 'Anne, would you like to apologise for Flossy and Keeper and then I believe we will have a full set.'

'This is interminable,' Anne said standing up abruptly. 'How can we just sit here as if nothing has happened, Charlotte. We simply cannot.'

'Anne, I don't think you know what you are saying,' Charlotte said very slowly, eyeing Ellen with all the subtlety of a West End dame. 'Perhaps it's the heat. Take a glass of water, why don't you?'

'I know the exact meaning of every word I utter,' Anne said, determinedly missing Charlotte's pleas to be silent on the matter of Mr Lowood. 'I say we should be done with rats once and for all and have nothing to do with them, whatever they might know.'

'Whatever could a rat know?' Ellen asked. Charlotte looked to Emily, helpless in the face of Anne's rebellion against polite pretences.

'I shall take Anne for a stroll,' Emily said, looking regretfully at the cake. 'We might meet a breath of wind if we are lucky.' She held her hand out to Anne. 'It will do you good, Anne.'

Anne stood for a moment, struggling with the indignity and injustice of it all, and then marched out of the room.

'That's settled then,' Emily said, and she took two pieces of cake from the table and popped them in her pocket.

CHAPTER

FOUR

Anne

They were confronted in the lane with the sight of Arthur Bell Nicholls engaged in an animated conversation with Mrs Bessy Lee, her basket of laundry held under one arm, propped on one jutting hip. It was clear there was a disagreement at hand.

'Oh dear, not this again,' Anne muttered, as they approached, Flossy dancing round her skirts. 'It is no wonder the village finds Mr Nicholls so disagreeable. He *is* a good man at heart, but seems intent on hiding his more redeeming qualities behind high-minded meddling and superior behaviour.'

'The man's intolerable,' Emily said, marching forward with Keeper at her heel, his nose intent on finding its way to where the cake was stored 'There is no amount of goodness that can address his resolute determination to be utterly unpleasant.'

'I do think that is a little unfair,' Anne muttered under her breath as they approached. 'He does his best; it is just that he does so with such very little charm.'

'Good day, Mrs Lee, Mr Nicholls,' Anne said pleasantly to the pair. Mrs Lee's face was knotted in a ruddy frown. Mr Nicholls blocked her path, his palms turned towards her, certain that his authority alone was enough to turn her from her purpose. It was as if he had never met a Yorkshirewoman in all his two years as a curate at Haworth.

23

'Not a very good drying day I'm afraid, Bessy,' Anne said pleasantly. 'Not felt a breath of wind this last week, and I'm certain that we are due a downpour sooner or later.'

'Right enough, miss,' Bessy said. 'Which is why I will lay out my sheets in the graveyard like I always have now, that I might have them dry by sundown. Wind or nowt.' Bessy attempted to sidestep Mr Nicholls, who promptly blocked her from passing him.

'Let her past, sir,' Emily sighed. 'What else do you expect her to do with her laundry? Let it moulder in the pantry?'

'There must be other areas for such things,' he told Emily. 'I shall not allow this practice to continue, it is ungodly.'

'So, Mr Nicholls,' Emily questioned him. 'Do you say that my father, who has allowed the local women to dry their laundry this way since he became parson of the village, is ungodly?'

Anne sighed; poor Mr Nicholls was about to be thoroughly discombobulated.

'N-no, I only mean that . . . Your father is a very busy man, and I mean only to assist him in—'

'Being more godly?' Emily said. 'Perhaps even as godly as you.'

'And besides, who are you to lay down the law?' Mrs Lee asked him. 'I'll not take orders from a curate when I scarcely do from my own husband. We've laid out our washing in the graveyard since I were a bairn, and shall long after I'm gone, unless the good Lord himself – or Mr Brontë – comes to say differently.'

'But it is not proper!' Mr Nicholls replied, indignantly. He turned to Anne. 'Miss Anne, surely you can see the impropriety?'

'It is clean!' Mrs Lee shoved her basket of white linen hard under his nose, forcing the poor man to confront a quantity of petticoats.

'Miss Anne,' Mr Nicholls turned to Anne. 'Surely you would agree that a person's . . . undergarments should not be left out to dry on the tombstones of the dead?'

'It's my own dead and they don't mind owt about it,' Mrs Lee said. 'And who are you, a young, unmarried curate to be talking to me about undergarments? It's a disgrace, I tell you, Miss Anne. A disgrace.'

'A disgrace,' Emily repeated, smiling at a flustered Mr Nicholls.

'It is true that the women of Haworth have been drying their washing this way since before we arrived in the village, Mr Nicholls,' Anne interceded to save the poor gentleman. 'While I do understand your position, it seems unlikely you will be able to change such a long-standing tradition over-night.'

'That's that settled then,' Mrs Lee said, moving Mr Nicholls out of the way with one firm thrust of her basket, muttering to herself furiously as she headed towards her family graves.

Just then Flossy darted after her, nipping one knitted stocking out of the basket and making off with it with much delight. Anne thought it was probably best not to alert Mrs Lee to the theft just yet. Not until she had had a chance to retrieve the item and assess it for repairs. It was possible that Flossy was single-handedly responsible for all of Haworth's cases of missing stockings and socks.

'Now then, Mr Nicholls,' Emily said. 'Surely there must be something more useful you could be using your time to attend to?'

'Miss Emily,' Mr Nicholls bowed curtly in response, first walking a few steps towards the parsonage, and then abruptly turning on his heel and disappearing into the Browns' cottage, where he was renting accommodation from the sexton.

'Emily, you mustn't be quite so hard on him,' Anne chided her sister as they walked, Flossy having disappeared to some secret den with her prey, and Keeper intent on the contents of Emily's pockets. 'Though he is stiff and a little awkward, he still means well enough.'

'A person should strive to do more than mean well,' Emily said restlessly as Mrs Lee laid out a sheet over an ancestor. 'A person should do good. Or at least I thought so until this very day. Now, I fear that all the good we have done will be our undoing.'

Anne was relieved. For a moment she had feared that Emily too was subscribing to Charlotte's method of pretending that all was well and that they had not been called upon by catastrophe earlier that day.

'Tell me truly, now Charlotte is out of earshot,' Anne said, catching her sister's hand and bringing her to a standstill in the relative shelter of the cavernous and ancient cedar tree. 'What do you think, Emily?'

'About what to do with Lowood?' Emily's eyes travelled over her shoulder, widening slightly. She tossed the cake slices into the roots of the cedar tree, whereupon they were pounced on by her ravenous dog. 'We should follow him.'

Anne turned to see where the unmistakable figure of Mr Lowood, as twisted and ragged as a moortop hawthorn tree, had paused briefly at a headstone before hurrying away from it, as if caught in a lie.

'It is broad daylight, he will see us,' Anne cautioned.

26

'Good,' Emily said. 'A man like that – a man who has become used to getting away with evil in plain sight – needs to know that he is seen.'

'I don't believe I agree with you,' Anne said as Emily began threading her way past the graves towards the gap that Lowood had vanished through. 'I suspect he is the kind of man who is even more dangerous when cornered.' Emily was already in pursuit, however, and as a good sister, Anne was obliged to follow her towards peril.

They hung back a moment, ducking low to find some cover from a crumbling tabletop tombstone, as they watched Lowood climb over the drystone wall that marked the border of the graveyard in one spindly legged leap, and begin to double back towards Main Street. The two sisters followed Lowood's path, pausing at the gravestone he had stopped by.

'Mary Martin 1782–1824.' Anne read the last name at the bottom of the weathered tomb. I do not recall any Martins in the village now. I wonder what this name means to Lowood?'

'I wonder.' Emily looked at the name for a moment. 'Perhaps he poisoned her too.'

'We should not make assumptions,' Anne said. 'A good detector does not guess or suppose. We should make a note of her name, and see what we can find about her. Tabby might remember her, though she died more than twenty years ago.'

'So, we are detecting once again?' Emily asked her. She sat down on the low wall that Lowood had vaulted over, and swung her legs over in one go, a feat that Anne repeated not quite so effortlessly a moment later, tearing her petticoats on the ragged stones.

'I suppose we are,' Anne replied, dusting down her skirts. 'I suppose we have no choice if we are to comply with Charlotte's wishes. They hurried down the lane to see Lowood turn up a narrow alleyway. In the distance, Anne heard Flossy and Keeper's barks and low growls, signifying a game of tug. She feared that Mrs Lee's stocking would be beyond repair.

'But must we, Emily?' Anne said, thinking of Mrs Lee. 'Or should we deny the vile creature Lowood and refuse to allow him any power over us, just as Mrs Lee refuses to let Mr Nicholls have any power over her? Why not tell Papa everything we have kept hidden until now? And as for the messrs Acton and Ellis Bell, what have their names to do with ours? They are free of our petty little lives and precious reputations, whether they be in a state of ruin or not. Would it really matter so much if folk around here knew how we had helped others with the power of our intellect and courage?'

Emily replied by abruptly dragging her into a doorway, out of sight of Lowood, just before he turned back to stare at the spot where they had been standing. Hidden by thick shadow, the two women watched as he leaned his whole frame into the steep incline of the hill, ignored and avoided by all those who passed him until he was swallowed into the always open mouth of the Black Bull.

'I commend your courage, Anne,' Emily said at last, turning back to her sister. 'But Charlotte is right. And you will soon be right too.'

'What do you mean?' Anne asked her, frustrated.

'Despite her chronic vision, our sister is the only one of us to see beyond the end of her nose. She envisages a future for us when our names and our reputations *will* matter.

A future where we are safe and secure, mistresses of our own destiny. That cannot happen if our adventures in detection come to light. Charlotte is protecting us for a time to come that you and I have not yet imagined.'

'I suppose,' Anne replied, rather begrudgingly, though she saw the sense of what Emily was telling her. 'And so how am I soon to be right?'

'Because you are Anne Brontë,' Emily said. 'Defender of the weak, poor and innocent. And you will soon come to the conclusion that in a world that hides its true face behind polite society and where justice can be bought and paid for, nothing is ever as it seems. You will conclude that simply because Lowood looks for all the world like a devil, and has by his own admission lived as one, it does not make him guilty of murder. Nor does it make him invulnerable to attack.'

Anne closed her eyes for a moment, seeing exactly how Emily was expertly shaping her thoughts. Yet there was no resisting it.

'Of course, we must meet with Lowood,' she said unhappily. 'We must establish the truth beyond any doubt when it comes to the death of his wife, and all of his poor children. We must hunt for evidence not yet discovered or hidden away and bring it to light. If he is innocent, we must prove him so. And if he is guilty, we must do the same. And . . .' She hesitated, the next words sticking in her dry throat. 'If he is the target of a killer, then we must protect him. For no other being will.'

'You are quite right, Anne,' Emily said, taking her shoulder in her hand and nodding her affirmation.

'In this instant it makes me feel quite sick to be right,' Anne said, unhappily. 'And sicker still that you saw it before me. As we seem to have lost Lowood to the Bull, may we go home? Or better still, up onto the moor to hunt down a whisper of air to cool our cheeks?'

'No,' Emily said, gathering her skirts. Anne followed suit as Emily hurried round to the back of the inn, which happened to be right up against the boundaries of the graveyard, and more or less at the point where they had begun their walk. Indeed, Keeper charged past, the poor unfortunate stocking trailing after him, as Flossy made a swift pursuit after the prize.

The foundations of the Bull were set several feet lower than the ground level of the graveyard, with the result that several of the interred were resting with their feet pressed against the wall of the pub, including the infamous highwayman James Sutcliffe who, legend had it, had been secretly buried there. Picking her way through the long, dry grass, Emily crouched down to the left of a single low dirty window and peered in.

'What do you expect him to be doing in such an establishment that we might not be able to reasonably guess whilst at home, with a cool drink of water?' Anne asked, fanning herself with her hanky.

'Well,' Emily said, pulling her sleeve over the heel of her wrist and swiftly rubbing clean a small circle to see better through. 'What I did not expect was to find him in conversation with our brother.'

FIVE

Charlotte

'You are here at last,' Charlotte said as she sat alone with Ellen in the dining room. 'I cannot tell you how it pleases me to have you near, Nell. I mean to spoil you and cherish you, and keep you as much to myself as I am able.'

'That would be perfect,' Ellen returned Charlotte's smile. 'Though I fear your sisters seem rather restless. Is there something amiss, Charlotte? More trouble with Branwell?'

Charlotte cast her gaze downwards as she returned her tea cup to the saucer. It felt morally dubious, to say the least, to use her brother's troubles as a mask for their own; nevertheless, it was an effective ploy. And there was a small part of Charlotte that supposed he owed them shelter at least, when he had done so much to tear down what little they had.

'Things have been very bad of late,' Charlotte said, speaking only the truth. 'He no longer makes the pretence that he is trying to reform. I'm certain Mrs Robinson was sending him money for a while, but now – he seems to have run up new debts on top of those he already owes. Poor Papa is beside himself with worry.'

Charlotte bowed her head as she collected herself, pressing her grief and anger firmly down into the centre of her chest where her passionate emotions were forcibly contained, always threatening to break her dam of composure and flood free.

'Papa's spirits were so raised after the restoration of his sight, but it has been restored to him to witness his dearest boy's destruction,' Charlotte went on. 'He goes about his work as diligently as ever, more so perhaps. And yet I see him pace his study, from window to desk and back again, and I know he is searching for a way to save Branwell. I do not have the heart to tell him I fear that time has passed. Branwell lost hope, and with that he ceased caring to live at all.'

Ellen covered Charlotte's hand with her own and squeezed her fingers.

'And your family?' Charlotte asked her. 'How do they fare?'

'Mama is . . . Mama,' Ellen raised her brows in all the explanation that was needed to accompany that phrase. 'Henry and his wife did naught but aggravate the parish of Hathersage, despite all the careful preparations I made for them. I don't know why I thought Henry might have heeded my advice, for I am only a sister, of course, and can know nothing of any consequence.'

'Of course,' Charlotte said, dryly. 'And poor, dear George?'

'He remains in York,' Ellen said, choosing not to elaborate further, though Charlotte knew that George was now permanently residing at an asylum. 'Now Charlotte, you must tell me what you are hiding. It is very impolite to keep secrets from your guest, you know.'

'Hiding?' Charlotte sat up quite straight, wondering what had betrayed which secret to her friend. 'Whatever can you mean, dear Ellen?'

'You are all altered,' Ellen said. 'You seem bright and so full of colour. Animated and conversational. It is quite unlike

Emily in particular, but you, my dearest Charlotte, are the most changed of all. As if a spark within has become a flame. Tell me, is it Mr Nicholls's attention that thrills you so?'

'Goodness no,' Charlotte said, springing up with a nervous laugh. Suddenly she found something outside terribly fascinating, which would also serve to hide her blushes from Ellen. 'No, you know perfectly well I cannot tolerate the thought. The very idea that rumours persist in linking us is humiliation enough. No, Ellen. We have no secrets in our little house. There is no room for them.'

Charlotte could not help but feel rather guilty as she returned to the table to stack the tea things onto the tray, wondering how she would be able to leave Ellen asleep in her bed as she stole out of the house for their covert assignation with a probable murderer.

'Forgive us, Ellen,' she pleaded in a heartfelt tone. 'For the three of us have been out of civilised company for so long that we have become like half-wild girls once more, talking riddles amongst ourselves and creating fictions wherever our gaze settles. We will do our best to reform, just for you, dear heart.'

'I don't wish you to reform,' Ellen smiled, holding her hand out to Charlotte. 'Just make me part of your games and let me play for a while, for I am so very tired of being sensible.'

'That I can promise you,' Charlotte said. 'Your visit shall be full of play and pleasure, and I shall not let one shadow cross your path, you have my word.'

Charlotte could only hope that she would be able to keep her promise.

Emily

'It couldn't have been, could it?' Anne joined Emily in the dirt, straining to get a look at the scene before sitting back on her heels. Emily remained focused on the apparent conspirators, Branwell's bright hair glinting through the grime-smeared glass, bent close to Lowood.

'That our brother has betrayed us for a little coin or a bottle of gin?' Emily completed the awful thought. 'I wish I did not believe it, Anne, but since he drank all of *that* woman's money, Branwell continues to find new ways to debase himself daily. I fear it *is* possible that he has sold our secrets to Lowood.'

'He would not. No matter how drunk or intoxicated he was, he would never . . .' Anne faltered to a stop.

The truth was that none of them were sure of what Branwell would or would not do any more. There had still been the barest glimmer of hope when they had returned from their last detection almost a year ago. If anything, it had been Emily who had found herself altered; changed to such an extent that she almost didn't recognise her own reflection. Branwell had seemed stronger, more purposeful, as if he had found a way out of his misery at last. Emily had cherished hopes for him as she swept away the ashes of her own. It was as if a layer of her skin had been flayed away by the rough edges of London. Since she had left that city behind, the whole world looked harsher, sounded louder and felt more intrusive. Emily had lost her certainty about her place in the world and, moreover, her previously unassailable sense of self as she had struggled to master this new rawness of heart. They had all dared to hope that Branwell would recover. Then something changed, and none of them knew quite what. In an instant, all Branwell's efforts to turn his life from the precipice ended abruptly. And still Emily would have trusted her secrets to her brother, for despite it all, she trusted his heart. Until this moment, that was.

Lowood appeared to slap Branwell hard on the shoulder and then slammed something down on the counter, probably some coin, before walking out. Branwell ordered another drink, clinging onto the edge of the bar as he lunged forward, his whole body following his desire for more alcohol.

Bitterness rose in her throat as Emily turned away from the window, offering her hand to Anne as they clambered to their feet.

'Charlotte must not know,' Emily told Anne. 'It would hurt her too much.'

'But why?' Anne protested. 'Charlotte deserves to know all that we do.'

'We do not know anything,' Emily said. 'Branwell is as likely to make conversation with a chair as a murderer in his present condition. It could be that in entertaining fellows with his tall tales, he has let a little truth add colour and spice to his stories, and that was enough for a man like Lowood. Besides Anne, have you ever known any person who has been obliged to bear disappointment as frequently and as well as our sister? She survived Monsieur Héger's indifference, and now she is bravely, cheerfully taking on the burden of our success with as much good grace as she can muster. It costs her dearly, I know that, Anne, because it would cost me dearly too. If we can save her even one jot of further distress, then we must. Especially while Ellen is here and she is so very desperate to be happy.'

'Very well,' Anne agreed with some hesitation. 'I would rather die than hurt Charlotte. We must protect her at all costs.'

'At all costs,' Emily said. 'Including this business with Lowood.'

'How can we protect her in our dealings with that monster?' Anne asked. 'When she is so determined to protect us?'

'Very carefully,' Emily said. 'Let her appear to have her head, and to lead us in decisions and we shall quietly go our own way. As for Lowood, I suggest we let him think he has the advantage, and use his misguided sense of control over us to allow him to reveal the truth of his crimes, whatever they might be.'

Anne nodded.

'God will be the final judge,' she said. 'But should the hangman bring him before the Lord's reckoning a little sooner, I should not mind it.'

'I must say I am surprised to hear you talk so,' Emily said as they began to make their way back to the parsonage. 'With such thirst for vengeance. It is most unlike you, Anne.'

'It is and it shames me,' Anne nodded. 'Yet I feel it so very strongly. A powerful hate towards Lowood and a firm wish to make that man pay for what he has done, for I am sure he has done *something*. Am I like your Heathcliff, Emily? Half mad and entirely poisoned by vengeance?'

'Not at all.' Emily dropped an arm around Anne's shoulders. 'You have a heart and a soul, and Heathcliff has neither. He is howling rage made human.'

Just then something small and hard flew through the dirty glass at high speed, whisking past Emily's skirts with a pistol-shot crack. A cry came from within, followed by a great cacophony of shouts.

'Branwell,' Anne and Emily said together, turning on their heels to run to the front of the inn.

Sure enough, Branwell was doing his best to fight his way back into the pub, throwing his small wiry body again and again against the bulk of Enoch Thomas, while others tried their best to drag him back and calm his fury.

'Time to come home, Branwell,' Emily called to her brother gently, as if he were an injured fox in need of aid. Sallying forth into the fray she attempted, and failed, to capture one of his wheeling arms. The back of his hand came into sharp contact with her left cheek and Emily was obliged to bite her lip to prevent herself from cursing her brother. At last she grabbed his wrist with one hand and pinned his arm under hers.

'Come on now,' she said, rather less gently. 'Time to sleep it off.'

'They're bastards!' Branwell shouted, breaking free of her grip and swinging towards Enoch Thomas once again in a sudden violent lunge, wrenching himself free of Emily's hold. She watched on, cheeks hot with shame, tears standing in her eyes. This time it was Anne who took a firm hold of his arm. Gravity swayed Branwell backward from his chaotic lunge, and he barrelled into Emily once again. By bracing herself for the impact of his weight, and with Anne at her side, Emily was just about able to stop all of them from tumbling onto the cobbles and her brother from hitting his head on the stone.

Humiliation and fury tore through her veins as she roughly wound his chaotic arms around her neck, and tried – along with Anne – to steer him away from the crowd.

'Apologies,' Emily nodded at Enoch Thomas.

'His account needs settling, Miss Brontë,' Mr Thomas called after her.

'Perhaps if you stopped selling him gin, then he wouldn't owe you quite so much money,' Emily said tightly.

'He's worse bother sober,' someone from the crowd muttered. 'Never stops going on about himsen', like we don't know it all and more. At least drunk he's amusing for a short while.'

Emily stopped, and turned around to scan the motley group of men. All eyes suddenly seemed to find the ground terribly fascinating.

'Look at you, drinking away your wages when you have a wife and hungry children at home,' she said. 'Shame on the lot of you. And as for you, Enoch Thomas, the account will be settled in full by tonight and I will thank you to serve my brother no more.'

'Told you they were bastards,' Branwell muttered as the three swayed and staggered their way back to the parsonage. Anne wept quietly as Branwell muttered a string of words that no gentleman should ever utter, and no lady should ever hear, each obscenity etching a further scar into Emily's love for her brother.

'We must take him through to the kitchen,' Emily said through gritted teeth. 'If we are fortunate, perhaps Tabby can help us get him to bed without bothering Papa, Charlotte and Ellen.'

'Bloody bastards!' Branwell shook his fist over Anne's head. 'Liars too!'

'Branwell, keep your mouth shut, for pity's sake' Anne begged him. 'You bring ignominy to us all.'

'Might I assist?' Mr Nicholls had appeared at the front door, and within a few steps he had intervened, removing Branwell from his sisters' shoulders.

'You have visitors,' he said pleasantly, as if the two women were carrying a rather large box, and nothing more. 'Let me take Branwell into my apartments for a while to recover from his affliction. I can return him to the house a little later when he is more fit for company. Perhaps after the household has gone to bed.'

'Thank you kindly,' Anne said, with heartfelt gratitude. 'Arthur, I cannot thank you enough.'

'He needs watching though,' Emily told Mr Nicholls, deadly serious. 'Take your eyes off him and he will escape. Or worse, stay.'

'I have work I can prepare while he sleeps,' Mr Nicholls assured her. 'You have nothing to fear, Miss Emily.'

'I only wish that were true,' Emily said, and then she thought for a moment. 'Thank you, sir.'

The sisters stood for a moment longer, catching their breath in the intense heat, as Mr Nicholls guided their now near unconscious brother out of sight into the Browns' cottage.

'I begin to fear that he will lose his life to the evil of drink,' Anne said, pressing the back of her hand against her hot cheeks.

'I believe that fear has long since been realised,' Emily said, darkly. 'Now that Mrs Robinson is done with him, death is his mistress. It only remains to be seen how long she will tarry before she comes to claim him. And I am so broken-hearted and full of hurt that I don't know if I wish her to hurry to his side or leave him be.'

The sisters took each others' hands and, holding tightly onto one another, made the short journey to their home as if it were one of a thousand treacherous miles.

Anne

The clock in the hallway had not yet even struck five as Anne and Charlotte tiptoed out of the front bedroom, leaving Ellen sleeping serenely, one cheek resting on the back of her folded hand.

Once downstairs they found Emily already up and dressed, sitting at the kitchen table reading. She waited for them to pull on their stockings, lace up and button one another's gowns, and lastly pin up their hair. Modest respectability was essential when one was meeting with a likely murderer.

The violet sky was already beginning to lighten to lilac with the promise of the sun. They wanted to be out of the parsonage when Lowood arrived, so that they could lure him as far as possible away from their home and prying eyes. By which they largely meant Tabby, and Ellen. Martha could come face to face with the devil himself and not pay him any mind.

It was a fine, still morning. Moisture misted in the air and Anne could feel the heat of the day approaching at pace. If their business hadn't been so very onerous, she would have been glad of an excuse to be abroad this early, when the grass was still bejewelled with dew and the touch of air on her skin felt like bathing her face in cool running water.

Lowood was waiting for them, leaning on a gate a little way up the lane, as if he had anticipated that they would come out of the house to meet him. The sight of him, gazing over the serene landscape, the smoke from his pipe twisting into the still air, only vexed Anne further. What right had such a man to one moment of peace? What authority did he have to summon them from their home as if they were beholden to him?

He ruined the beauty of the world simply by existing in it, and yet she was powerless to resist his demands. Such was this world of Man that even the lowest of his sex knew he could threaten and cajole them based on something as slight but as sacred as a woman's reputation. That was why, though she knew that Emily spoke right when she talked of fairness and justice, Anne could not accept these principles when it came to Lowood. The sight of him enraged her with a brutal, instinctive hatred that she was powerless to quell. That he invoked such a strong reaction from her only distressed her further. Anne had always thought herself better than this, but he brought out the worst in her.

'What a pretty posy you are this morning,' Lowood greeted them with a crooked smile. Emily rolled her eyes in disdain, crossing her arms. Half turning away from him, she tapped her foot on the dusty road in impatience. Anne, on the contrary, made herself look at him, searching his gaunt face for any sign of humanity. The merest hint that a Christian soul still inhabited the desecrated tomb of his body that might dilute her unrelenting disgust for him. He must have been handsome once, how else could he have charmed so many women under his spell? Or perhaps it was that particular way he looked at a person, as if he knew you inside and out just from a single glance. He made Anne feel uncertain and afraid, and the sooner she was out of reach of his gaze, the sooner she would feel restored.

'Tell us what you want from us, sir,' Charlotte said abruptly, looking off to the horizon rather than gazing upon him directly.

'Firstly, I wish you to find out who it is that tried to kill me,' Lowood told her. 'And see they face justice for it.'

Anne could not help the bark of a laugh that escaped her lips.

'She don't like me much, that one,' Lowood said, addressing Charlotte, whose expression was impassive. 'Shame, because she hasn't lost her bloom, like you other two. Still worth a look, that one.'

'None of us like you at all, sir,' Charlotte said. 'You can hardly expect us to when you have threatened and blackmailed us. And if you wish us to help you, you will refrain from speaking of my sister in those terms again.'

He touched the rim of his hat in assent.

'You said "Firstly",' Charlotte said. 'What is the second request?'

'That you clear my name, for I did not murder my wife. The court saw the truth. And now the people of this village and all around must follow. I will not be moved on again.' Anne detected the stress in his voice. While he had wrangled his way loose of the grip of justice, it seemed to really matter to him that those around him believed him innocent too. It would be onerous indeed to help him clear his name when she felt certain he had done exactly what he was accused of.

'And if in fact we find the very evidence that damns you to hang?' Anne asked him, archly.

'You will not,' Lowood said. 'No such evidence exists. I am not guilty.'

43

'With regards to the attempt on your life,' Anne went on, 'did you not see your assailant when they attacked you?'

'No,' Lowood winced, as if remembering pain. 'I was poisoned with arsenic. Same as did for my wife. It's my belief that whoever tried to make off with me, made off with her too and it's them that should be at the end of a rope.'

Anne huffed and shook her head.

'You may hate me,' Lowood said, taking a few steps towards her, obliging Anne to stand her ground, 'and I may deserve it. But still, someone attempted to murder me, the same person that killed my wife. They will try again. I would rather know who they are before they are successful in their venture.'

'Mr Lowood,' Emily said. 'Your actions in recent years alone have caused harm and pain to so many that you must realise you have countless enemies who would gladly see you dead? A brutal workhouse master, with a fearsome reputation. A wife-beater. A philanderer, with amoral appetites. Sir, are there too many who hate you for you to keep track of?'

'I thought I knew of all that wanted me gone,' Lowood told Emily, untroubled by her sharp assessment of his character. Even so, Anne noticed how his dark eyes darted around constantly, never still, as if he expected an attack from any direction and at any moment. He might act like a brute, but he was capable of fear. Anne was glad of it.

'I keep all of them that might want to harm me under the heel of my boot,' Lowood said. He ground his boot into the rain-starved earth. 'I beat 'em down, I hold them down by the neck so that they can't move or breathe without me knowing about it.' He paused for a moment, drawing the stump of his wrist across his forehead. 'Whoever this is that has attacked me, I don't know who it is. I half think . . . I half think it's her.'

'Who?' Anne asked, tilting her head as she tried to make sense of the wary expression on Lowood's face.

'Mrs Lowood,' he muttered. 'My Barbara. I still hear, you see. I hear her in my lodgings, though she never lived there a day. I hear her step on the stair, the sound of her skirts. Her cries in the night; that woman wailed like a banshee when she was upset.' He shuddered, in an attempt to shake himself loose of the image. 'I know she's waiting for me in hell. That much is true beyond doubt. But sometimes I wonder if she hasn't found her way back to me, come to speed me on my way.'

Anne suppressed a smile. So, this monster was afraid of death. More specifically, he was afraid of hell and the justice that was sure to be meted out to him there for all eternity. Before her eyes, Lowood's mystery and power ebbed away.

'But if you were not your wife's murderer, why would she seek revenge against you?' Anne asked sharply.

'Because she was a very stupid woman,' Lowood said with a sneer. 'And because I told her I'd kill her without a second thought if she gave me too much trouble. She believed that to be true while she was living, I made sure of it. So why wouldn't she think it dead?'

'I would certainly seek vengeance on you from beyond the grave,' Emily said. 'But as much as I would enjoy your assailant being the ghost of your poor murdered wife, I suspect it unlikely that spectre would be able to administer arsenic with such ease. More likely it is a living soul seeking vengeance. One you have yet to identify and keep 'under your heel' as you so charmingly put it. Which does make this all quite interesting.'

'And you'll find them then,' Lowood pressed them urgently. 'Whether they be flesh and blood or . . . something

45

else.' He shivered, even in the mounting heat of the day. 'You'll find them out, and stop them. I heard what you did at Chester Grange, and up at Top Withens. I know you been down in London . . .'

'How?' Charlotte asked him flatly.

'It doesn't matter how,' Anne interjected hurriedly, afraid that Lowood would reveal their brother's name and distress Charlotte. 'All that matters is that you accept our terms, sir. For be assured *we* will not be kept under your heel.'

'What are your terms?' Lowood said, bemused by the idea that they might have power of their own.

'We will investigate for you, as you have specified, in return for your complete discretion,' Anne told him. However, you must know two things. Firstly, you will stay away from our home and family and you will not make our association known to anyone. Do you agree?'

'I do,' he said. 'You have my word of honour. And the second thing I should know?'

'That we will find a way to use whatever evidence we gather to secure a conviction in regards to the attempt on your life, and the death of your wife. And if that points to you, then so be it. Do you accept our terms?'

'I accept them,' Lowood said. 'I have nothing to hide.'

'That seems very unlikely,' Anne said.

'It's other people's secrets that leave them open to enterprise,' Lowood said. 'As for myself, every detail of my life has been laid bare both in court and in the press. The whole world knows what sort of man I am. Help or condemn me, once this matter is settled, I shall leave you be.'

Charlotte glanced towards Emily, who turned to Anne, the three of them making a silent pact of strength and dignity.

'Then we shall do our best to discover the truth of what happened as soon as we are free of other commitments.'

'That will not do, miss,' Lowood told her, urgently. 'You'll begin this day.'

'We have a guest at the parsonage,' Charlotte went on. 'Our father is at home, the curate always underfoot, our brother . . . indisposed. It would be very difficult to make any headway without attracting unwanted attention.'

'You will surely attract attention when the world finds out about your exploits,' Lowood said, reminding them – as if they needed it – that for now at least he held all the cards in the grimy deck.

'Very well,' Charlotte said stiffly. 'We begin today. The sooner it is begun, the sooner it is finished with.'

The three turned on their heels, walking in silence back towards the parsonage, each unable to articulate their thoughts on the devil's deal they had just struck. That was until a fearful sight stopped them in their tracks.

'May the good Lord protect us,' Emily said heavily. 'For we are in for it now.'

Tabby Ackroyd was waiting for them by the back kitchen, her arms crossed under her bosom and her eyes blazing with fury.

'You three will be the death of me,' she told them as they trailed towards her. 'Now get inside at once and explain yourselves before I take a broom to your backsides.'

EIGHT

Emily

'You must do no such thing!' Tabby hissed as she took a fresh loaf of bread from the oven, turning it out onto the newly scrubbed table where a freshly churned pot of butter waited to be spread on it. 'You must go after him now, Emily, and tell him straight that you will have nowt to do with him. He's the devil. And you are parson's daughters. You will tell him that he must not darken this door again, nor even look at you, let alone speak your names. You tell him!'

'Why me?' Emily asked attempting to pull a chunk of crust free, only to have her hand slapped away. 'Why are you always sending me out to deal with the forces of evil?'

'Because you are a terrible wilful savage,' Tabby said. 'And I'll thank you to wait for that bread to be sliced.'

'If we could just send him away, Tabby, we would,' Charlotte said gently, as she brewed tea and Anne set out the breakfast things on a tray to be taken into the dining room. 'But if we did, he would tell the whole town about Chester Grange and Top Withens, and more. Imagine if all of Haworth knew that we went to visit the Witch of the Wage of Crow Hill.'

'She's a wise woman,' Tabby muttered, touching wood and throwing a pinch of salt over her left shoulder just to be on the safe side. 'Then you must go and tell Mr Brontë all of it, now. Though the shock of it will surely kill him stone dead, at least then you will no longer be beholden to that . . . that *man*!'

'Come now, Tabby,' Emily said. 'We all wish to keep Papa in good health. Branwell's affliction already takes its toll, we can't add to that. Perhaps once it is all done and settled, but not now.'

'You girls, you think you are clever as sixpence and know best, but I'll tell you this now, you are woolly-headed fools, every one of you. Your father is a wise and brilliant man, and he would know what you should do, if you would just *talk* to him. I had thought you had given all this nonsense up after you came back from London so altered, Emily. Never been the same since, you haven't.'

Emily was caught off guard for a moment, so certain was she that she had smoothed all trace of what had taken place in London out of her mind and complexion. That Tabby had seen it, saw it still, troubled her.

'I am perfectly well, and just exactly as I always was,' Emily insisted, deciding not to notice how knowingly Charlotte and Anne looked at one another. 'And we *had* given it up entirely, Tabby dear. We have had much more important business to occupy us. But somehow Lowood has come across this information about our adventures and is determined to make it pay in his favour. There is very little we can do about it without risking even more harm to Papa and the family name than our brother has already inflicted. Truly, we have no choice in the matter. And as such I am determined to enjoy this detection. It is fascinating, after all. A man who readily admits he is guilty of so much, refusing to admit he is guilty of the crime that so many – save corrupt lawyers – believe he perpetrated.'

'I must agree,' Charlotte said thoughtfully as Anne wrinkled her nose in disgust. 'As repellent as our situation is, there is much to be learnt here about the nature of man. Lowood's hateful and malign character is all there in his face and skull bones, you know. A phrenologist would be able to minutely discern his dissolute nature all from the contours of his head and features.'

'And his lengthy career as a criminal,' Emily added, dryly.

'You mock me, Emily,' Charlotte said. 'But phrenology is a fascinating science. And though it might be too late for the likes of Lowood, imagine if we were able to identify and treat such afflictions before they took hold, from childhood even. Perhaps we could have foreseen Branwell's troubles, if we had had his head felt.'

'We took dear George to see a phrenologist,' Ellen said as she entered the kitchen. 'It did him no good, I'm afraid.'

'But if your family had been able to know from boyhood that George would be so troubled with low mood and such,' Charlotte said, her enthusiasm for her subject making her less than tactful, 'then perhaps you might have been able to prevent his decline in some way.'

'I expect you're right, Charlotte dear,' Ellen said mildly. 'Now, I'm vexed that you all rose so early and left me to sleep on. It is not my way to rest while others toil. You must let me be your sister while I am here, and take equal part in your daily duties. Here, let me take the tray through. Will your papa and Branwell be joining us for breakfast? I do hope so, I do so enjoy your father's company.'

'Branwell has not risen before noon of late,' Charlotte began as she followed Ellen. 'And Papa has taken to eating all of his meals alone, though I am sure he will wish to see you, Ellen.'

'Do you think Ellen heard our talk of Lowood?' Anne asked as soon as Charlotte and Ellen were out of earshot.

'She was singularly unperturbed if she did,' Emily said, turning to her younger sister. 'And what of you, Anne. Will you be able to stand being of aid to Lowood?'

'No,' Anne said, flatly. 'But I do believe in the truth. I am willing to do my part in discovering it and I hope that in doing so we can bring that brute to justice.'

'And if we cannot?' Emily asked Anne, knowing all too well that justice was rarely so cut and dried.

'But we shall,' Anne said. 'I am determined. If this is to be our last detection then it must succeed, it is vital. Not just for our sake, but for poor Mrs Lowood. Her memory deserves not only the truth of her death to be heard, but the circumstances of her tragic life. Too many women die at the hands of their husbands, perhaps not in such sensational circumstances. Often quietly and behind closed doors. I want to make enough noise about their murders so that the world will finally see this injustice, and tolerate it no more.'

'Then that is what we shall do,' Emily said, touching her palm to Anne's fair cheek. 'My dear warrior Anne.'

As Anne went to breakfast, Tabby caught hold of Emily's hand, keeping her behind.

'I always send you to vanquish evil,' she told Emily, 'because you are the only one in this family that sees the world for what it is, like I do.'

'And what way do we see it, Tabby?' Emily asked, though she already knew the answer.

'That the world is full of death and ghosts,' Tabby said. 'And both want us in their grasp.'

CHAPTER

NINE

Charlotte

'A walk? May we not accompany you?' Ellen asked as Emily and Anne tied on their light summer bonnets, making excuses about errands that Charlotte and Ellen need not trouble themselves with.

'Oh, you would not wish to,' Charlotte said. 'Emily and Anne are going into Keighley to pay a visit to the workhouse on Papa's behalf.'

'What did you say?' It just so happened that this was the precise moment that Charlotte's father emerged from his study, and the first time she had set eyes on him since yesterday. One might have thought it impossible to avoid a member of one's own family in a home as small as the parsonage, but Papa had always been so very good at withdrawing and making himself invisible at will. There were times, and always had been, since Mama had died, when he did not wish for any company but that of his own thoughts. The last few days had been such an interval, devoted to duty and prayer. Charlotte had almost forgotten he was at home. Which was rather inconvenient when caught in the middle of something adjacent to the exact truth.

'What are you doing on my behalf *now*, daughters?' He peered at them over his glasses. 'I do not recall dispatching you so?' He turned to Ellen, his newly clear eyes twinkling with pleasure at the sight of her. 'And dearest Miss Nussey, please do forgive me for not greeting you the moment you arrived. Somehow it escaped me! You are, as ever, so welcome in our humble home.'

'It is a delight to see you, Reverend Brontë.' Ellen bobbed a curtsey as their father returned a stiff bow. 'And that your sight is now so restored – what a miracle.'

'I thank God daily for his benevolence,' Papa said. 'I am so grateful for the return of my sight.' He levelled his gaze at Charlotte. 'For I fear I missed rather a lot when it was compromised.'

He looked sternly from daughter to daughter, who each lowered their lashes under the scrutiny. Charlotte could feel little spots of guilty pink bloom on her cheeks.

'You did not dispatch us, Papa,' Emily said, hooking her arm through her father's and leading him into the dining room, where she pulled out a chair for him and poured him a cup of tea, before taking a seat at his side. Charlotte, Anne and Ellen followed suit. 'We took it upon ourselves to visit the workhouse on your behalf to save you the trouble. You see, yesterday, Mr Lowood, the recently disgraced workhouse master, came to see you. His complaint was that – since his acquittal on charges of murder – he remains shunned by the parish and seeks your advice, supposing, I imagine, that your approval would lead to folk accepting him once more.'

'Ah yes, I see,' Papa nodded gravely. 'You might think that after such dreadful trouble a man might move on and change his name. That Mr Lowood is unwilling to do so shows either great character or great hubris. It is a conundrum indeed.'

'Exactly,' Charlotte continued. 'And we know that you are currently deeply committed to other matters.' She referred of course to Branwell and his ever more complicated debts and difficulties, as well as her father's usual work. 'So, we conspired to relieve you of some of the load. We thought if Emily and Anne were to pay a visit to the workhouse, we might see how the inmates are faring, particularly now the poor unfortunate Tolliver family is overseeing the place. We thought we could interview a few who had dealings with Mr Lowood and return the intelligence to you so you might decide how best to proceed with his concerns. After all that went on there, behind closed doors, so to speak . . .' Emily looked acutely uncomfortable when alluding to the particularly explicit nature of the revelations that had emerged during the trial, 'it might be that the best thing for all concerned would be a fresh start.'

'A thorny issue indeed,' Patrick said, looking at Ellen. 'And not one that I would wish any young ladies in my care to be speaking – or even thinking – about. I have always let you have free access to the newspapers and such, but in this particular case I do wonder at the wisdom of that liberty. I believe I should have put my foot down and shielded you from the—'

'Papa, we are all old maids now,' Charlotte said, serenely. 'There is little that quells our maiden hearts. You have no need to fear for our morals, for you are our compass and, if we follow you, we can never steer wrong.'

'Well, then I steer you away from making such a visit. I do not believe it would do you good even to be heard talking of the matter, never mind visiting the scene of the crime, so to speak. You are right that Lowood's grievances should be addressed, and that I should stand aloof from it, so I may maintain distance. However, a gentleman must be dispatched. Martha, fetch Mr Nicholls for me.'

'No need!' Charlotte called into the hallway, resting her hand on her father's sleeve. 'No need to trouble Martha, Papa. We will walk out anyway on such a fine afternoon, and can tell Mr Nicholls you require him on our way to town.'

'Take your brother with you,' Papa asked her. 'Female company and fresh air would do him the power of good.'

Charlotte had not seen her brother since Emily and Anne told her Mr Nicholls had taken him back to his room yesterday, and she had no idea where or what sort of state he was in now, but she very much doubted it would be one that would crave fresh air. Besides, the last thing her brother needed was to be in the vicinity of another lurid scandal, even if he had not been directly involved, for once.

'Branwell is still rather poorly,' she said tactfully, glancing at Anne. 'But we will call on Mr Nicholls for you, Papa.'

'Yes, send him to me and I shall instruct him. You must stay away from the whole sordid business, are we in agreement?'

'Of course, Papa,' Charlotte nodded, Emily and Anne adding their assent in similar obedient tones.

'Then amuse yourselves with more fitting pastimes while Miss Nussey is with us. Emily, did I not give you an allowance for new material for garments and such? Perhaps Miss Nussey might accompany you to the clothiers and lend you some of her exquisite taste, for she is always so picturesque.'

At least Papa must be feeling a little more himself if he was flirting again, Charlotte observed with a small smile.

'You are too kind, sir,' Ellen fluttered her lashes to please the old gentleman. 'Such an excursion sounds delightful. I must say, I have not heard of this Lowood person, and I think, from what you have said, I would rather not. Charlotte, Emily and Anne – can I not tempt you to spend some time amongst ribbons and lace with me?'

'Of course, dear,' Charlotte said. 'What could be more delightful?'

It was their own brother who answered the door of John Brown's cottage, looking more dead than alive. Charlotte was silently horrified to note that his skin was so pallid, it seemed almost blue, and sunken close enough to the bone for the outline of his skull to be visible. His eyes were shot with blood and a sort of grey sheen had settled over the entirety of him; a layer of grime that was not dirt but airless misery that had become engraved into his skin. His decline in recent months had been sharp. For the first time, Charlotte had begun to have doubts that Branwell would recover himself eventually. For the first time she saw the pallor of death on his hollow cheeks.

'Ah, why are you knocking on your own door?' He peered at them, apparently still not entirely in possession of his wits.

'You have passed the night in John Brown's cottage,' Charlotte told him reproachfully. 'You were too difficult to bring home yesterday at noon. Fortunately, Mr Nicholls took you in.'

'That does make more sense, now that I think about it,' Branwell said, blinking at the unfamiliar lintel he stood under. 'So, I awoke in the curate's bedroom. What did I do?'

'It is probably easier to consider what you have not done,' Emily said, coolly. 'You were too intoxicated to take home yesterday so Mr Nicholls took you in to save Papa the worry. You are also barred from the Bull. Again.'

'Ah,' Branwell said. Noticing Ellen standing just behind his sisters, he stood up a littler straighter, running his fingers through his bright red hair.

'Ellen! What a delight!' he said, as he stepped out into the summer morning.

Ellen curtsied, 'I hope you are well, sir.'

'Well, I live, still,' Branwell said.

'Do you know the whereabouts of Mr Nicholls?' Charlotte asked him, keen to get her friend away from her brother as soon as possible. He still reeked of the pub and she feared that just standing near him would render her unstable.

'The school room, I think,' Branwell said, with a shrug. 'I only stayed one night in his room, Charlotte, we are not married.' He chuckled in amusement, but his sisters and Ellen did not.

'Go home, Branwell,' Charlotte said. 'Wash and change your clothes. Do your best not to cause our father any further pain for today at least.'

''Tis a shame that a woman can never be a parson, Charlotte,' Branwell said, tucking his shirt into his breeches as he stumbled towards the parsonage. 'You do deliver a sermon so very well.'

TEN

Anne

Mr Nicholls had been located, and asked to attend on Papa at his earliest convenience that afternoon. The difficulty they faced was how to carry out their required trip to the workhouse without Papa discovering they had disobeyed his direct instruction *and* with Ellen in tow. The problem quietly dawned on each of them at the exact same moment.

This resulted in an uneasy silence between the sisters and an obliviously cheerful Ellen, commenting on the larks in the sky or the wild flowers in the hedgerows as they made their way into Keighley. The dry, dusty road was hard and rocky beneath the thin soles of their summer boots. At least today there was a slight movement in the air, enough to almost be called a breeze. It meandered its way over the hillsides, giving a little relief from the oppressive heat. Anne searched the blue sky for anything more than the wisp of a cloud in hope of a promise of rain, but there were only the sparrow-hawks hanging in the sky, riding the hot air and poised for the kill. Emily had been right when she said that a storm was building in the air: if one couldn't see it in gathering clouds, one could feel it in the thickening air. The only question was how long it would be before heaven broke this drought with a mighty deluge. Not today, Anne wagered.

Besides, there were other, more pressing matters to be considered. Like what to do with Ellen while they visited the workhouse, and how to discreetly ask those they spoke to at the workhouse not to mention that they had visited to Mr Nicholls. How they were to circumnavigate this difficulty, Anne could not imagine. She only knew that the solution would need to present itself, as they were but yards away from the crux of the matter. Deception did not come easily to Anne, and she looked forward to the day when there would no longer be any need of it.

'Anne and I must go this way,' Emily said, stopping abruptly and demonstrating her planned departure by pointing in the direction she intended to walk, rather like Flossy did when she'd sensed a nesting curlew, but with significantly less grace. 'Good day to you, Charlotte, Ellen.'

'But why?' Ellen asked, stopping Emily in her tracks, which didn't surprise Anne. As plans went, it was far from elegant or subtle. 'Why must you go that way, and we this? What prevents us from going together?'

Emily frowned deeply and, as Anne had no ideas of her own to extricate them from the situation, she remained silent and enjoyed Emily's rather flailing efforts.

'Our errand, that is to say mine and Anne's . . .' Emily looked up at the sky for inspiration. 'Is a dull affair. We simply need to fetch . . . books . . . that we have ordered from the stationer's. So . . . uninteresting.'

Emily faltered and shuffled, and looked at her sisters for help, though none was forthcoming. It was usually Emily who was the best of all of them at falling on a plausible lie at a moment's notice, but today that dubious skill seemed to have deserted her. The reason, of course, was Ellen. Honest, straightforward and decent Ellen, who had always been so kind and loyal to them all, and especially Charlotte. Emily hated to lie to Ellen, and Anne felt exactly the same.

Ellen gazed at Emily, her mild blue, trusting eyes conveying some surprise. 'Books, uninteresting?' Ellen looked from Emily to Charlotte, perplexed. 'We are at leisure, are we not? I should very much like to come to the stationer's and see the books you have ordered.' She smiled sweetly. 'And besides, if memory serves, I rather think the stationer's is this way.'

She pointed in the opposite direction from the one Emily had declared she was travelling – Emily whose hand, until that very moment, had still been wavering in mid-air. Now it flopped heavily to her side.

'Oh no, why on earth would you be interested in dusty old books?' Charlotte said, somewhat hysterically. Ellen's serene smile set just a fraction more firmly in her round face.

'It's just that . . .' Anne began, hoping that some brilliant thought would occur to her before she reached the middle of the sentence. It did not. This was most galling; she had thought herself in possession of a nimble mind, but it was powerless in the face of Ellen's trusting serenity.

'What Emily and Anne are trying to say is that I long to have you to myself, dear,' Charlotte rescued them at last. 'I told them to make an excuse and leave us at the crossroads.'

'What nonsense, really,' Ellen said sweetly, tilting her head to one side as she regarded them all with a faint air of disappointment. 'I must admit to wondering if any of you know me at all. For you certainly must think I was born yesterday. I have eyes in my head, Charlotte dear. And ears either side of it, Emily. And between those organs a functioning brain that has learned almost as much as you, Anne.' She lifted her chin. 'Now what are you really up to, and what has it to do with the depraved Mr Lowood?'

'Corrupting influence? You, Charlotte Brontë, did not wish to be a corrupting influence?' Ellen laughed dryly, some minutes later, after Charlotte had explained the tale of Mr Lowood to her. 'I would have thought better of you, Charlotte, than that you should make the same assumptions of me that you abhor others making of you.' She paced up and down on the path. 'Of course, I know who Abner Lowood is, and all the despicable sins he has committed,' Ellen went on. 'I read the papers. Mama had the maid cut out all the reports from the trial in a bid to protect me. But I have feet and money of my own, and a brain that is not addled yet, despite the family propensity for madness. I do not like to be censured, so I sought the information out myself. Though I am appalled and horrified by the whole business, I have yet to explode in a puddle of feminine incapability.'

Ellen puffed her chest out a little, a flush of indignation spreading across her nose.

'Ellen . . .' Charlotte attempted to catch her friend's arm but it was snatched away before she could. Ellen in a justified rage was really rather impressive, Anne thought guiltily, for she had done exactly as Ellen accused; assumed that the gentle spinster simply would not be able to cope with the truth of the world and all the evil in it.

'You forget, Charlotte,' Ellen upbraided her sister, 'that I have been your confidante, and you mine. I know you don't share all with me that you do with some and that you think me too seemly or polite or conventional, perhaps. But I am not a porcelain doll to be kept in a cabinet, Charlotte. I have my own mind and a resilient soul that has endured and witnessed at least as much unpleasantness as you in my life, if not a little more.'

'Unlikely,' Emily muttered. Anne kicked her under her skirt.

62

'Was it not I who saw my dear sister Sarah waste away to death? Who did my best to care for her needs, and keep her out of the asylum, knowing that – although her person was failing – her mind was as sharp and bright as a butterfly until the last? It was I who sat next to her until every mouthful she took would have choked her. I who could do nothing but watch on while she wasted away and Mama called her passing a blessed relief. A blessed relief! It was no relief to have such a soul taken so soon, when her only fault was to be born misshapen, as if that somehow made her less than the brilliant human she was.'

'Ellen dear, please.' This time Charlotte caught Ellen's hand and rooted her to the spot. 'You are quite correct. We are full of shame. Will you not—?'

'Have I not seen my brothers suffer and go mad?' It seemed that now the gates had been opened to Ellen's disquiet, there would be no stemming the flow until her frustration with them was fully purged. 'George is languishing in an asylum even now, and it was I who had to tell his fiancée that he would never be able to marry her. It is I who tries to mend all the fences that Henry and his wife broke in his parish, though that was all for naught. I who care for Mama, though she has not one jot of love or gratitude for me, only an ever-increasing list of things I cannot do to her liking. It is I who walk into the village and buy my own paper and know all about the Lowood scandal. And I who do my best to be polite, and to ignore the panoply of things that you are patently hiding from me. But no more! I shall not be sent off to look at ribbon and lace while your mind is somewhere else, Charlotte, and your sisters are off doing whatever it is they are doing. I am here with you. I am sister to each of you for as long as I stay, and beyond, at least I thought it so. I demand you treat me as your equal in intellect and fortitude from this moment forth.'

Anne watched Ellen's form seem to shrink a little as the last of her fury was cast out. It seemed that Ellen had been silently carrying that frustration with her for much longer than today, and they three had been the straw that broke the camel's back.

'Darling Ellen,' Anne said, taking Ellen's other hand. 'I beg you to forgive us. You are quite right on every count. We made assumptions, and as detectors we should have remembered that assumptions only ever lead a curious mind astray. We failed you, and ourselves.'

'It was Charlotte's idea not to tell you,' Emily said.

'Emily, cease,' Charlotte said. 'Anne is right. How could we even consider attempting to conduct this detection under Ellen's nose without her realising we were keeping something from her? We must be honest. We must tell her all. Everything, from the very beginning, and let her then decide if she will join us or return to Brookroyd.'

'What in all of creation is a "detection"?' Ellen asked.

'It began with a vanished bride,' Emily said. And for the rest of their walk to the workhouse, they regaled her with a more-or-less unabridged account of their adventures to date.

Emily

At first glance one might have thought one was visiting an elegant manor house, rather than an institution to reform the poor, as the workhouse was cloaked in grandeur.

Once inside the gates, it was possible to see the remains of the former farmhouse and outbuildings, around which the rest of the establishment had been constructed. The farmhouse and adjacent cottage provided a home for the workhouse master, and senior staff, and other existing buildings had been adapted into a variety of uses that ensured the workhouse was not only self-sufficient but profitable.

The courtyard they entered was neat and orderly, with silent women working in the laundry, hanging sheets out on a line that ran from one side of the courtyard to the other. Male inmates loaded sacks of grain, harvested from their own fields, to take to the mill for grinding into flour. To a casual observer it would have looked almost utopian, this haven for the poor. Emily, however, knew of the cruelty and shame that hid behind the whitewashed walls; the ignominy and sacrifice that every person who crossed this threshold endured in order simply to survive. Man and wife parted, mother and child torn asunder.

Emily resisted the idea that poverty was a sin that could be purged from the weak and hungry. Recent years had seen the end of many a skilled profession, as cheaper machines had steadily replaced man. It seemed that the more the world progressed, the more it divided into the ever-increasing privilege of the upper echelons, and the broad expanse of those who would never have enough, no matter how hard they strived.

As Emily recalled it, Mr and Mrs Lowood had been appointed as master and matron of the workhouse from the start, although neither seemed particularly qualified for the job, Mr Lowood having been a druggist, a travelling circus hand and a house painter, before somehow securing himself that position. In addition, another family, the Tollivers, had been taken on to run the farm and orchard. They could not have known when they took the relatively well-paid and secure position what horrors it would lead to.

'The place seems very well kept on the face of it,' Ellen said as she stood in the centre of the courtyard, turning around to observe the hive of industry. 'I see a laundry and a bakehouse.'

'There's farmland, and an orchard too, beyond,' Anne told her, gesturing past the grand central building where the women and men were kept on opposite sides.

'And a mortuary and a graveyard,' Emily added, a little less enthusiastically. 'Where all who die here are buried in unmarked graves. Many who enter those gates in search of relief are never to leave this place again.'

'It was a hopeless and unkind place under Lowood,' Anne said. 'Perhaps now, in the new hands of the Tollivers, it has seen an improvement?'

'Ladies, I am afraid we are not open to tours at present.' A stout, well-kept woman of middle age emerged from the laundry, shielding her eyes against the sun to observe their group. From the dark gown she wore, topped with a pristine white cap and apron, not to mention the chatelaine of keys that hung around her waist, it could be supposed that this was Mrs Tolliver.

'Mrs Tolliver,' Charlotte said with a smile. 'How pleasant to see you again. It is Charlotte Brontë and my sisters.'

'Oh! It is the misses Brontë,' Mrs Tolliver said, somewhat aghast as she hurried to greet them. 'I should have known you from your distinctive appearances if it had not been for the addition of a fourth lady! I beg your forgiveness. We have not had respectable visitors at the workhouse since . . . Well . . .'

Her tone was cheerful and keen to please, but Emily noted how she nervously patted at her hair and smoothed her apron, untying and retying it at the back. Here was a woman who had been set adrift on a sea of scandal and infamy. A woman who was desperate to make a good impression in the hope of getting at least one toe back on the dry land of respectability.

'Have you come to see the poor, Miss Charlotte?' Mrs Tolliver asked her.

'We have not, precisely,' Charlotte said. 'More to visit you, in actual fact, if you will have us, Mrs Tolliver?'

'Me? Oh dear,' Mrs Tolliver went pink. 'Have you come to see how Mr Tolliver and I are faring as Master and Matron? You may tell your papa that we are so grateful he interceded on our behalf when the guardians wanted us removed. Without his standing up for us, we would have been put out on the street.'

'Papa would not have allowed that to happen,' Charlotte said.

'But I am not fit for visitors,' Mrs Tolliver said. 'If you would return perhaps tomorrow, or next week, we could demonstrate to you that we have made many changes for the better.' She gestured at a circle of female inmates darning sheets in silence. 'See how I bring the women out to sit in the sun as they work. I do believe it does them good to see the blue sky, and hear the birds in the trees.' She nodded, adding as an afterthought, 'And more pieces are sewn to boot. You will tell your father that, won't you?'

'My father intends to send a curate to look into the matter, as it happens,' Emily said pleasantly. 'I'm sure he will find the work you are doing favourable.'

It really was very much more difficult to investigate on one's own doorstep. As recognisable as they were, it was impossible to assume identities and invent convincing reasons to be in places they had expressly been told not to go. The only way around the matter was to be perfectly frank.

'To be entirely honest, Mrs Tolliver,' Emily said, 'we have come here without our father's knowledge and would prefer it if you would keep our visit to yourself for the time being, as he told us not to come.'

Mrs Tolliver looked uncertain. 'I should not like to lie, Miss Brontë. We are a decent family, despite our recent . . . troubles. And your papa has been so good to us.'

'No, of course not. I would never ask you to lie,' Emily said, waiting for one of her sisters to step in and speak of 'complicated emotions' and 'delicate difficulties' in that intense confiding way they had, which made strangers tell them their deepest secrets at a moment's notice. Today, however, it appeared that they were content to let her blunder on. 'More just refrain from mentioning that you have seen us. The truth is, we are concerned for you and your daughter, Mrs Tolliver. We came to offer our support and to see if we can't find a way between us towards her rehabilitation.'

Emily was unprepared for the effect her words would have on poor Mrs Tolliver.

'Oh dear,' Mrs Tolliver said, tears rolling down her cheeks in an instant, though she did her best to mop them with her apron. 'I did think that we would never know such kindness ever again.'

'Well,' Emily said, rather embarrassed, 'It is nothing at all, really.'

'Then you will come into our cottage and take tea with me?' Mrs Tolliver smiled and wept in unison. 'Though Rosalyn is not at home. It is impossible for her to be seen in the town at present, and so she often goes to the orchard where she can find a little peace amongst the bees and birdsong, you see. There's an old oak tree there, with a seat, and she likes to sit there and daydream about all the things a pretty young lass like her should have to look . . . to look . . .'

Mrs Tolliver blew her nose on her apron instead of completing the sentence.

'She is not the same as she once was,' Mrs Tolliver said. 'The change in her, since the trial and the revelations, is very marked. Sometimes I fear for her sanity.'

'Perhaps Miss Nussey and I will take tea with you,' Charlotte said kindly. 'You may confide in us. Emily and Anne shall locate Miss Tolliver and see how she is faring. They are a little closer to her in age, and I suspect the last thing she would enjoy is a great gaggle of well-intentioned spinsters descending on her.'

'You are too kind, too kind,' Mrs Tolliver said, anxiously. 'I fear our little cottage is not suitable for company.'

'Mrs Tolliver, I am sure your home is delightful,' Charlotte said. 'Any home to a decent and tidy woman always is.'

'You let me talk on and on to the poor woman,' Emily complained to Anne, as they left Charlotte and Ellen walking towards the Tollivers' cottage, and headed for the orchard.

'There came a point of no return,' Anne said. 'Besides, Charlotte will truly comfort Mrs Tolliver; she must be in powerful need of it. And we will find a way to help Rosalyn.

Perhaps between us we can find the family a new situation far away, where no one will know their name.'

'I am not sure that place exists, within the shores of England, at least,' Emily replied. 'It seems that every lurid detail of the trial was reported in every newspaper across the nation.'

They wove through the lines of white linen, swaying gently in the still, hot air and out to an open stretch of meadow. Butterflies and bees darted and flitted in amongst the long grass and wild flowers as they followed a mown path towards the orchard, comprised of rows of squat and gnarled apple trees that must have been planted decades ago by the folk who used to farm this land. The further they got from the confines of the workhouse, the more Emily felt her body release a long breath, and with it all the disjointed and awkward discomfort of being amongst so much collective unhappiness.

Standing proud at the centre of the fruit trees was the ancient oak that Mrs Tolliver had spoken of. Tall and full canopied, its mossy trunk was so thick in circumference that it must surely have seen the Civil War fought under its boughs, and perhaps even the Wars of the Roses too. A few feet from the base of a tree a fair-haired young woman, who could only be Rosalyn Tolliver, dawdled contentedly as she collected fallen apples in her skirts.

Emily did not recall meeting the nineteen-year-old previously. However, thanks to particularly detailed descriptions of her person in the press, she would have recognised her anywhere. It seemed to thrill reporters that Lowood's young mistress bore such an angelic appearance. They wrote paragraphs devoted to her golden hair and creamy complexion, her soft girlish voice, generous bosom and lithe waist.

Indeed, it had been a particular sport of theirs to contrast her faultless beauty with the base and vile lustful acts of debasement she had confessed to, with a particular kind of judgemental glee.

The moment Rosalyn became aware of their approach, she clasped her skirt to her and froze like a rabbit or a deer, too uncertain to escape the predator.

'Miss Tolliver?' Anne spoke her name gently. 'How do you do?'

The young woman started, so that the apples she had collected tumbled onto the grass. Straightening her shoulders, she began to walk past them as if they did not exist.

'Rosalyn,' Anne tried again. 'It was your mama who told us you were here. We have come to visit with you, we mean you no harm.'

'I do not wish for visitors,' Rosalyn said, without turning to look at them. 'I have said what I was obliged to under oath. I told the truth, and was damned for it. I will never say more and wish to be *left alone*. Do not associate with me, misses. You will regret it.'

'Miss Tolliver, please wait. We mean only to be your friends,' Emily said in the soft soothing voice she reserved for an injured animal. Slowly she approached the young lady, holding her palms before her as she might when approaching a skittish horse. 'We are Anne and Emily Brontë, visiting from the parsonage in Haworth. We have just come to see how you are.'

'How I am?' Rosalyn appeared perplexed by the question as she turned her luminous blue-eyed gaze upon them. 'Why should you wish to know that? It is all done now. I told the truth and I must pay the price for my honesty. I beg you, leave me be.'

71

'It *is* all done with, Rosalyn,' Anne said. 'We only want to offer you our friendship and support.'

'Why?' Rosalyn asked. 'Don't you know I am a pariah? Loathed; an object of disgust to all respectable people?' She clapped her hands together as she gave a hollow laugh. 'You should leave now, if you know what's good for you.'

Emily and Anne exchanged a glance.

'Great harm has been done to you,' Emily said. 'And I won't spin a tale or attempt to deceive you. We are folk who can see the injustice of your suffering. You are unable to leave the grounds of the workhouse, while Abner Lowood walks free.'

Rosalyn's expression altered for a moment at the sound of Lowood's name, but Emily could not be sure if it was fear or longing that flitted across her face.

'We want to bring clarity to this matter once and for all,' Anne said. 'We have been tasked with establishing who did kill Mrs Lowood. And if indeed it was the same person who in turn attempted to kill Mr Lowood.'

'Tasked?' Rosalyn asked. 'Two ladies have been tasked with such a matter?'

'Somewhat unofficially, yes,' Emily said. 'We are rather good at solving mysteries, you see. We are sure that we will be able to help you, and we hope that you might be able to help us. Though the one does not depend on the other.'

'I see,' Rosalyn said, her eyes wandering over their faces in turn, as if she were trying to discern their characters purely from intense observation. It made Emily's skin prickle with intense discomfort. 'Please believe me when I say that I regret I cannot help you. I do not know the answer to either question, you see.'

'You do not know if Lowood killed his wife?' Anne asked, unable to hide her surprise.

'I know that he did not,' Rosalyn said, suddenly fierce with passion. 'I love Abner. And I know he would never have killed Barbara.'

'And yet,' Emily struggled to hide her incredulity, 'he beat her, and tortured her in body and mind. He made her life a living nightmare. There are many witnesses that attested so, including you.'

'Abner never lies,' Rosalyn said. 'And I always speak the truth, believe me. He can be cruel, and violent. But for all that he is an honest man. He saw me for who I truly am and taught me more than I can ever give thanks for. You see, the others, they didn't understand him like I do. They let him smother them. I let him lead me to the truth. He is my dear love, and still, though we are parted, I would call him to me in a heartbeat with my eyes wide open.'

'You still care for him?' Anne asked. 'Even after all that has happened because of him?'

'I do,' Rosalyn said simply. 'And if you cannot accept that, then I am certain you will not be able to help me.'

When Rosalyn lifted her blue eyes to meet Emily's, they were full of such an intensity of longing that it was almost as if she were mesmerised into seeing some other kind of reality, as if the hold Lowood had on those who fell under his spell was immutable.

'I can see that the deeper you consider me, the more you must think me weak-minded and foolish beyond rescue,' Rosalyn continued, turning back towards the gate and home. 'In the night, when the past comes to shake me awake, I think so myself. It is true that I sometimes fancy that perhaps he put a hex on me; a curse I can never escape from, ruined as I am.'

'You are not ruined, Rosalyn.' Anne said. 'Whatever went before, you are not to blame for it. It might take time, perhaps, to fully understand all that you have lived through. To separate yourself from the feelings you have for him. But if you will allow it, we shall do our best to aid you. Wouldn't you like to be free of him, of all of it, for good?'

'Perhaps,' Rosalyn said after a moment of thought. 'And it is true that it would please my mama. I would so very much like to please my mama again. She is so proud of her position here, and I should hate her to have to leave it, even if *she* wishes it. The more I try to do better, the more deeply I hurt her.'

Emily would have thought that Rosalyn was talking only of her mother, if the girl had not continued. 'Every night she returns,' she whispered, as the hum and buzz of wildlife around them suddenly fell away to nothing. Rosalyn put her left hand on Emily's shoulder, as she looked into her eyes. 'Believe me, Miss Brontë. I do wish she would not come back. She truly frightens me so. Much more than Abner ever did.'

'Who comes back?' Emily asked, caught fast in her gaze. 'Who frightens you?'

'Barbara Lowood,' Rosalyn said, biting her lip. 'She digs her way out of her grave every night, and comes to stand under my window. And every time she visits, she takes one step closer to my door.'

CHAPTER

TWELVE

Charlotte

'You chose not to take the master's house when it became available?' Charlotte asked as Mrs Tolliver set down a small wooden tray carrying a simple white teapot and three china cups and saucers. Aunt Branwell had taught her always to judge the character of a person, at least in part, by their neatness and cleanliness. Mrs Tolliver stood up well to this kind of scrutiny in both her home and appearance. Her collars and apron were starched a pristine white and her home, though a small cottage consisting of two rooms upstairs and two down, had been recently swept and polished until it glowed with pride.

Charlotte knew better than many that outward appearances didn't always reflect the rotten secrets that could hide within a person. Yet, there was nothing about Mrs Tolliver, whose hands trembled as she poured tea for Ellen and Charlotte, that would suggest she would have raised a daughter prone to depravity. That such unspeakable scandal had torn into her neat, ordered life was very difficult to understand.

'We did not,' Mrs Tolliver responded, her expression telling Charlotte the very thought disgusted her. 'He was still there, after the trial. Took a full week for them to get rid of him, and then he reckoned he'd been poisoned, and hung on another week until he could walk again. All that time trying to persuade the guardians that he should be kept on!

I cannot tell you the relief I felt when he finally went out of those gates. Where he is now, I do not know. I do not care to know, just as long as it is far from my Rosalyn.'

The poor lady shuffled uncomfortably in her seat, as if making a concerted effort was required to keep her composure. 'Mr Tolliver wanted us to leave all together, after the . . . proceedings. And perhaps we should have.' She shook her head, considering the prospect. 'But what did we do wrong, Miss Brontë? Miss Nussey? I think of it again and again. What did we do wrong? We are good people, God-fearing people. We raised our Rosalyn with high hopes. A girl as pretty and amenable as her, we thought she'd make a good match, and she would have, if he hadn't . . . We did nothing wrong. Why should we have to move on?' Mrs Tolliver stopped abruptly to stifle a choke of misery.

'We quite understand,' Charlotte nodded, taking a sip of her tea. 'I, for one, applaud you for refusing to be bullied away. If the world was a just place, it would be quite right to stand your ground.' Mrs Tolliver nodded emphatically. 'But I wonder if it might be easier for you all somewhere where people don't know your faces?'

'Perhaps,' Mrs Tolliver conceded. 'We do good work here, though, Miss Brontë. We are fair and not cruel. We make a profit for the parish and when we can get people back on their feet, we do it. If we were to start again, there'd be no cottage, no home for my Rosalyn.' Tears sprang into her eyes. Ellen reached across the small table and patted the other woman's hand. 'You do right to stay here, and more importantly, people do forget. There will be a time, perhaps sooner than you think, when all that has passed will not matter any more – to you or Rosalyn.'

'Do you really think so?' Mrs Tolliver asked, and Charlotte marvelled at how Ellen was able to pour her particular kind of soothing balm onto Mrs Tolliver's troubled soul.

'I do,' Ellen said. 'Before you know it, there will be some other poor unfortunate who has become the talk of the county. Gossip is a fickle thing.'

'And, if it is any consolation, Lowood's life is entirely miserable despite his acquittal,' Charlotte continued, gauging that now was the moment to ask the really pertinent question. 'Do you believe he poisoned his wife, Mrs Tolliver?'

'No doubt in my mind,' she replied so promptly that Charlotte must have looked a little sceptical.

'I know what you are thinking, that after what he did to Rosalyn I am bound to think him guilty of every crime, not just the ones he admitted to. And I am. But I saw with my own eyes what he did to Barbara, before I knew anything was amiss with my daughter.' Her face crumpled. 'I saw, but I said nothing because it was no business of mine, and anyway, who would I tell? A man may beat his wife if he wishes, may he not, Miss Nussey? But if I had, if I had told someone – anyone – how very cruel he was to Barbara, unnaturally cruel, I might have saved my Rosalyn from this torment.'

'We are taught not to question, or to interfere,' Ellen said, taking a small pencil and a notebook from her reticule, much to Charlotte's surprise. 'You are a well-bred woman, doing what you thought was best. Who amongst us could say we would have done anything differently? Would you mind terribly if I made a note of anything you say I think might be important, Mrs Tolliver?'

'You will not pass on anything I say?' Mrs Tolliver pressed her.

'I promise you I will not. My notes are only for myself and Miss Brontë. You have my word.'

Charlotte's eyes widened. Ellen was clearly more suited to the business of detection than she had given her credit for.

'The thing is, it was more than just violence though,' Mrs Tolliver went on as Charlotte sensed she would. For here was a woman who longed to tell her story, longed to be heard and, crucially, forgiven. A tumult of emotions was bottled up inside her frame straining for release, and, Charlotte guessed, theirs were the first sympathetic ears she would have encountered since the trial. 'He was cruel, terribly cruel. He made sure she lived almost every moment of her life in fear, so that in the rare moments he was kind to her, she would do anything for him even . . . even accepting my daughter as his mistress. As her mistress too.'

'And how did he go about this tyranny?' Charlotte asked, determined not to look as queasy as she felt about this whole sordid business.

'Barbara was fearful of the dead, you see. The bodies, I should say. We have our fair share of the passed here at the workhouse, less these last few weeks. But it seems that when Barbara was a girl, her ma had told her stories of revenants; that the bodies of those who had been wronged in life would raise themselves up from the grave and seek out revenge on those who had harmed them. Lowood made Barbara bitter and cruel. She wronged many, hurt many in her turn. She'd come from a good home, I think, was raised decent, and there was a time when she might have had a good life. But Lowood got into her like rot into wood. He dragged her down into his hell, like it was his calling. She was exhausted from the constant hate and fear. There'd be days she'd come here just to rest – from herself, even. I'd let her take refuge by my fire, and bring her tea never knowing, never guessing what she was party to . . . well you wouldn't, would you? What good

78

Christian woman ever could imagine such a thing? The short of it is that I felt sorry for her. Especially after the dead house.'

'The dead house?' Ellen asked, turning a page.

'The workhouse mortuary,' Charlotte told her.

'Like I say, she was afraid that some of them she helped drive to the grave would come back to punish her. Well, last winter was a hard one at the workhouse. There were three little girls, sisters, not one of them older than ten. All sick with a fever, but Barbara still sent them out to the field in the cold, even when the ground was too frozen to dig and their little fingers were blue and stiff. Three little sisters, all dead within a week of each other. I helped Barbara lay out their little bodies in the dead house so she wouldn't be alone in there. But before it was done, Rosalyn called me away to attend to another matter. I realise now, Lowood sent her, so that Barbara would be abandoned. As soon as I left, he locked her in there with the three little dead girls.'

Though the room was bright and sunny, and a glass jar of yellow meadow flowers sat in the window, it suddenly felt as cold and dark as the heart of winter. Ellen's complexion had gone quite pallid, Charlotte noted, the roses in her cheeks fading to nothing. Still her pencil diligently moved across the page.

'I went to let her out, but he told me to leave her be. Told me I'd get a thick ear if I didn't do as he commanded. I sent for Mr Tolliver, and they almost came to blows over it. Lowood said she needed a lesson learning and this was how he'd do it. Mr Tolliver said there was nothing he could do about that.'

Mrs Tolliver shuddered, rubbing her forearms as if against the cold.

'I could hear her screams all night as I lay in my bed. Crying and screaming that the little ones were rising up and grabbing at her, set on doing her harm. If she'd died of fright before dawn, I would not have been surprised. Lowood had a bottle of drink, and he just sat there, with his back to the door, and drank and laughed, until he passed out, right there in the yard. Soon as the sun was up, I went down to let her out and I shall never forget the sight I saw, try as I might. It will haunt me till the day I die.'

'What did you see, Mrs Tolliver?' Ellen asked, her tone querulous.

'I don't think I should talk of such things, not to ladies like you.'

'You can be assured that we are both capable of hearing whatever you witnessed,' Charlotte said. For a moment Ellen seemed in two minds, before steeling herself, pencil poised in readiness.

'Barbara was cowering in the corner, hand over her head. She'd torn out great chunks of hair, scalp and all, rent and ripped at the neck of her dress till it'd come half away. And her forearms, legs and face were covered all over in scratches she must have given herself. You couldn't get a sensible word out of her, just gibberish, cries and mutterings, like she'd gone quite mad in those hours in the dead house. But it was worse than that, Miss Brontë.' Mrs Tolliver's expression was very grave. 'She must have moved the children's bodies. In her hysteria, I mean. She must have picked them up and thrown them around, for none were laid out as they had been when I left. Instead, they lay around her, reaching towards her as if she had been their prey.'

Mrs Tolliver drew back as she whispered the word.

'I see.' Charlotte closed her eyes for a moment, in an attempt to rid the image from her mind. She was not successful.

Ellen stood up abruptly.

'Are you quite all right, Ellen?' Charlotte asked her.

'Yes, quite all right,' Ellen said bravely. 'I just need a little air. Good day, Mrs Tolliver. It was such a pleasure to meet you. I will wait for you outside, Charlotte.'

Charlotte could not reproach her friend for her need to be outside in the warm sunshine once again. When they had begun these endeavours, more than two years ago, she had hardly realised what terrors and treachery they would come across. What awful deeds and blackened souls she would come face to face with. Had it altered her? She could only suppose that it had, though she could not quite fathom yet exactly how.

'I should not have spoken,' Mrs Tolliver said unhappily. 'Please forgive me, miss. Only it haunts me, you see. To speak of it out loud – with the sun shining and to a kindly ear – lessens the fear of it a little.'

'It is quite all right, Mrs Tolliver,' Charlotte assured her. 'You have done no harm.'

'Anyway, he did worse to her than that,' Mrs Tolliver said. 'But I will not talk of it. It was all in the papers, if you care to read about such things.'

Charlotte had cared to read of such things or, more accurately, she had not been able to stop herself. At first, she had read the reports furtively, with a sickening feeling in the pit of her stomach, a guilty unease that she was being entertained by such horror. Then one morning she had come across Emily and Anne, reading in the cellar, Anne holding aloft a lamp. The expressions on their faces told Charlotte at once that they were reading about the Lowood case. After that they had read the news together, behind a firmly closed dining-room door.

So, she was aware of the chains that Lowood kept secured to the marriage bed, and how he would chain Mrs Lowood there, often forcing her to crouch or stand for hours until she fainted away. And that he had forced her to allow Rosalyn Tolliver into his marriage bed, and to consent to whatever it was that went on between the three of them. Whatever else Mrs Tolliver might be alluding to did not bear thinking about.

'Anyway, you asked if I thought him guilty of murdering her,' Mrs Tolliver went on, 'and I answered yes. I answered yes because Barbara told me herself that he meant to do her in. She came to me, the week before she died, and told me that if owt happened to her in the days that followed, then it would be him that had done it. Now, he told her every day he'd see her dead one day, but something must have made her certain the day was nigh. Within the week she was dead. It was not a quick death, Miss Brontë. How she suffered, that poor woman. Some might say she deserved it, but I say she was a victim just as much as any of those that she hurt.'

'Quite,' Charlotte said.

'Then he tried to do away with himself, and even the devil didn't want him,' Mrs Tolliver spat.

'You think he took the poison deliberately?' Charlotte asked her. 'Not that he was attacked by an enemy as he claims?'

'I do.' Mrs Tolliver stood up. 'I do not believe he was attacked. I say it was all a charade, an attempt to try and stay on here. And as for what he's done to my Rosalyn's mind . . . Now, if you will excuse me, miss. I do not think I can talk of it a moment more. I must get on.'

That Mrs Tolliver had brought the conversation to such an abrupt end, and whilst they were on the subject of people who might wish Lowood harm, did not escape Charlotte. For who would have a better motive than the parents of Rosalyn Tolliver?

'Of course,' she said, 'thank you for your hospitality, Mrs Tolliver. And your discretion. You may be assured of ours.'

Mrs Tolliver had been about to close the door, when she paused, and spoke once again.

'And thank you, miss, for hearing my woes with such kindness. You have done me the power of good, Miss Brontë.'

'I'm glad for it,' Charlotte said. 'And before long my sisters and I will do our best to help you further.'

'Goodness,' Ellen said, as she waited for Charlotte under the shade of a spindly tree. 'I don't think I was quite as prepared as I thought I was.'

Charlotte raised her hand to Emily and Anne as they approached, young Rosalyn walking beside them for a few steps more before returning to her cottage.

'I almost feel as if he has got me in his grip,' Ellen said. 'As if just saying his name evokes him.'

'This is the trouble with detections,' Charlotte said, as her sisters fell into step with them and they made their exit through the workhouse gates. 'It is rarely the decent and moral people who need such close examination.'

Charlotte took her friend's hand.

'Your inclination to make notes was a very sensible one, one we have not thought of previously.'

'Well, I do so like to have a written record,' Ellen said. 'After all, recollections can fade, and memories misalign. I thought it prudent, though the words I wrote down were so very upsetting.'

'Will you be well, Ellen? Or shall I take you home and read to you until all memories of the last half an hour have faded away like a bad dream gone with the dawn?'

'Certainly not,' Ellen said, stoutly. 'There is no turning back from this, I see that now. We must pursue the truth until the very end, even if the result is that I shall never sleep again.'

Anne

'A revenant.' Anne repeated the word thoughtfully.

'Dear Lord, what have you sent to test me now?' Tabby asked the ceiling as she kindled smoke from a bunch of dried sage and wafted it around the already hot kitchen. 'And me planning a pork roast and all.'

'There were many tales of such horrors, in medieval times,' Emily said, warming to the subject, which she had read about in great detail from some of the histories contained within Ponden Hall library. 'It was often thought that those who had been mistreated in life would return from the grave, in the period between burial and decomposition, to wreak vengeance on those who had harmed them – especially children. No wonder Mrs Lowood feared the dead house so.'

'If she hadn't done wrong, she'd have nowt to fear,' Tabby said primly.

'Also, it was believed that sinners and evil men would be more likely to rise from the grave rather than face the judgement of the Lord. They say that if villagers or townspeople feared such an occurrence, they would disarticulate the limbs and behead the corpse to prevent it wandering about.'

'Heavens,' Ellen muttered, her hand fluttering to her chest, as Charlotte poured her a strong cup of tea.

'Marvellous, isn't it?' Emily said happily. 'History, I mean. That only a little while ago man could believe such outlandish things as walking corpses to be unassailably true. For there is no such thing, is there, Tabby?'

'I wouldn't say no such thing,' Tabby replied, just as Emily must have known she would.

'Shall we retire to the dining room?' Charlotte said, attempting to intervene before Tabby found her stride with her particular brand of tales of terror. 'I have a little writing to do, and perhaps you might find some sewing calming, Ellen?'

'No, Charlotte dear.' Ellen was as firm as the grip she had on her tea. 'You cannot be removed from such a vital conversation, not when you are the lead detector. What would Emily and Anne do without your insight?

'Lead detector?' Emily asked, quizzical.

'Lead indeed,' Anne said quickly, shooting Emily a look to remind her of the publishing contracts that they had but their sister did not. 'Charlotte, do stay. We need to collate all we learned today, to look over Ellen's excellent notes if we are to discern our next direction. And we cannot hope to do so without your guidance.'

'We certainly cannot,' Emily echoed rather flatly.

'Very well.' Charlotte pursed her lips, but a ghost of a smile remained. Perhaps Charlotte preferred it when she and Emily were teasing her to the great care they had taken in her company of late, Anne thought. Of course, Charlotte would find it more of a humiliation to be coddled and protected than anything. But to be put in charge over Emily was something of a tonic, it seemed.

'The trouble would be,' Emily went on, loading her plate with a thick slab of bread oozing with strawberry jam, 'that after a few days a corpse becomes putrid. So, in historic times, when frightened souls dug up a body to check if it was truly at rest, they were often confronted with that they feared the most. The natural state of decomposition would make it seem engorged with fresh blood, as if they actually might still be able to rise from the grave and feed on animals or humans at night as they wandered the earth.' Emily took a great bite of her bread, leaving a good deal of jam dribbling down her chin. 'Ancient peoples who didn't understand scientific reasoning were very disturbed at the thought, leading to the beheadings and stakes driven into the body and such.'

In the firelight of the small kitchen, it wasn't too hard to imagine Emily as her very own Cathy Earnshaw, risen from the grave and come to find her Heathcliff once more. Anne shuddered, preferring to think of her own tale of redemption, persistence, kindness and – after all – love. It must be somewhat exhausting to live in the perpetual storm of Emily Brontë's mind.

'You go on about so-called "science",' Tabby said. 'Like there had never been such a thing as a corpse rising from the grave, when it is well known there is and there has been, and I have heard of it with my very own ears.' She spoke as if hearing a tale told was just as good as seeing a thing happen which, in all honestly, when it came to Tabby and her endless store of spoken histories, it almost always was.

'There was such an occurrence not far from this very spot. There is precedence,' Tabby said very gravely.

'Precedence?' Emily said, with a smile.

'What do you mean, Tabby?' Anne said, perching on a stool.

'I do not mean to tell you of it, 'Tabby lifted her nose in indignation. 'You young ladies will use what I tell you to tease me and then as an excuse to do something terrible, as you always do. Before I know it, you will be off to consort with travelling folk, or witches, or dead folk.'

'We promise we will not tease you,' Anne coaxed her. 'And I can't think of anyone we could consort with in the instance of revenants. Unless of course you know of an expert?'

'I do not,' Tabby said staunchly. 'Not this side of Bradford, in any case.'

'And let us hope they stay the other side,' Ellen said, holding out her cup for more tea.

'Of course, in these modern and enlightened times it seems impossible that anyone even moderately educated could believe in a corpse rising from the grave to walk and talk, but if you know of a case it might give us some insight,' Charlotte coaxed the older woman. 'For it seems that both Rosalyn and Mrs Lowood were and are very afraid of the idea of a revenant. That Rosalyn claims to see Mrs Lowood in the form of one every night. The one thing they had in common was Lowood's influence. It might prove vitally important, Tabby.'

'Very well,' Tabby sighed, 'but you'll give me that chair, Emily. I've been on my feet all day, and every bone is aching.' Emily stood up at once, leaning on the back of the chair, her chin on Tabby's shoulder as she listened.

'There was a fellow in York. His name was William Deers, and he was unfortunate enough to love another man's wife. I don't recall her name, but they say she was uncommonly beautiful. Other men's wives always are, are they not? William could not let go of his desire for her, no matter how he tried. And so, he would creep into the rafters of her house at night and watch her in bed with her husband.'

'He should have had a cold bath instead,' Charlotte said. 'Why is it that the superior sex is unable to master its longing sufficiently? I shall always wonder why God made them with such a weakness.'

'Yes, one really does wonder at the idea that man is made in His image, doesn't one?' Ellen said.

'Perhaps She thought it would it be amusing,' Emily said, quietly.

'Well one night, this Deers fellow fell out of the rafters and landed on his head and died,' Tabby said so matter-of-factly that Anne had to stifle a laugh. 'It was a shock to the poor couple he had been spying on, as you can imagine, to discover what had been going on under their very noses.'

'Over their heads more like,' Emily muttered as she rubbed Tabby's stiff shoulders.

'Still, he paid the price for his lust and was buried in the graveyard on the north side, as is the custom with sinners and a good deal more than he deserved if you ask me.' Tabby shook her head, as if recalling the person in question. 'Drinking, and lewd behaviour. Never went to church. Not unlike your brother.'

'And then?' Anne prompted her before she forgot her subject and turned to her fears for Branwell and What She Thought Should Be Done About Him.

'Well, the night after he was buried, people start to hear dogs barking and howling. When they went to look, there were dozens of the creatures, like they've come from all over. Like they've been summoned. They follow the dogs and what do they see?'

'William risen from the grave,' Anne replied on a single breath.

'With thirty or forty dogs at his command,' Tabby nodded. 'As real as me or you, standing there clear as day. The whole village saw him.'

'Or thought they saw him,' Charlotte said. 'Was it not more likely a drunk, perhaps with a particular fragrance that attracted scavengers? Like Emily going about with bits of mutton in her skirts for Keeper.'

'Are you implying that I smell like a corpse?' Emily asked.

'Wrapped in his shroud he was,' Tabby said, giving Charlotte a look. 'Marked with a cross on the back.'

'Still,' Charlotte reached for Ellen's hand and patted it, 'I'm sure that it was a mistake, or too much wine had been taken. Or grave robbers, I expect.'

'How comforting,' Ellen replied dryly.

'They go to his grave at dawn and it is covered with fresh earth.' Tabby crossed her arms as if resting the prosecution in a court of law.

'I suppose he was only buried the day before,' Anne countered. Now it was her turn for Tabby's look.

'But that is not where it ends,' Tabby told them. 'On the second night he rises up again, goes to the woman's house, breaks down the door as if it were made of straw, and throws himself on top of her!'

'Goodness me,' Charlotte said.

'Try as she might, she could not throw the beast off her. Her husband stuck knives into him, but it had no effect. They say a revenant has the strength of ten men.

'The wife begins to pray and the husband too, and this is the only power they have against the corpse. For it climbs off her, and returns to his grave, covering himself with earth once again.'

'Very tidy of him,' Emily commented, winking at Anne, who had to press her lips together to prevent a giggle escaping.

'On the third night, local folk gathered together, armed themselves with whatever they could and waited at the poor unfortunate couple's home. Sure enough, just after midnight he rose again, went directly to the woman's home and tried to batter his way in. The abomination throws himself at the door, again and again. Imagining it, this sickening thud, bones cracking, softening flesh bruising and tearing.'

'Why don't the people stop him?' Ellen asked, pushing away her own plate of bread and jam.

'Fear,' Tabby said simply. 'Disbelief and fear. They prayed, but it seemed like the monster had become stronger, for prayer moved him no more. Just before the dawn, he ceased his battering. One arm hanging off, head all of askew, and went limping back to his grave. Well, the whole town went after him. As soon as the sun was up, they drove a stake into his chest, and they say he sat up and gasped, bringing forth great gouts of blood. So, they took his head off for good measure, and still more blood, as if his heart had still been pumping or as if he had been feeding on flesh.'

'Putrefaction,' Emily said.

'How horrifying,' Anne gasped. 'When did this happen, Tabby? Perhaps we could interview witnesses?'

'Oh, about three . . .' Tabby mumbled the rest of the sentence.

'I beg your pardon?' Anne prompted.

'Around three hundred years ago,' Tabby said. 'But my ma heard it from hers, and so on and so on, all the way back to the very person who saw it all with their own eyes. So, it is as real as you and me.'

'This does reveal something,' Charlotte said, thoughtfully. 'We know that the local folk have yet to fully embrace the age of enlightenment. Though they pray to a Christian God, they pay their respects to ancient traditions too. The story of William Deers has persisted for so many centuries because

A Gift of Poison

even if a man may not survive beyond the grave, fear certainly can and does.'

'What if Lowood knew the story too?' Emily questioned. 'And he used it to frighten and control Mrs Lowood and Rosalyn. Made them believe it was in his power to raise the dead, or to come after them if they ever betrayed him, somehow?'

'I would say that would be entirely possible,' Charlotte nodded.

'There is another possibility,' Anne said thoughtfully. 'One that could explain everything: the attempt on Lowood's life, Rosalyn's visions of a revenant.'

'What is it, Anne dear?' Charlotte asked her.

'That Barbara Lowood is not dead after all,' Anne said.

FOURTEEN

Charlotte

'I shall write to Mrs Crowe,' Charlotte said after dinner when the four women were seated around the table. Emily and Anne sat heads together, scanning pages of fair copy, though of course neither one mentioned to Ellen that the pages they read came from a novel called *Agnes Grey*, or that her sister Anne hid behind the pen name of Acton Bell. 'If there are any more recent reports of revenants then she will know of them.'

Charlotte had met the prolific and hugely successful novelist, Mrs Catherine Crowe, during the ill-fated London detection. It was one of the rare bright moments of that dreadful week. Mrs Crowe had another interest besides her novels, and had taken up a scientific investigation of 'supernormal' occurrences, as she often referred to them in her letters to Charlotte. She believed that eventually science would demystify every dark corner of the human experience, and that which many considered to be superstition or fantasy should be treated with exactly the same rigour and discipline as the other sciences. Charlotte had to admit that Mrs Crowe made a compelling argument. Her most unconventional assistance when they were in dire need of it had perhaps even saved Emily's life.

'And I propose that we pay a visit to Celia Prescott,' Anne suggested very sensibly, talking of the doctor's wife, who was just as qualified as her husband. They had first met Celia during the Chester Grange detection, and her expertise had proved invaluable on more than one occasion. 'I am certain she will be familiar with the details of the case and will know a good deal about the effects of arsenic poisoning, and the likelihood of a person surviving burial.'

'Excellent idea,' Emily said.

'We shall go in the morning,' Charlotte agreed. 'I believe we have laid good groundwork in solving these mysteries, sisters three,' she nodded at Ellen. 'For the rest of this evening, though, let us indulge in a little quiet repose, for I feel certain our souls and hearts would benefit from a respite from such darkness. Are we agreed?'

All agreed, and set about their usual evening work.

Though she was certain that Ellen indeed needed a break from all the gruesome talk, the truth was that – for perhaps the first time – Charlotte was not as fascinated nor distracted by a detection as she was by her own work. Every minute of every day that she was not at her writing slope, it called to her like a siren, demanding her utter dedication. And if she but could, she would sit at the table all day, every day, never pausing to eat nor sleep, so consumed was she with one particular person named Jane Eyre.

This new work of fiction absorbed her so thoroughly that whenever she set her pen to paper she stepped into another life. One where she walked alongside Jane Eyre at her shoulder, in her mind, their hearts beating in unison. As Jane suffered injustice and indignity, so did Charlotte. As

Jane feared and thrilled, so did Charlotte. As Jane remained unbending and unbreakable in the face of tremendous pressure, so did Charlotte.

It was not that Jane was a version of her, that was not it at all. Jane was her own creation, half changeling, half fairy: a living being that lit the way from word to word. As she committed Jane's story to the page, Charlotte felt as if her mind were on fire, scorching the world with her words. She knew they were good. She knew they were better than anything she had ever written before. Somehow, she knew, even then, that these words would outlive her, would outlive them all. That Jane would light the way from word to word for many more souls yet to come.

Yet when she set her pen down, and came to her senses, shame and doubt washed over her and she became convinced that she was deluding herself. Perhaps it was so. But even if it was, Charlotte determined that she would allow herself to believe for one more day, and one more, and so on, until she confronted evidence to the contrary. A writer could not live any other way.

Yet before she could properly settle at her desk, Keeper lifted his head off his paws and whimpered at the window, before hauling himself to his feet and giving a little yip at closed shutters.

'Come away, Keeper,' Emily said, distracted.

The dog responded with a deeper bark, and a low growl.

'Perhaps he scents a fox or badger,' Ellen said, getting up to go to the window. She opened the shutter half an inch, and then snapped it shut at once, backing away into the table, upsetting Charlotte's ink. Charlotte snatched up her new pages in the nick of time.

'Oh dear!' Ellen said, anxiously, her hand pointing towards the closed shutter. 'I'm rather afraid there is a revenant in the garden.'

Sighing heavily, Charlotte put down her pen once more.

'We told you not to come to the house again,' Charlotte told Lowood after leading him through the gate to the graveyard, where the shadows were a little darker and more dense.

The trouble with summer was that the evenings remained light so very long. If anyone were to pass by now, they would be able quite clearly to see her in conversation with a suspected murderer and known scoundrel. And yet, Charlotte could not bring herself to travel with him any further from the path.

Only once she had let herself quietly out of the front door and gone to meet him, did she realise that he fascinated her as much as he terrified her. It was that air of otherworldliness about him, or rather underworldliness. A sort of diabolical magnetism that once, before his body and visage had been so ravaged by near-death, must have had the power to draw many near to him, just as flame lures a moth to its death. The idea that he had some power that could cause the unwary to see and feel things that did not exist. For all her education, there was a part of Charlotte that believed in other realms, and fairy folk come to steal your soul away. It was this part of her that was striving to make her feet run, even as she composed herself.

'You told me not to draw attention to your business,' Lowood told her. 'And I am not. You could have invited me in and none would have seen me then, but you'd rather risk being seen out here, than to invite me into your parlour.'

Charlotte glanced down the lane, and then up at the blue face of the clock below which a pair of white doves nestled.

The bell ringer would be in the tower already; if he should come out before she had departed, there would be nowhere to hide from his scrutiny. It was true that the possibility of being attacked by Lowood was slightly less awful than the idea of him crossing the threshold of their home, however. She had a notion that once you had invited him in, it would somehow be impossible ever to truly rid the place of his presence again. As it was, timing was everything.

'You have until the clock strikes nine,' she said, showing not one atom of the unease that consumed her. 'Be quick about it.'

'You were at the workhouse this day,' he said. 'What did you discover?'

It was unsettling, though not entirely surprising, that he knew their movements.

'Nothing that we did not already know,' Charlotte lied. 'Nevertheless it is important to get an independent view on all matters before we can proceed.'

'Did you see Rosalyn? Did she speak of me?' Charlotte repressed a shudder at the young woman's name in his mouth.

'I did not,' she said, which was not a lie, as it had been her sisters who had met with the poor young woman.

'You should see her,' Lowood said. 'You should talk to her. She knows all. Rosalyn knows I did not kill Barbara. Ask her.'

'Why?' Charlotte said. 'Her testimony was well documented. Was it false?'

'No, but you will see that she was willing.' He smiled faintly. 'That she came to me of her own free will, they both did. And I had no cause to murder my wife. Why would I, when she made no objection to Rosalyn?'

The bell rang heavy and loud, and Charlotte turned away from him in relief, pausing for a moment to speak over her shoulder.

'If you return to the house, we will cease to aid you,' she instructed him. 'Do not approach us again. When we have discoveries to share with you, we will find you.'

As she turned towards the sanctuary of the house, Charlotte expected him to call after her with threats and dark promises, or even to leap upon her, dragging her down into the earth with him. But when she turned back to where Lowood had been standing moments before, he had vanished into thin air.

'Miss Brontë?' Charlotte started as Mr Nicholls stepped out from where the side of the house had been shrouded in shadow, seemingly checking his pocket watch against the tower clock. How long had he been standing there, Charlotte wondered anxiously? Had he seen her with Lowood?

'It is very late to be out alone,' Mr Nicholls said, concerned. 'Is everything quite well?'

'Mr Nicholls,' Charlotte said, taking a step closer to him, tipping her face up to his. 'Arthur. My sisters told me of the kindness you did for Branwell, for us all yesterday. You have my gratitude. It really is unbearable to see Papa made so unhappy by my brother's dissolution.'

'I hope you know I would do anything to ease your troubles, Miss Brontë,' Arthur said, following her lead. 'Charlotte. You, your family, means a great deal to me. You must know that?'

Charlotte looked up into Arthur's dark, intense eyes. Emily thought him impossibly dull. Anne found him rather grey, almost invisible. Yet there were moments when Charlotte caught glimpses of a soul that was altogether more passionate than the mild-mannered, nervous man they had first welcomed at the parsonage two years ago. Mr Nicholls had grown in stature and in courage in her eyes. That he had developed a fondness for her was becoming ever clearer, though Charlotte could not think why, when either one of her sisters had more beauty or more charm than she. It might take another two years, perhaps even more, but Charlotte was certain that – one day – Arthur would declare himself to her. The question was how best not to break his heart when he did. For though he was kind, and not at all unpleasant to look at, she could not imagine a world where she could love him in return.

'Your service to this family is greatly appreciated,' Charlotte said warmly, hoping that – as he had not brought the subject up – he had seen nothing untoward. 'I really should return home. I came outside hoping for a breath of air, that's all. But I see there is none to be had in this heat.'

'I visited the workhouse this afternoon, as your father asked me,' he said.

'Indeed, and how do things fare at that establishment?' Charlotte asked him.

'Well,' he said, 'the Tollivers have made many improvements, despite the unpleasantness their family has endured of late. I talked to some of the inmates, also.'

'Oh?' Charlotte said, knowing exactly what he was about to say. For they had not troubled any of the poor unfortunate souls who relied on the workhouse to keep silent about their visit.

'Yes, on the whole their lot is improved.' Mr Nicholls searched her face with his dark eyes. 'They told me four ladies had also come to visit that day; one believed them to be the Misses Brontë and a companion. I told them that was, of course, impossible.'

'Quite!' Charlotte said. 'How peculiar.'

Arthur regarded her upturned face for a long moment, during which Charlotte could not tell what he was thinking. He was infuriatingly implacable.

'May I escort you to your door?' he asked. Charlotte took his proffered arm, which was strong beneath his coat sleeves.

'Goodnight, Mr Nicholls,' she said as she came to the door. 'I believe Papa has already taken to his bed so I must be quiet going in.'

'Goodnight, Miss Brontë,' Mr Nicholls said, letting go of her hand with great tenderness. 'I shall hope to see you again on the morrow.'

Just as Charlotte was about to open the door, Mr Nicholls caught her hand in his.

'Charlotte, if I may?'

'Go on,' Charlotte said.

'If you need assistance, whatever the matter might be, I beg you, don't be afraid to come to me. I would always help you, and never betray you.'

So, he had seen her then.

'Sir, I—'

Emily opened the door, releasing Keeper onto the steps, where he leapt around Mr Nicholls's legs, unsure as to whether he should greet his good friend, or give him a nip to see him off.

'Charlotte, there you are,' Emily said. 'I thought you said you would just be a moment.' She regarded Mr Nicholls as if troubled by the sight of him. 'It is not proper for you to be dallying on the doorstep at such an hour with a gentleman, Charlotte. Not even Mr Nicholls.'

'Arthur was seeing me safely home,' Charlotte said as she mounted the last step to safety. She turned back to Mr Nicholls, her eyes meeting his. 'He is our friend, Emily, we can trust that he would never do us harm.'

Charlotte could only hope that she was right.

FIFTEEN

Emily

'What a joy to find a collection of Brontës on my doorstep!' Mrs Celia Prescott proclaimed as she caught sight of the sisters peering round the rather substantial bulk of her housekeeper, Hattie. 'Hattie dear, do stand aside and let the ladies in, it's not as if they are strangers to us!'

'There's a new one, ma'am,' Hattie said, narrowing her eyes at Ellen, who shuffled a little to her left so as to hide behind Emily. 'We don't know this one.'

'We are not acquainted with this lady, is how one might put it, dear,' Celia explained to Hattie. 'Even so, your duties do not require you to bar entry to a lady, especially not when she is accompanied by dear friends of ours.'

This altercation on the doorstep was nothing new to Emily or her sisters. Some years previously, after a rather dangerous entanglement with a certain nefarious gentleman the sisters would later come to know, Dr and Mrs Prescott had taken it upon themselves to give a safe home and decent employment to as many women and girls who had found themselves in straitened circumstances as possible. Women came and went, usually only staying with the Prescotts long enough for them to find their feet and move on to longer-term employment elsewhere. Hattie, who had been the very first woman that

Mrs Prescott had taken in, remained, and though she had what many might consider flaws, she was fiercely loyal and, Emily thought, probably capable of seeing off the most rabid intruder if so minded. Hattie was, Mrs Prescott often liked to say, a work in progress.

'Celia, did you receive the letter we sent yesterday?' Charlotte asked her, taking Celia's hand as the lady led them within. 'I trust we are not inconveniencing you?'

'I was just reading it as Hattie answered the door,' Celia told her. 'The post is not what it was, Charlotte. Only two deliveries a day these last few weeks. In any case, a visit from you can never be an inconvenience.' Her eyes were alight with curiosity. 'You always bring me something fascinating to ponder, and I confess to being in the grip of tedium and quite beside myself with boredom. Your visit is most welcome. And you bring a new fourth?'

Celia smiled warmly at Ellen who dipped a curtsey.

'May I introduce our dear friend, Miss Ellen Nussey.' Charlotte completed the niceties, as they removed their bonnets, grateful for the shade of the cool hallway.

Celia led their party, hot and exhausted from the ten-mile walk, into her darkened parlour, where the air was cool enough for it to feel as if they were stepping into refreshing waters. Charlotte took the seat nearest Celia, with Ellen at her side, Anne the overstuffed chair. Emily, though she liked Celia Prescott very much, retreated into the corner, seating herself on a piano stool, where she might observe without being observed quite so much.

Celia looked as becoming as a summer rose in her pink satin wrapper dress, which was reflected in the glow of her cheeks. Her dark hair was worn loose down her back, and there was a shine to her eyes that spoke of a secret delight.

Emily realised at exactly the same moment as her companions that Celia Prescott was with child.

'My dear,' Charlotte said, taking Celia's hand and kissing it. 'You expect an addition shortly?'

'I do,' Celia beamed. 'I had rather thought that after so many years of marriage such a blessing would never be ours, but at last the time has come.' She glanced up at Hattie, who hovered in the doorway. 'Tea, please Hattie, and some iced water for the ladies?' Celia returned her smile to her guests. 'I am very well, perfectly healthy, and the child seems to thrive and grow as expected. Dr Prescott has employed the finest midwife within a hundred miles to deliver the baby, and we are confident that all will be well.'

The women nodded, smiled and muttered their soft congratulations. Beneath it, all thought there was an undercurrent of unease that walked arm in arm with the joy and hope of pregnancy. Though none acknowledged it, they each knew all too well that the very event that Celia had prayed for could very well be the same that robbed her of the world. Suddenly the formidable lady looked so fragile, so transient, in the watery light of the darkened room that Emily felt a strong urge to protect her from any intrusion on her happiness and stop time itself in order to preserve her forever.

'Perhaps,' she said, 'we should not trouble Celia with our questions on this occasion.'

'I quite agree,' Charlotte said at once with a decisive nod, turning to Ellen. 'Mrs Prescott studied to be a physician, and we have consulted her on her extensive medical knowledge more than once in the past, each time on matters that would not be suitable for a person of a delicate disposition. Now Celia, dear. You are that person. We cannot in all good conscience trouble your tranquillity with talk of the macabre.'

Only Charlotte could take so many words to repeat what she had already said in a handful, Emily thought.

'Nonsense! Of course, you may "trouble me", as you put it!' Celia said, with a dismissive wave of her hand. 'I am still myself, I am still a woman of science, and medical training, and most of all I am so very, very bored. I beg you, you will not frighten me one whit, so proceed.'

'Listen to the ladies, please, ma'am.' Hattie made a rare interjection, as she carefully put down a large tray laden with tea and a jug of water before straightening. 'Dr Prescott said that on no account was you to be upset, or too excited, too hot, or too cold, or hungry or overfed.' Hattie ticked off the list of instructions on her fingers. 'You should not be talking of such particulars in your condition, ma'am. The child will hear and feel everything you hear and feel, and these ladies never speak of anything suitable for a baby.'

'Oh dear,' Anne said. 'I rather fear that is true, Celia.'

'Old wives' tales,' Celia laughed, taking Hattie's hand. 'You are a dear friend to me, Hattie, but I am still a person with a mind of her own and I shall decide for myself what is right and proper, are we in agreement?' Reluctantly Hattie nodded, curtseying before taking her leave. But just before she left the room, her eyes met Emily's, and in them was a warning that should any harm come to Mrs Prescott, it was her and her sisters she would hold accountable.

'I admit I rather thought you had ceased having any use for me,' Celia remarked as she poured the tea. 'As much I enjoy your letters and social visits, it's been almost two years since you last brought me a more challenging matter to mull over. I thought perhaps you'd found another medic to make your enquiries to.'

'We had determined to cease our involvement in such matters,' Anne said. 'Until recent circumstances meant that was no longer possible.' She glanced at Charlotte, whose downcast eyes seemed determined to avoid getting to the point of the matter, and naming the devil.

'We are looking into the murder of Barbara Lowood,' Emily said, with a small shrug. Celia's eyes widened at the name.

'Well, as far as I knew that awful matter was closed when the fiend escaped justice,' Celia said. Despite what she had said just a few minutes ago, Emily noticed how her hands unconsciously rested on her abdomen.

'It was Abner Lowood himself who came to us,' Emily went on as Charlotte coloured and Anne's lashes remained downcast. 'He wishes for his name to be cleared.'

Celia gasped, 'The gall of the man!'

'There is more,' Emily told her, getting up from the piano seat and positioning herself on the arm of Anne's chair. It seemed that her sisters were still too squeamish about their enforced involvement with the beast to yet be able to speak his name aloud. 'Lowood claims an attempt was made on his life, by the same means as his wife was killed, though he survived. He believes that whoever tried to kill him might have been the true murderer of his wife.'

'It's all nonsense, of course! The fantasies of a narcissistic mind,' Celia exclaimed. 'Ladies, why are you countenancing his claims?'

'It's rather delicate,' Charlotte said, finding her voice at last.

'We would really rather have nothing to do with him, of course,' Anne added.

'He is blackmailing us,' Emily said.

'Blackmailing you?' Celia was stunned.

'He found out about our detections, in great detail, from an unknown source,' Emily told her. This time it was her turn to lower her eyes, as the picture of Branwell in close quarters with Lowood came into her mind. 'We don't know who betrayed us, and though we have no shame in the work we have done, we decided that this was not the time to stand against his demands. You will notice Branwell is not with us, his condition deteriorates by the minute. It takes a great toll on our Papa, and we would not give him a further reason to regret his children.'

'Of course,' Celia said, gently. 'I understand. You will, of course, continue to enjoy my utmost discretion.'

'Thank you.' Charlotte was heartfelt. 'He has forced our hand. However, it may be that between us we women are able to discover a truth that implicates the very man who wishes to be cleared.'

'Well, we could not do worse than the gentlemen,' Celia said. 'For myself, I am certain that he used the same tactics to sway the coroner and the judge to change their mind about his guilt.' She sighed. 'Well, the pursuit of justice is a noble one. However, on no account must my husband know that we have discussed the case. He attempted to prevent me from reading any coverage of the trial, and barred me from all the discussions he had with his colleagues. However, Hattie and I have become very adept at listening at doors, have we not, Hattie?' she raised her voice slightly.

'Yes ma'am,' came Hattie's voice from the other side of the door.

'You might as well come in if you are going to eavesdrop,' Celia replied.

Hattie opened the door where she stood like a child about to be scolded, her hands folded together in her apron.

'Very well, Hattie, you may stay, on the understanding that you will keep your counsel.'

Hattie nodded, standing at the door like a sentinel.

'There is more,' Emily went on. 'A strangeness around the whole business that was not mentioned at the trial and yet seems key, somehow.'

'A strangeness?' Celia asked, intrigued.

'In the days before she died, Barbara Lowood claimed she had been molested by revenants. Not ghosts, you understand, but corpses come back to animation. She said she had been attacked by children who died in her care, and there is an eyewitness account that at least supports that the poor souls' remains were interfered with.'

Hattie took a step forward, but though Celia frowned deeply at Emily's words, she held up her hand to stop an intervention. Though every word seemed heavy with dirt and darkness, Emily pressed on.

'You will remember the young lady involved in the case,' Emily said. 'We went to visit Miss Tolliver. She claims that she has seen Mrs Lowood standing below her window on several nights, face turned upward, as if she is waiting for Rosalyn. Each night she takes a step closer to the house.'

'I see,' Celia said, sitting back rather astonished. 'How fascinating. A delusion, perhaps brought about by a broken mind. After all, the girl suffered beyond even her own comprehension by all accounts.'

'We hoped there might be another explanation, though it is rather an extraordinary theory,' Anne said, finding her voice when there was a chance her ideas might be appropriated by Emily.

'Is there any possibility that Barbara Lowood could still be alive? That it might in fact be her appearing under Rosalyn's window? Perhaps even poisoning her husband as a direct act of vengeance when her first plan to have him hang for her murder did not succeed?'

'What a wonderful proposition,' Celia said, thoughtfully. 'A remarkable tale that would make, to be sure, exactly the sort of story you might read in a novel.'

'Too fantastical an idea, then?' Anne questioned.

'There are documented cases of poor unfortunate souls being interred alive,' Celia told her. 'There was a spate of cases in America only a few years ago. One in particular always stuck in my mind. A woman thought to have died from a broken heart after the loss of her infant was buried by her husband. It was only when neighbours also began succumbing to a condition that rendered them utterly unconscious for prolonged periods that the poor man feared the worst and had her coffin opened. Indeed, it appeared that she had scratched her nails bloody in attempting to escape her casket. They say her face was frozen in a scream of perpetual terror.'

'Madam,' Hattie murmured.

'It is terrible, Hattie,' Celia said. 'But no such fate shall befall me, I assure you. Just last year a French physician, Eugène Bouchut, suggested that the new stethoscope technology could be used to determine the absence of a heartbeat in the deceased before interment. Rest assured that Dr Prescott would perform all the necessary checks on me, should the need arise, which it will not.'

There was a moment of silence where everyone present silently added a prayer to Celia's assertion.

'Mrs Lowood was buried in the workhouse graveyard,' Emily went on. 'We have yet to visit the dead house there, but I imagine the coffins are cheaply made, of poor materials. And that the graves are not as well dug as they might be. If there was any possibility of a similar fate befalling her, if she awoke from oblivion, it would not be impossible for a strong and determined individual to fight her way out of the grave. And perhaps from that moment concoct her plan to see her husband pay for all he has done to her.' Emily paused for a moment. 'It must be remarkably freeing, in a way, to leave all the shackles of life behind you. To roam the earth as a ghost, entirely liberated from the dull business of living.'

'It would not have been completely impossible if such a situation had arisen,' Celia said, blinking away Emily's morbid moment. 'However, Mrs Lowood does not live. Some weeks passed after her death, weeks full of rumours and accusations, before the Crown decided to bring a prosecution against Abner Lowood. Her body was exhumed, and a post-mortem conducted. Unless she placed another in her grave to cover her deceit, she is very much late of this world.'

'I see,' Anne said, regretfully.

'The girl's visions will be some kind of hysteria, I expect,' Celia said. 'What that young lady has experienced would be enough to damage any mind. It could be that her guilt about her part in the sordid business manifests in hallucination. It is as yet an unproven thesis, but I have been reading on the science of the brain, and I do give credence to the theory of the duality of the mind, as described by Dr A. L. Wigan. It really is fascinating, the notion of our present functioning mind, that directs us to breathe and speak, and think and feel, but also a second hidden mind that reveals itself when influenced by disease or a distressing event, either direct or sympathetic.'

'So, there can be no doubt as to the cause of Mrs Lowood's death, then?' Emily asked before Charlotte fell onto the subject of phrenology and they were trapped all day listening to invented sciences and improbable theories, none of which were as straightforward as the most likely and obvious explanation, as far as Emily could see. Which was that Rosalyn really had seen the risen corpse of Barbara Lowood, compelled to come from her grave to deliver an omen of doom.

Celia thought for a moment.

'There is no doubt that arsenic was present,' she said. 'The testing for arsenic poisoning is remarkably precise thanks to advances of recent years.'

'So, she was poisoned by someone,' Charlotte mused.

Celia paused for a moment, sucking in her bottom lip, as she gave the matter further consideration.

'Not necessarily,' she said. 'I read the court transcripts, the first autopsy and the second vastly amended version. I am in no doubt over what kind of man Lowood is, and the likelihood that he poisoned his wife, and at least some of his poor children, is not in doubt. However, I would not be honouring my profession if I did not raise the possibility that her poisoning could have been accidental.'

'Accidental?' Anne asked. 'How could that be?'

'Arsenic is all around us, Anne,' Celia told her. 'Since the industrial age began, it has been an increasingly abundant by-product of coal, used in a dozen industries or more. In printmaking, in fabric dying . . . in the medicines that your doctor prescribes to you, and in the preparation and the preservation of the dead. You will find it in my kitchen and, I'm sure, in yours, carefully labelled and kept away from other foods. But not all kitchens are as careful and well-regulated as my Hattie's.' Hattie nodded gravely. 'Contamination occurs often, and regularly. It is possible, I'm afraid to say, that the presence of arsenic in Mrs Lowood's remains does not suggest conclusively that she was murdered. Indeed, the effects of arsenic poisoning are virtually identical to the symptoms of cholera. The presence of the former does not mean she could not have contracted the latter, and that was her true cause of death.' She paused once more. 'In fact, that Lowood himself fell victim to the same poison weeks later, only lends credence to his denial of any guilt. There is reasonable doubt if one does not dwell on the proven monster that he is.'

'Therefore, it is entirely possible—' Charlotte began in dismay.

'That Abner Lowood is innocent after all,' Emily finished.

Anne

'I suppose one should not be disappointed that a person was not buried alive, purposefully or otherwise,' Anne said, a little gloomily, 'but I did so warm to my idea that the poor unfortunate Mrs Lowood was the secret mastermind of a diabolical plot.'

Anne smiled as Flossy rushed out of the parsonage to greet her mistress home, printing her paw on her already dusty skirts.

'There now, Flossy. Isn't it wonderful how a dog will always urge one to rejoice?' Anne said, scratching the spaniel under her ear so that her tail thumped happily.

'Not my dog, it seems,' Emily said, looking around for Keeper, her hands on her hips. 'Either Tabby is preparing mutton or he is up to no good again.'

'I fear you have caught the sun, Emily,' Charlotte admonished her sister as they stepped into the hallway. 'This is what happens when you refuse to wear a bonnet at midday! You will be as brown as a nut.'

'Good,' Emily said. 'I prefer it; it shows I have walked under the sun and greeted the skies with my whole heart, instead of paling into insignificance in dreary parlours.'

'Looking after one's complexion has precisely no relation to how dreary or insignificant one is,' Charlotte said, stoutly and rather offended at the implication.

'No indeed,' Ellen agreed. 'I think the best thing a woman can do for her visage as she ages is to wear a bonnet and eat a little cake to plumpen her cheeks.'

'I do agree with the cake part of your advice, Ellen,' Emily said, continuing, 'I should have liked a fiendishly clever revenge plot too, Anne. I suppose the trouble is that, as imaginative souls, we are somewhat prone to conjuring up a story that would be far more satisfying than reality. The worst of it, though, is the notion that Lowood might actually be what he says he is: an innocent man. It is hard to reconcile such a notion with how the mere sight of him makes me feel.'

'He may not be guilty of his wife's murder,' Anne said. 'But that man is no innocent. However Mrs Lowood died, he still beat her and seduced poor Miss Tolliver out of her right mind. One less charge on his soul makes very little difference.'

'You are back, I see,' Tabby said, emerging from the kitchen with a devoted Keeper at her side, who was gazing adoringly up at the keeper of the buns. 'Your meal is almost ready.'

'Tabby, you are too kind to us,' Charlotte said, perhaps detecting the same stiffness in their housekeeper as Anne. 'What should we do without you?'

'Go off and about pursuing all manner of dreadful things, I shouldn't wonder,' Tabby said, adding with a pointed look at Charlotte. 'I spent a very enlightening ten minutes with Mr Nicholls today.'

'And you an unmarried woman,' Emily joked, receiving a cuff around the back of her head for her trouble. What was that about, Anne wondered.

'Now, wash your hands and faces, make yourselves at least look something like ladies, and go and take a seat at the table,' Tabby told them. 'Before I send you all to bed with no supper.'

Anne was taken aback to see that the dining room was already occupied. Branwell lay curled up on the sofa, his legs drawn up under his chin, muttering fitfully in his sleep.

'Oh dear,' Ellen said as she gazed upon him. 'I see he is still not yet himself. Perhaps we should eat in the kitchen?'

'No, we shall not,' Emily said, firmly kneeling on the floor before her brother and peering into his waxy face. 'Branwell is in dire need of a decent meal. I can't remember the last time I witnessed him ingest anything solid.'

Ellen absented herself with an excuse of helping Tabby, as Anne took a seat on the edge of the sofa and gently shook her brother's narrow shoulder.

How ill Branwell looked, and how very small. He had always been slight in stature, but his force of personality was such that he filled every room he entered. Now he seemed less than a child, frail and translucent as a shell.

'Brother?' Anne said softly. 'Will you take a meal with us?'

She was obliged to repeat herself more than once.

His expression tightened, before his blueish eyelids fluttered open and focused on her as he groped around his person for his spectacles.

'Anne,' he blinked. 'Emily. What time is it? I recall sitting down for a moment to rest when I came home this morning . . .'

'It's time for supper,' Anne said. 'You were not home at all last night?'

'It was a warm night,' Branwell said. 'The stars so bright, I thought I'd stay out to admire God's work. I'm afraid I rather forgot to come home at all.'

'Branwell, this is not good for you,' Charlotte said unhappily, taking a seat at the table. 'To lead such a disorganised life. You must find purpose and routine again, before you are lost to your habits, never to return.'

'I have routine and purpose,' Branwell said, sitting up, rubbing his hands roughly over his skin so that a little blood rose to its surface. 'My purpose is to get routinely drunk.'

'You are not amusing,' Emily said, her face set like stone. 'Do you care nothing for anyone but yourself?'

'It is that I care too much for others that has killed me,' Branwell said. 'Love dealt the mortal blow and I am fated to wait until the infection of caring finally carries me away.'

'You speak of dreams and fantasy. I talk of the flesh-and-blood people who stand by you in your stupor. Did you truly think we would not discover what you had done?'

'What has he done now?' Charlotte asked, alarmed.

'Emily,' Anne cautioned her sister, hoping it was enough to remind her that they didn't want to trouble Charlotte with their suspicions. Emily would have been silently nursing her resentment at seeing Branwell in close conversation with Lowood, and the likelihood that it was he who had put them at Lowood's mercy. Now was not the time to vent those feelings, however. Charlotte, at least, could be spared the betrayal.

'What have I done?' Branwell asked, seemingly genuinely perplexed. 'I confess there are large swathes of yesterday, and the days before, that I do not recall precisely at all. If I have offended you, Emily, or anyone, I am sorry. I seek to inhabit a haven of oblivion, and as a necessity this means I am not always in possession of all my wits. Or indeed any of them.'

'You see he does not know what he has done,' Anne told Emily, hastily. 'Let it be, it's of no import now.'

Emily scowled deeply, but withdrew from her brother to take a seat next to Charlotte.

'What has he done?' Charlotte asked once more, her alarm growing. 'Branwell, have you incurred yet more debt? You know that the woman has cut you off, and Papa cannot afford to continually meet your costs. Have you no soul?'

'I do have a soul,' Branwell said wearily. 'A heart and a soul, each one in torment for every moment of every waking hour.' He looked around him. 'I have been conscious but a few minutes and already I wish with all my heart that I was not.'

'Don't think of anything,' Anne said, taking his hand, which seemed as cold as ice, even on this warm day. 'Think only of sitting at the table, and a nourishing repast, with those who love you.'

'Though it should be noted that love is not a bottomless well,' Emily muttered, her arms crossed. 'It can, and does, run dry.'

Anne led Branwell to his usual chair, Emily pulled it out for him, and he sat just as Martha, Tabby and Ellen entered with a veritable feast of pie, buttered potatoes, summer vegetables, and a seed cake for dessert.

'Your father is taking his dinner in his study,' Tabby told them, looking askance at their brother. 'It's probably just as well.'

'Here,' Anne cut a piece of pie for Branwell, and then once it was on his plate began to cut it into smaller pieces. Emily added a spoonful of potatoes, and Ellen filled his glass with water.

'How are you faring, Branwell?' Ellen asked him, bringing a fresh air of cheerfulness. 'It has been an age since we have been able to truly talk to one another.'

Branwell took the forkful that Anne had raised to his mouth out of her hand, and took a bite from it.

'Well, I am not two or ninety-two years old, and I can still feed myself, that much I know, Ellen. And you, tell me how you are faring?'

'I have been extremely busy,' Ellen said. 'It seems to be a spinster sister's lot to travel between her siblings to put their affairs in order, before beginning the whole process anew. It is fortunate I have not married; I do not know how they would manage without me.'

'You might yet marry,' Branwell said, a flicker of his old mischief in his eyes. 'For you are awfully comely, and utterly charming. Perhaps you would marry me?'

'Perhaps I would if you brushed your hair and tucked your shirt in,' Ellen said lightly.

At least Branwell was eating, Anne thought she saw him rally for Ellen's sake. Perhaps a fresh face at the parsonage was exactly what her brother needed to help him see himself afresh once more. He might yet find a shred of pride in amongst the tatters of his remains and begin to make himself anew. Anne needed to believe there was another chance for Branwell. That she was not witnessing the end of her brother. Each day she sought any shred of hope she could find and wove it into a rich tapestry full of hope and promise.

Tabby entered the room again, coughing and waggling her eyebrows at Anne.

'What is it, Tabby?' Anne asked her.

Tabby pulled a face and jerked her head back, as if indicating there was someone she would rather not mention in present company waiting to be seen. Surely not Lowood again?

'I'll see what the matter is,' Charlotte began, but it was Anne who rose from the table first.

'I'll go,' she said. 'I'll be but a moment.'

Rosalyn Tolliver was standing in the kitchen, looking anxiously at the hems of her skirt, while Martha made it her business to sweep around her, gradually backing the poor unfortunate woman further against the sharp edges of the table.

'This one's here,' Tabby told her, with a disdainful sniff, making it no secret what she thought of Rosalyn, which was that she was no better than she should be.

'Miss Tolliver,' Anne said, glowering at Tabby and Martha, 'thank you so much for coming to call on us. We are just taking supper. Would you do us the honour of joining us?'

'Oh no, I couldn't, miss,' Rosalyn said, as Martha jabbed the broom at her feet, making her scuttle backwards into the sink. 'It wouldn't be right.'

'Nonsense,' Anne said. 'Nothing would please me more.'

Everyone but Branwell was surprised to see who the uninvited guest was. Her brother, it seemed, was the last person on earth not to know who Rosalyn Tolliver was.

'Why this table grows lovelier by the moment,' he said as Anne pulled a chair out for Rosalyn, and returned to her own. Seeing how the young lady was all but paralysed with anxiety, Charlotte took a plate and piled it high with a selection of bites for Rosalyn, while Emily poured her a glass of water. Not one of them would have her feel like an outcast at their table.

'I did not mean to cause such inconvenience,' Rosalyn said, her eyes travelling around the table and back towards the door again. 'It was only that you said I could call, and to tell you at once if I remembered anything that could be of help. My pa did not want me to come – he insisted on bringing me himself and is in the lane waiting – but I had to, Misses Brontë. In case what I recalled was of any importance.' She glanced at Branwell, her cheeks reddening. 'But I don't rightly know if I should speak of it now.'

This poor girl, who had stood before a court packed full of men and reporters and, under oath, had been obliged to tell her intimate dealings with Lowood, was still just a girl, still caught firmly in the web of all that her mother told her made a young lady respectable. Still trying to please the world, when the world had already deemed her ruined.

'You need not be shy of me, my lady, I am but a husk of a gentleman, more of a ghost in reality,' Branwell told her with a flourish of misery. 'As for my sisters, they may look like fierce old schoolma'ams, but they are kind of heart.' He paused for a moment. 'Well, Anne is.'

'Rosalyn, you are amongst friends,' Charlotte said, ignoring Branwell. 'You need not fear my brother, for anything you say today it is likely he will have forgotten by tomorrow. Shall I send Martha to fetch your papa in?'

'Pa won't come in, miss,' Rosalyn said. 'He was certain that you would not admit me. As for him, he says that – on account of what I've done – he can never look God in the eye again. He says he'd rather see me dead than bring him one more moment of shame.'

'This may be a parsonage, but God does not live here,' Emily said. 'And as for our brother, as you can see, he is in a slough of despond. It's terribly dull.'

'Abner got like that oftentimes,' Rosalyn said softly. 'When the black dog got hold of him. Restless and full of rage, needing something to take away all the pain.'

'I know that dog well, madam,' Branwell sighed. 'It gnaws at the flesh of a man, driving him to madness.'

'You would do better not to compare yourself to . . .' Charlotte stopped abruptly.

'To whom?' Branwell asked her.

'Abner Lowood,' Emily told him.

'You knew the poisoner?' Branwell asked Rosalyn, suddenly alert with interest. 'How fascinating. But tell me: why would such a pretty young thing as you have anything to do with that infamous gentleman?'

Rosalyn bent her head low, her hand trembling in her lap.

'Oh,' Branwell said slowly, as he realised who was seated at the table. 'I see.'

Shame had stalked her every step since the trial, Anne realised. Every breath she took, every step, every action was tainted now by what she had done. By what she had confessed to the court in the name of truth. But Anne was certain that Rosalyn hadn't realised the trap that she had been led into. Like the children of Hamlyn charmed by the piper, she had been unaware that Lowood was leading her far from the path of righteousness. Rosalyn had been fooled, tricked and conned into her involvement with Lowood. And now she would forever have to own his vile actions as her own. It hardly seemed just.

'I shall depart,' Rosalyn said. She began to rise but Anne's hand stayed her.

'Don't feel any discomfort because of my brother's words,' Anne said. 'He himself had an involvement with a married woman. One that has cost our family dear in both reputation and coin, and him his dignity and sanity. No one at the table is better than you, Rosalyn, least of all him. We are all equal in the eyes of the Lord; he will redeem us all in the final hour.'

Unshed tears intensified the blue of Rosalyn's eyes as she looked up at Anne.

'Thank you for your kindness, miss,' she all but whispered. 'There aren't many that would speak my name, let alone invite me to sit at the table with them.'

'You will find safe haven here,' Anne promised her, encouraging her to eat. 'Now tell me, are you sleeping well or are your nights still disturbed?'

'I sleep passably well, miss. Until she comes calling,' Rosalyn told her.

'You have seen her again?' Anne asked, doing her best to keep her voice light. It was likely that Celia was correct, and that the visions Rosalyn had each night were some kind of reflection of what she had endured, a kind of delirium. And yet Anne could not help but feel there was more to it than that. That the appearance of someone or something pretending to be Mrs Lowood would unlock the whole sordid tale.

'Yes, miss. Always at the witching hour.'

'Three in the morning,' Emily clarified.

'And you are sure you are not dreaming?' Anne asked her. 'Sometimes a dream can feel very real.'

'I'm not dreaming, miss,' Rosalyn said. 'If I was dreaming, I could wake myself up and be safe in my bed. I awake, and climb out of bed, as if I must. As if I am being called to the window. And though I try with all my might not to go, I cannot resist the urge. She is always there in the courtyard, looking up at me. Her clothes ragged and filthy, her skin shrunken and grey. Each night she takes one step closer to the house, and I fear the hour when . . .' Rosalyn bit her lip hard.

'When she reaches your door,' Emily said, glancing at Anne. They had both heard similar tales before; the revenant as an omen, forewarning of a death. If the legends were true, and Tabby swore they were, then it would be Rosalyn herself whose fate hung in the balance.

'Do you know, miss,' Rosalyn asked Anne, 'what will become of me?'

'I do not,' Anne said. 'But we are going to help you, Rosalyn. I promise, in this matter and all else.'

'And Mr Lowood?' Rosalyn asked, hopefully. 'Will you help him too, as you promised?'

Even now, despite everything she had lost because of him, it seemed that Rosalyn was still in Lowood's thrall. As repellent and disgusting as she found Lowood, he held an undeniable attraction for some; Anne knew it was imperative not to frighten or alienate Rosalyn now.

'Just as we've promised,' she said with a smile.

'Only I thought of a name that I believe might be important,' Rosalyn said, putting her hand on Anne's, locking eyes with her. 'Mrs Lowood told it to me once, when she was lamenting her lot as a wife. She told me that once she had been betrothed to another. One Peter Wilson. And that she wished with all her heart that she'd married him and not Mr Lowood, and then her life would have been peaceful and content. But you never can go back, can you?'

'Do you know where this Peter Wilson is now?' Anne asked.

Rosalyn shook her head.

'I believe he worked in service, not far from Keighley, but I don't know exactly where,' Rosalyn said. 'I suppose she thought he might still be there.'

'We shall seek him out,' Anne assured her. 'Thank you for coming to speak to us, Rosalyn. You have given us valuable intelligence.'

'I will take my leave,' Rosalyn said. 'I mustn't keep my pa waiting any longer. Thank you for the refreshments.'

'Then let me see you out,' Anne said, all too aware of the deafening silence that swelled in their wake. A silence filled with the death of promise.

SEVENTEEN

Emily

Emily rose an hour before dawn, dressing silently before she crept downstairs in her stockinged feet, with a docile Keeper at her hip. This was not the first of their solitary expeditions, and he had learned through some trial and a good deal of error to keep his excitement at the promise of open moors and rabbits to himself, at least until they were out of earshot.

It felt to Emily as if she had lain awake, fighting against the weight of the heavy air and even the light pressure of her sheet, waiting for the very first moment when she might reasonably get up. Sleep came and went in fevered fits and starts, bringing with it fractured dreams of dark places and hard-forgotten faces, until she had been obliged to abandon it entirely or drive herself mad in search of rest. Now all she wanted was to be alone and in the cool, quiet air of the last minutes of night.

Solitude had been a near impossible treasure of late. The absence of any proper length of time to herself, outside of her tiny room, had begun to weigh as heavily on her shoulders as the weather. It had begun to feel that with every step she took she sank a little further into the unending weariness of always being polite, always being interested, always being alive. Until now, that was, or at least so she thought.

The dining-room door was open a crack, just enough for her to see Charlotte sitting at the table in her nightgown, lit by a single candle burned down almost to the wick. She was bent closely over her writing slope, nose hovering just above the paper, writing furiously. Every few seconds, she paused only to dip her nib in the ink, and then on she went. Emily thought for a moment about making herself known, but she knew exactly what it felt like to be in such a moment of creation that nothing around you seemed real.

She left without making a sound.

As Emily and Keeper hurried up and out of the village, onto the moors behind the parsonage, the sky above their heads turned from inky blue to pale violet, as yet unobliterated by clouds. The mist that had lain dormant in the hedgerows and heather slowly began to rise, like a mass of ghosts emerging into thin air. Even this early, the promise of heat could be felt in the air, like a memory. Still, nothing could prevent woman and dog breaking into a trot as they approached Waters Meet, Emily rolling down her stockings and tucking them into her pockets as she walked ankle-deep into the freezing, fast-running waters. They stayed there for a moment, Keeper dipping his head into the stream and lapping at it, and Emily marvelling at how the running water could transform the dullest of stones into shimmering jewels. Above them, the valley climbed towards the heavens, a sparrowhawk wheeling in the deepening day.

Emily shivered with delight as she climbed out of the icy beck, and they continued their journey ever-ascending. Each bracken curl they passed was bejewelled with rainbowed droplets. The ground underfoot was pliant and warm. As Emily pressed her toes into the soft earth, she felt its gentle embrace in return. Here she was not a sister, not a poet nor an authoress. Here she was nothing, as light and free as the air.

Finally, they reached the goal that Emily had had in mind since she'd left her bed two hours earlier: Ponden Kirk, the great shelf-like rock that jutted out over the valley below; where a person could feel about as close to God as any mortal could. It was only then, with the warmth of the rock beneath her bare feet and her arms flung wide to embrace the valley, that Emily felt at peace. For a moment or two she leaned into the drop, letting the wind buffer her against falling, until Keeper's nervous whimper told her to take a step backwards. To cling onto the earth because God had not granted her wings.

Everything had altered since they had concluded the London investigation last summer. The world had changed around her, and she within it. Half-baked hopes and dreams, which had always seemed more Charlotte's than hers, had become reality the moment *Wuthering Heights* had been accepted for publication and had become a real, living thing, untethered from its mistress, soon to be free of her control entirely. Emily was in no doubt that her novel was perfect. It had arrived on the page exactly as she had imagined it, a noisy cacophony of torment, darkness and rage. What would the world think of it, though? And what the world would think of her – even cloaked, as she was, behind the name Ellis Bell – was another matter.

The truth was that she could live the rest of her days quite happily if no one read a word of her work, or formed any opinion about her at all. That was the difference between Emily and her sisters. For Emily the act of creation was enough. For Anne her writing had to have a purpose, an ambition for good that was larger than itself. And for Charlotte it had to conclude in recognition and admiration to mean anything of worth at all.

It was not just the prospect of having her work published that had changed Emily, though. Last summer she had gone to London full of hubris, feeling invincible. Scornful of her brother's weaknesses and Charlotte's doomed attachments. Certain that her own cleverness would be a more than proficient weapon against the darkness that infested the city streets. Her longing for adventure and never-sated curiosity had made her fearless in the face of terror. What she had not accounted for – what she could not have prepared herself for – was the consequence of letting another get close enough to her so that now they were gone it took every little bit of her strength to prevent her from mourning them. Theirs was a name that would never be spoken again, not even in the silence of her own mind. She would refuse the thought of it before it had even begun to form. Even so it was always with her, in the breath of the wind against her cheek and whispering grass under her fingertips. It was here where the sky was within touching distance and thin air was only one footstep away.

So, Emily had risen before the dawn, and all but run through the rising heat and lowering bank of suffocating cloud to be here to meet this very moment, in this very place. Where she could, if not remember exactly, allow herself to feel all the ways her soul was scarred, just for one beat of her heart.

The church bell struck seven as they wound their way back down to the bottom end of the village, where Emily picked her way through the fields that ran along the back of Main

Street, in search of Benjamin Cross, the groomsman at the Fleece coaching inn. As she expected, Benjamin was in the stables giving the horses their morning feed. From what she knew of him, which was little, he seemed like a gentle young man who took good care of his charges. Though Emily scarcely had reason to converse with him outside of church, she had noticed his determined kindness towards all creatures. They would never encounter cruelty under his watch.

'Good morning, Benjamin Cross.' She announced herself in the doorway of the stable in order not to startle him, but somehow it seemed to have the opposite effect. Emily had forgotten until that moment that she must look half savage, with her hair tangled and loose, her skirts still damp and – worst of all – her feet still bare. Well, she couldn't very well put her stockings on now, so she supposed the thing to do was to behave as if she were perfectly seemly and hope Benjamin Cross would soon forget that he was looking at a hoyden.

'Um, good morning, Miss Brontë,' Benjamin said, his eyes dropping to the ground where, upon seeing her toes, they turned back towards the horse and stayed there. 'Are you well, miss?'

'I am quite well, thank you,' Emily said, curling one foot over the other, and nudging them under Keeper's behind. 'I came to ask for your assistance, if you would be so willing?'

'I'd be glad to help you, if I'm able, miss,' Benjamin replied a little fearfully, Emily thought.

'You may have noticed that we have a guest staying with us at the parsonage at the moment, and she is in need of a good, reliable groom at her mother's residence at Brookroyd. I believe that the gentlemen of your profession all know of one another, and I wondered if you might have a name you could recommend?'

If Benjamin Cross thought it odd that Emily had come to him with such a request at that hour of the morning, he was at pains not to show it. Emily was immensely grateful.

'I know it cannot be me, Miss Emily,' Benjamin said. 'I'm to be married this September and we have a cottage already set.'

'Of course, of course you are.' Emily had entirely forgotten. 'Which is why I knew better than to ask you directly, though of course you would have been the first choice. We have had the name Peter Wilson mentioned to us, and I wonder if you know his name at all?'

'Peter Wilson out at Harrowings?' Benjamin frowned. 'No, miss, no – I don't like to talk out of turn but it wouldn't be right for me to recommend his name to you.'

'Really?' Emily asked. 'May I enquire as to why?'

'I shouldn't say, miss . . .' Benjamin hesitated, his colour deepening.

'I completely understand,' Emily said. 'No need to say. I will take you at your word. Thank you for your help. I wish you a good day.'

'What I will say,' Benjamin blurted, just as Emily was about to leave, 'is that Wilson is good to his animals, that much is true. But he's afflicted by the same poison as . . . well, as Master Branwell, miss. If it weren't for his father having worked so long for the family, I am sure he would have been let go by now.'

'I see,' Emily said, reaching down to rest her hand on Keeper's head. 'I shall strike his name from the list at once.'

Of course, in reality Emily had discovered all she needed to know and more. The location of this Peter Wilson, and what kind of man he was. Could a man who cared for his animals and his wine equally be minded to murder? It did not seem out of the question.

On her way back home, Emily paused in the cavernous branches of the great graveyard yew to discreetly reinstate her stockings and tidy her hair into a knot secured with a pencil. Which was just as well, as the moment she emerged from the shelter of the tree she saw that there was yet another visitor arriving, and at such an early hour too. A carriage had stopped on the lane outside the schoolhouse, and a lady was being handed down. Under normal circumstances the sight of another guest would make her run in the opposite direction, but not on this occasion. As soon as Emily realised who the visitor was, she broke into a run, smiling broadly from ear to ear. This visitor was sure to bring interest and vitality.

For Mrs Catherine Crowe, novelist, playwright and ghost hunter, had come to call at the parsonage.

Charlotte

'Why, Mrs Crowe, what an unexpected pleasure!' Charlotte exclaimed as she rushed to greet her friend, profoundly relieved that she had made herself break away from her work when she had, in order to wash and dress for breakfast. A little extra trouble had been taken that morning; she had chosen a neat grey silk dress for the day ahead, anticipating making excursions and enquiries with Ellen and her sisters, and always keenly aware that when one did not have the easy resource of an abundance of natural beauty, one had to do what one could. It was fortunate indeed that she had taken such care, for what she had not expected was Mrs Crowe arriving at her door before the tea had had a chance to brew in the pot.

'Catherine, my dear, please call me Catherine,' Mrs Crowe told Charlotte as she took Charlotte's hands, clasping them warmly. 'Of course, I realise it is a terrible intrusion to turn up unannounced like this, but you see, by the time your letter caught up with me I was mid-transit between Edinburgh and London and realised that I could be at your side by dawn, if I left at once.' She laughed with delight. 'And so, I did.'

'You could never be an intrusion, Mrs Crowe – Catherine,' Charlotte told her warmly, before glancing up at their little home. 'I am not entirely sure how we will accommodate you, as all my siblings are at home, and I have a friend already visiting. But I am certain we will find a way.'

'Catherine can have my room,' Emily offered at once. She had appeared as if from thin air, looking, to Charlotte's great distress, as if Keeper had just dragged her up and down the moors by the hem of her skirt. 'It is but small, Mrs Crowe, but comfortable enough, particularly if you do not mind the chances of a great hound leaping upon your chest demanding his breakfast.'

'I should mind no such thing!' Mrs Crowe said, embracing Emily before bending down to fuss Keeper. 'Such a noble beast! But of course, I can't expect to impose upon you, my dear Brontës, I shall stay at an inn. I'm sure there is one nearby that you can recommend.'

'We simply couldn't allow that, Mrs Crowe,' Anne said, joining the party on the doorstep, but soon making her way to receive a kiss on each cheek from the older woman. 'Nor can we allow you stay out here in this heat a moment longer. Come in, I beg you, and take some refreshment.'

As they entered the rather congested entrance hall, Ellen hovered on the bottom stair, her head tilted in enquiry.

'Ellen, come let me introduce you to Mrs Catherine Crowe, the author of *Susan Hopely.*'

'*The* Mrs Catherine Crowe?' Ellen said, going rather white.

'I do believe so,' Mrs Crowe said with a small smile.

'And this is my dearest friend, Miss Ellen Nussey,' Charlotte said, looking from one to the other, rather bemused as to what was taking place.

'Why, Mrs Crowe,' Ellen said, her voice trembling. 'I don't know quite what to say. I have read all of your novels, and I find them so very invigorating and thrilling! I never thought I should have the opportunity to stand before you and profess my deepest admiration. I find I am rather over-come!'

Charlotte looked from Emily to Anne; not one of them had ever seen Ellen so affected by an introduction before. It did not seem to be an extraordinary occurrence to Mrs Crowe, however.

'Why, Miss Nussey,' she said with warm largesse. 'You have no need to feel so afflicted or reverential in my company. Naturally, I am delighted beyond measure that you enjoy my writings, for indeed I do pour a good deal of my soul into each. But though my name may be known the width and length of the country – and on the continent too – I am but a person, just as you are. And we shall be great friends, the spirits tell me so. Now, will you escort me to the table?'

Charlotte's mouth fell open just a little more than was seemly, as Ellen – bursting with a curious combination of pride and admiration – led Mrs Crowe into the dining room.

'So that is what it is like to truly be famous,' Charlotte said, as her sisters stood at her side.

'Indeed,' Emily said. 'Let us pray such celebrity is never ours.'

Mrs Crowe had taken what seemed like her natural position at the head of the table, where she was surrounded on all sides by her universally admiring and attentive audience of four women and two dogs.

'Revenants,' she said. 'The risen dead. Such a fascinating subject, and as you mentioned in your letter, Charlotte, the meat of folklore all across the world, in multiple civilisations.' Catherine took a sip of her tea, beaming at them all. How happy she was, Charlotte thought, to be living her life exactly as she chose, at no one's beck and call but her own.

The sight of such a rare being both thrilled and made her feel sick with longing at exactly the same moment. 'Lately, I have been embarking on my own scientific investigation of otherworldly occurrences of multiple varieties. Investigating incidents such as your revenant, by travelling to the location of the alleged happening and undertaking a series of rigorous tests with specially devised scientific instruments. These I use to collect irrefutable information that can be analysed, in order to conclude as to the veracity of the phenomena once and for all.'

'Quite brilliant,' Emily breathed, clapping her hands together.

'Needless to say,' Mrs Crowe told them, 'There are a great many charlatans, frauds and frankly gullible individuals making reports. Nevertheless, to date I have succeeded in collecting more than fifty such noteworthy cases for study, which I intend to publish in a book as soon as my research is complete. A veritable multitude of ghosts, a series of doppelgängers, half a dozen wraiths, countless omens, visions and prophecies, one rather terrifying incident of what I can only refer to as 'possession', and a handful of curious instances of an altogether more elusive phenomenon that I have adopted the German term "poltergeist" to describe.'

'Poltergeist, a rumbling spirit?' Emily questioned, leaning her chin on her hands, fascinated.

'Yes, exactly. A noisy and disruptive presence, but not one born of a human soul. More, it seems to be a manifestation of powerful emotions, formed by the thoughts and feelings of living humans. I notice they are quite often present as a young person transitions to adulthood.'

'How marvellous,' Emily all but swooned with admiration. As much as she admired Mrs Crowe, Charlotte had to admit to feeling rather put out. No one, not even her sisters, had ever looked at her the way everyone in this room was gazing at Mrs Crowe.

'Now you will know, as ladies of intelligence – ' Ellen giggled liked a flattered girl, as Mrs Crowe went on – 'that we live in the world of Man. And as such, Man is apt to try and make the world in his own image, as if it cannot possibly exist in any form outside of the scope of his understanding. Such arrogance, in the face of Our Lord's mysteries of creation! What did Man know of the power of steam or the potential of electricity fifty or a hundred years ago? Why nothing, ladies. Nor did Man believe the earth to be spherical in nature for the first greater part of our existence. We live amongst miracles, yet because we see them every day, we treat them as if they are commonplace events. They are not. Everything, from the flowering of a daisy, to the flight of a lapwing, is a wonder.' She tapped the table with her fork to emphasise her point. 'My goal is not to attempt to teach or impose my own ideas upon the world of men, but if my efforts can inspire one or two men of science to treat the subject of the supernatural with the same inspired thought and determination as they have other much better understood realms, then I will have achieved my target.'

'You are a true marvel,' Charlotte said, unable to hold on to her churlish mood in the presence of such inspiration. 'I truly believe that nothing frightens you.'

'Well, that is not exactly accurate,' Catherine confessed, buttering herself another slice of bread. 'There have been moments in the past when I have both feared and had to run for my life. But that time is past now, never to return. Now I am captain of my own ship, creator of my own destiny. And I do hope you will allow me to aid you in your detection by discovering, with your help of course, if the sighting of the revenant reported to you can either be proved without a shadow of a doubt or discounted.'

'We could not be more delighted, Mrs Crowe,' Charlotte said.

'I see once more you have invited guests into the house without alerting its master.' Papa arrived in the doorway, peering over the rim of his glasses at the, admittedly, rather excitable gathering. 'It seems you are having quite a party.'

'Reverend Brontë.' Mrs Crowe stood, her hand flying to her bosom as she made her way around the table, offered their papa a deep curtsey, and in the process revealed rather a lot of her generous décolletage. Papa bowed and the two shook hands. It was quite clear even before Mrs Crowe spoke one word that her father was rather taken with the comely lady who was approaching the age of fifty, Charlotte supposed. Mrs Crowe's dark eyes sparkled with delight as she regarded their papa; her glossy black hair was threaded with strands of silver that she wore like a crown. And yes, Mrs Crowe was generously made, her figure presenting a somehow all-encompassing flourish of comfort that Charlotte imagined no gentleman could help but appreciate. Judging by the light in Papa's eyes, she was not incorrect.

'I must say what a great honour it is to meet the gentleman who has brought up, after the tragic loss of your marvellous wife, such truly brilliant daughters. You are a marvel, sir, one of a kind. There is not another man on this earth who could have produced not one but three such talents. I bow to you.'

'Oh, come now, madam,' Papa said, blushing and beaming with pleasure. 'I have only done my Christian duty, though I do believe, as any man would, that my children are destined for greater things.'

'Oh, not any man, Reverend Brontë, no, sadly, not any man at all. Now, I'm afraid I must reveal that your daughters invited me to stay a night with you in your charming home, but as I told them, I am perfectly happy to take a room at the inn.'

'No such thing will occur,' Patrick said sternly, still holding on to Mrs Crowe's hand. 'You are most welcome to stay with us, madam. Charlotte, tell Tabby I shall take dinner with you ladies tonight. It seems churlish indeed to deprive myself of the delight of such agreeable company.'

'Sir, you honour me,' Mrs Crowe bowed again. Papa bowed again. Many more minutes of such appreciation and Charlotte feared that Mrs Crowe might be receiving a proposal.

'Well then, Papa, if you will excuse us, we should like to take Ellen and Mrs Crowe—'

'Catherine,' Mrs Crowe reminded her.

'Catherine, for a tour of the area.'

'I shall pine until we meet again,' Papa said, his Irish brogue becoming suddenly a good deal broader. He kissed Mrs Crowe's hand and closed the door behind him. Charlotte could hear him humming as he crossed the hall to his study.

'What a wonderful gentleman,' Mrs Crowe remarked.

'You do realise he is in love with you now?' Anne said. 'Poor Papa. He has hoped to marry more than once since we lost our mama, but he has always been rejected.'

'And I am afraid that I am not the lady to change that,' Mrs Crowe said. 'One husband was more than enough to last me a lifetime. Now, my carriage is at your disposal, my comrades. Where do you propose we begin?'

NINETEEN

Anne

There had been quite a disagreement.

Charlotte had proposed that Anne should accompany her and Mrs Crowe to the workhouse, as Anne had such a natural rapport with Rosalyn. And that Emily and Ellen should walk to Harrowings Hall to interview Mr Peter Wilson, in the event that he might be able to shed more light on the occurrences. In the normal scheme of things this would have been quite suitable. After all, it had been Emily who had discovered the whereabouts of Mr Wilson, working for the son of the family his father had worked for at a new, yet wonderfully Gothic castle of a house, and Emily was usually very possessive of her discoveries. However, the difference on this occasion was that all of them, including an admiring Ellen, each longed to be at Mrs Crowe's side as her chief and best assistant.

'But I wish to come on the supernatural investigation,' Emily said. 'Charlotte, you cannot bar me from witnessing such a wonder! I long to see Mrs Crowe's equipment and how she makes her determinations!' Emily stamped a foot hard enough to start Keeper from his slumber. 'I swear I shall die if I do not, and I shall haunt you, Charlotte. I will spend the rest of eternity interrupting your writings.'

'I also would like to be present for Mrs Crowe's examinations,' Anne added, calm but firm. 'I am particularly interested in learning more about the psychic resonance of certain kinds of bedrock, and whether they might act to amplify uncanny occurrences.'

As was often the case with the sisters, it had been Charlotte who had befriended Mrs Crowe and so could reasonably exert some ownership of her, but Anne was not about to give up the best seat in the theatre to go and speak to some dull old groom who may or may not know something about the murders.

'My dears,' Mrs Crowe had said, clapping her hands together in delight. 'How it warms my heart to see such enthusiasm from young women for science. But fear not. During daylight hours the work is quite dull. Taking base-line measurements and mapping out the area, for example, so that one might have a clear picture of the geographical nature of the landscape and surroundings, despite all being obscured by dark, particularly when the atmosphere is so charged with the threat of a storm. In truth, though, the essential work always takes place at night.'

'Because ghosts and spirits only walk the earth at night?' Anne asked.

'No, not at all, they are with us at all times,' Mrs Crowe said cheerily, and Ellen glanced nervously around. 'But at night the world is a quieter place, more tranquil and still. Closer to the paradise that God created, and the intuitive spirit part of our brain becomes alert and more attuned to sensing and accepting what in daylight hours we simply might be too distracted to notice, do you see?'

'I do,' Emily said enthusiastically. 'We shall have to creep out after Papa is abed.'

'Your papa does not know of your detections?' Mrs Crowe had asked them, and as one they felt like schoolgirls caught in a lie. Anne blushed deeply.

'We do mean to tell him,' Anne told her. 'Once we are done with detecting and they are far in the past and there can be no inconvenience to him. We fear our . . . exertions might trouble his heart, you see. And he already has so much to contend with, with the parish, and our brother.'

'Beloveds, I will not betray your confidence,' Mrs Crowe told them solemnly, with the faint air of a disappointed mama. 'But I urge you to share the truth with your papa. Time on this earth is short, and if he truly loves and knows you, as I am sure he must, then there is nothing you can do that will estrange him. I adore my son, I would kill for him. From time to time he gives me a little trouble, as young gentlemen are prone to do, but I could never cease to care for him. A mama's love is infinite.'

For a moment the sisters felt – very strongly – all that they had lost when they lost their own mama.

'It is true that Branwell has tried very hard to drive us all away, and Papa still loves him,' Emily said. 'We will talk to him, Mrs Crowe, you are quite correct. It is time for the end of secrecy between us. At least on the detecting matter.'

'What other matter is there?' Ellen asked.

'Nothing at all,' Emily said, sweetly. 'Just a turn of phrase.'

'Well then,' Ellen said, 'May I just say that, though I do so admire Mrs Crowe, I do not mind being absent from the night investigation. Indeed, I am sure my strengths are much more suited to assisting the esteemed Mrs Crowe today in the organisation of the matter, measuring and taking notes and so forth, if I might be so bold as to offer my services. I should be quite glad to stay behind during the night hours and hear tell of it afterwards, perhaps in one of Mrs Crowe's most excellent novels.'

'Well then,' Charlotte said. 'Ellen and I shall accompany Mrs Crowe in her carriage . . .'

'Charlotte does love a carriage,' Emily muttered to Anne.

'Anne, you and Emily will visit Mr Wilson. It is not too far a walk, I believe. If you begin now, we can all be at home in time for dinner with Papa.'

The younger sisters exchanged a smile. It had been an age since they had had such a wealth of time together. Not one step would be taken without it being lit up by stories.

Harrowings was a remarkable house, the like of which neither of the sisters had seen before, and neither one of them could determine if they were attracted to or repelled by it. They were used to the old kind of manor houses, built of grey stone, often long and low to begin with and then adorned and prettified with additions, crenellations and carvings as their owners came into increasing wealth. Those kinds of houses seemed steeped in the landscape, somehow. As if it were not man who added to them, but the earth and water of the moors themselves, pushing great buildings out of her own flesh.

Harrowings, however, despite its rather ominous name, came straight from the pocket of newly found wealth and was scarcely two years old, though it wore the pretence of the medieval like a young maid might wear a costume at a summer fête. As they approached the great house from one end of a long drive, Anne noted that the house seemed to feature at least one example of every fashionable architectural motif, from turrets to towers, Venetian balconies perfect for a Juliet and, most notably in Anne's mind, a large and curiously organic conservatory, which seemed to her like a cathedral in full bloom, its metal and glass petals creating sweeping arches and domes that looked on the verge of flowering outwards at any moment.

Anne decided to like Harrowings. Yes, it was new and immodest, but it was somehow hopeful too. It had that irrepressible joy of beauty for its own sake, and she could never frown upon such a thing. Emily, however, was of another opinion entirely.

'I do believe that after things rather went wrong with his monster, Victor Frankenstein came to Yorkshire and built a house.'

'Don't be such a snob, Emily,' Anne told her.

'I? A snob? Take that back, I am the least snobbish person I know,' Emily grumbled. 'I just believe that there is nothing so beautiful or worthy of admiration as the countryside that this abomination blots out with its very existence.'

'Allow it its moment,' Anne said. 'The moors will always be here, houses fall away and crumble to dust, as do the people within them.'

'That is a cheering thought,' Emily said, and Anne knew she was not being sarcastic.

'We should go to the servants' entrance,' Anne said. 'It would be preferable if the family never knew we had visited.'

'And perhaps the rear of the house will be altogether more aesthetically tolerable,' Emily commented.

It was not.

They came upon a girl who was polishing silver at a table that had been dragged out onto the courtyard so that she might sit in the sun as she worked. A sign of a good family,

Anne thought. And a kindly housekeeper who would afford an under-maid such a treat.

Emily muttered darkly about the practical purpose of external spiral staircases and what kind of fool could possibly consider a dome as an appropriate adornment to a country house.

'Good day,' Anne greeted the child warmly. 'My name is Miss Anne Brontë, what is yours?'

'I'm Helen, miss,' the girl said. 'I'm no one important.'

'I am certain that is not true,' Anne smiled. 'We are in search of a Mr Peter Wilson, would he be about the place?'

Helen stood up nervously, smoothing down her skirts.

'He's nowhere near here,' she said. 'But Mrs Wilson is in the kitchen, I can fetch her for you?'

'That would be most kind,' Anne said. 'Would you mind telling her that the Misses Brontë of Haworth have come to call?'

'To call on Mrs Wilson?' the girl asked again, clearly feeling the need to be certain, before she delivered her message. Perhaps Mrs Wilson was not fond of having her time wasted. 'Not the master or the missus?'

'No, Mrs Wilson please,' Anne said again with a smile and a reassuring nod.

The child disappeared within.

'A minaret,' Emily said. 'I have honestly never seen such nonsense. The whole confection is a whimsy, and parody. There is no history here to bind the place together. No story that shows you how it grew from its roots. Take Ponden Hall for example. There you can see the age, trace the story from the oldest part to the new. This house is like an architect sneezed. A drunk architect.'

'May I help you, Misses Brontë?' A strong-looking woman nearing middle age appeared in the doorway of the kitchen.

Anne noticed her swift appraisal of them, deciding they were well-to-do enough to be tolerated, but not so grand that she had to affect any airs and graces.

'Mrs Wilson? So pleased to meet you.' Anne and Emily dipped a curtsey, and Mrs Wilson responded in kind. 'You might be familiar with our name; we are the daughters of the parson at Haworth.'

'I have heard of the Reverend Brontë,' Mrs Wilson nodded, guarded.

Anne glanced at the young maid who had returned to her polishing, head down, intent on looking occupied, before asking, 'If we might have a moment regarding a rather delicate matter?' nodding pointedly at the oblivious child. 'That is perhaps not suitable for tender ears.'

Mrs Wilson sighed deeply, as if she now knew precisely what the sisters wanted with her husband.

'A moment is all you may have,' she replied sharply, leading them away from the girl and across the cobbled courtyard, where the stable door stood open, showing it devoid of any inhabitants. 'I am busy preparing this evening's meal, and not free to be at the beck and call of passing strangers.'

'Madam,' Anne said, determining that Mrs Wilson would prefer a direct approach. 'You will have heard of the Lowood poisoning case?'

'What is that to do with me or my husband?' she asked.

'We are aiding a young woman by the name of Rosalyn Tolliver,' Anne began, deciding that perhaps it was better not to mention their interest in murder. 'You may recall that she gave evidence as to her involvement with—'

'I know who she is,' Mrs Wilson all but spat, clearly distressed by the subject. 'What have I to do with that harlot,

Miss Brontë? Speak now or begone with you, otherwise –
parson's daughters or no – I will put you out myself.'

Instinctively, Anne rested a calming hand on Emily's arm,
stilling her sister. It was not them that Mrs Wilson was angry
with, she supposed, but her husband, and his former links to
Mrs Lowood.

'Rosalyn is greatly troubled by the events that took place,'
Anne said. 'She was no older than your girl polishing silver
over there when she was first influenced by a man with no
moral compass. You know of whom I speak: Abner Lowood,
who worked for your master's family for a short time.'

'Not at this house,' Mrs Wilson said, as if she were determined that her new kingdom would not be sullied by any such
association. 'He was employed by Mr Blackford, the elder,
to paint Blackford Hall. And the few weeks he was there, he
ruined many a life, including mine, though I did not know it
then.'

'How so, Mrs Wilson?' Anne asked her gently.

'I don't have time to tell you my private business,'
Mrs Wilson said. 'If you want to know the ins and outs of it,
you must find my husband. If he has a mind to, he can tell
you, though I cannot swear to what sort of temper he will be
in.' She gestured at the empty stalls. 'You will find him out at
the back pasture, exercising the horses. Be warned, you will
not likely find him sober. And you will be gone before lun-
cheon is over; I won't have my people disturbed by the sight
of you. Do we understand one another?'

'We do,' Anne said, gently grasping Emily's wrist. 'Which
way is the pasture?'

Mrs Wilson nodded in a direction away from the house
and turned her back on them.

'Why would you not let me speak?' Emily said. 'Hateful woman. I should have given her a piece of my mind.'

'Unhappy woman,' Anne replied. 'Trapped in marriage to an unhappy man. If the little power she has is to treat us with such disdain, then I for one do not begrudge it her.'

'You are too good, Anne,' Emily said. 'You should do more wrong, otherwise God might be tempted to take you for an angel.'

'I am not afraid of death,' Anne said, and she meant every word. 'I only wish that I will be able to improve the lot of others in the time I am given.'

'Like I said,' Emily replied fondly, her arm winding around her sister's waist, 'too good by far.'

Charlotte

Wherever Catherine Crowe went she created something of a commotion. Charlotte realised this as her carriage drew into the central courtyard of the workhouse, and people appeared from everywhere to see what sort of grand personage it might contain.

She was not a noblewoman, nor someone born into wealth, and although Charlotte had not enquired as to the nature of Mrs Crowe's marriage, or the death of her husband, she knew that Catherine relied entirely upon herself and herself alone for her income. It was her novels that had made her a fortune. Her talent, resilience and determination alone had earned this kind of attention and respect. If Catherine could achieve so much on this basis, then Charlotte was sure that she could follow suit. If she could just keep a firm grasp on her courage, she was certain that *Jane Eyre* was good. That it was very good. That it could help her break free of the fear and uncertainty of life as an unmarried woman, just as Mrs Crowe's novels had helped her do the same, and even to go and pursue her more 'unusual' interests. Catherine was a beacon of freedom and Charlotte intended to follow her light as far as she was able. Perhaps, one day, she too might offer that hope to other women in search of an example that such things were possible.

Mrs Tolliver had soon emerged from the women's half of the main workhouse building, and tasked the inmates to bring down a large wooden chest from the back of the carriage, which Mrs Crowe asked to be brought into the Tollivers' cottage.

'The date of the buildings?' Mrs Crowe asked Mrs Tolliver as she took herself directly to the first floor in search of Rosalyn's bedroom.

'This cottage is old, ma'am,' Mrs Tolliver replied, a little breathless, as she hurried after Mrs Crowe up the steep stone steps. 'As is the laundry, the dead house and all the buildings across the courtyard. They were part of a farm once, I do believe, and that stood here for three hundred years or more.'

Mrs Crowe lifted up her hand for a moment, and listened. Charlotte thought she saw Catherine nod slightly, as if she had heard something whispered in her ear.

'The fate of the farmer and his family that last lived here?' she asked abruptly.

'Cholera, ma'am,' Mrs Tolliver said. 'Took a great many that year. As for the other buildings, they were added about a dozen or so years since, after the parish acquired the land. But it being public money, they made use of what was already here.'

'I see,' Mrs Crowe said, thoughtfully.

'Your daughter has told you of her nightly visitations, madam?' Mrs Crowe asked Mrs Tolliver, who had given way to her demands without a moment of hesitation before she even truly knew what Mrs Crowe's purpose was. 'About seeing the revenant of Barbara Lowood.'

'She did yesterday, after meeting with the other Misses Brontë,' Mrs Tolliver said anxiously. 'Mr Tolliver wanted to take her directly to an asylum, but I said no. I said that tonight we will all sit up with Rosalyn and keep watch, and if there is nothing there for her to fear, we will be able to reassure her.'

'Excellent,' Mrs Crowe said, 'And how did the night pass?'

'The clock struck three,' Mrs Tolliver said, glancing anxiously at Charlotte. 'And sure enough, there she was. Looking up at my girl's window. Terrible disfigured, bone showing through flesh, but I would have known her anywhere. My Rosalyn is telling the truth, Mrs Crowe. Will you be able to help us?'

'Certainly,' Mrs Crowe reassured her.

'What will you do?'

'Well, that is to be determined, but I promise I shall not leave you until I am sure that the matter is properly resolved. Do you believe me?'

'I do, ma'am,' Mrs Tolliver said, now quietly weeping. What the poor woman had endured over the last months must have been sufficient to test the sanity of the most sensible person, Charlotte thought. This had to be some shared hysteria, surely? For it certainly could not be a risen corpse come to seek revenge, could it?

'And where is the young lady who is suffering the sightings?'

'I am here.' Rosalyn, whom Charlotte had not seen when she entered the cottage, had appeared from somewhere, and must have been the last to follow Mrs Crowe. She hovered on the small landing, her eyes wide as she observed the great lady with a certain degree of mistrust. Hardly surprising, Charlotte thought. When a person had been so roundly damned by all and sundry, she must surely expect each new acquaintance to be her enemy.

'Come here, my child,' Mrs Crowe requested gently, holding out a hand to Rosalyn. The young woman crossed to her side. Taking her hands, Mrs Crowe invited Rosalyn to sit on the bed with her, rather cleverly creating a sense of intimacy and trust, Charlotte thought. Catherine scanned the girl's face, her head tilted slightly.

'Mrs Tolliver,' she said, glancing up. 'Would you mind giving us a moment alone with your daughter?'

'I suppose it will be all right.' Mrs Tolliver looked to Charlotte and Ellen for reassurance. 'Mr Tolliver will return soon, though, and he has a great deal of views about outsiders looking into our affairs and might seem rather . . . inhospitable.'

'Naturally,' Mrs Crowe said. 'Of course, any father would feel the same, fear not, madam. I was married to a soldier.'

That revelation seemed to settle Mrs Tolliver entirely.

'Would that be all right with you, Rosalyn?' Mrs Tolliver asked her daughter.

'If Miss Charlotte is near,' Rosalyn nodded, reaching to gently lay her hand on Charlotte's shoulder. 'I believe no harm will come to me with her close.'

Charlotte felt a swell of tenderness towards the poor girl. In recent years they had helped many women who had been done wrong by a world that prized purity and beauty in womanhood and precious little else. Perhaps Rosalyn was not the worst case she had seen, but she had the least hope of recovery. What she had done, she had done willingly, at least as she and the world saw it. She would never be forgiven for that.

As soon as Mrs Tolliver had departed, Catherine, with Rosalyn's hands still in hers, closed her eyes. Outside, the usual noise of the workhouse could be heard, but within all was silence.

'Yes,' Mrs Crowe murmured, nodding once again, as if listening. 'Yes, yes, I see.' After a moment more she opened her eyes once again, and smiled.

'There is a great deal of disruption around your spirit,' she told Rosalyn gently. 'An alteration – I sense a great deal of manipulation has taken place. Not only bodily, but also of the mind . . . Yes, there has been a campaign of influence waged about you, it is no wonder your mind is so open to the nether realms.' Mrs Crowe pursed her lips as she scanned Rosalyn's face for a moment more. 'Very well, we shall proceed. My dear, this is nothing to be afraid of, I see it all the time. You have undergone a great trauma, and such psychical assault can take a great deal of time to heal.'

Rosalyn said nothing, her blue eyes fixed on Mrs Crowe as the older woman elaborated.

'Traumatic events have the effect of heightening the senses of the afflicted to the supernormal world. This is often a temporary state of affairs but, quite honestly, given all that you have endured, I am not in the least bit surprised.'

'You believe that I am seeing her then?' Rosalyn asked her. 'You know I say true when I see Barbara's corpse walking. It is not just my imagination. Or my mind gone broken? The revenant is really there, is she not? As real as you and me.'

'Well now,' Mrs Crowe said, sitting back a little. 'When an individual has suffered a great deal, and gone on to endure further indignities due to the nature and prejudices of society, there might be a temptation, a perfectly understandable desire, to manufacture some extraordinary event, perhaps an illness or an unusual happening, in order to deflect attention away from themselves. Even having your parents as witnesses does not preclude a kind of hysterical vision, because they – more than anyone – want to believe you.' Mrs Crowe leaned in a little closer to Rosalyn, as if she were her confidante. 'As do I. However, we must be rigorous. You are among friends here, my dear. No one outside the room will know your answer, so tell us true.'

Rosalyn waited, gazing at Catherine with her wide blue eyes.

'Are you being honest about what you have witnessed?' Mrs Crowe asked her. 'Or are you perhaps inventing a story that might protect you from further scrutiny?'

'I only tell the truth, ma'am,' Rosalyn said. 'I swear it upon my mother's life. Believe me, I have no wish to see the horror of that rotted corpse come after me. No wish for her to come in my house. No wish for her to . . .' Rosalyn snatched her hand from Mrs Crowe's and held it over her mouth. 'I do not know what she might do. She might do terrible things ma'am, with her snapping teeth and clawing fingers.'

'If she is indeed what you think she is, then she will do you no harm,' Mrs Crowe promised Rosalyn. 'It is very rare the dead have the power to harm us. But first we must discover the nature of this creature. Charlotte, Ellen – to my trunk! We have much work to do to prepare for tonight's events.'

'We begin with the very basic tools,' Mrs Crowe said, handing a large tin of flour to Ellen, who took the heavy object with some confusion.

'You say you see her figure across the courtyard, drawing ever nearer? Can you tell me from which building she seems to appear?'

'From the dead house, ma'am,' Rosalyn said. 'After Abner was poisoned, I first saw her at the door. And each night since then, she's come a step closer. She's almost at our house now.'

'Mrs Tolliver, you must close the courtyard off to any inmates or workers between now and the dawn,' Catherine said. 'I shall have my carriage wait for us without the gates. Is that possible?'

'Mr Tolliver won't like it. It will mean giving half of them the afternoon off from their labours,' Mrs Tolliver said. 'But if it must be done, it must be done. Rosalyn, run and find your father and tell him what's needed and see he keeps the courtyard entirely clear.'

'Very good,' Catherine said, once the girl had departed. 'Mrs Tolliver, might you make us some tea?'

The good lady bustled off to do so at once, and Catherine lowered her voice.

'No matter how good they seem, we must treat all, even Mrs Tolliver, as suspects in creating a fiction. They must not be privy to our checks and balances, lest they should use that information to circumnavigate them.'

'I see,' Charlotte said, glancing at Ellen. 'This must be a very different excursion to the one you had envisaged, Nell.'

'I do not believe I could have imagined this in my wildest dreams,' Ellen agreed cheerfully. 'I am having such an entertaining time.'

'Now, Ellen.' Ellen jumped to attention as Mrs Crowe spoke her name. 'Once the courtyard has been closed off, I wish you to cover every cobble between the dead house and here in flour. It will be sparse enough not to be noticed in the dark, but should it be a creature of mass and form, the flour will record its footprints, and the size of its feet, whether booted or bare, not to mention the stride. This would then help us determine height, and if such determinations meet expectations in respect to Mrs Lowood's person.'

'Ingenious,' Ellen said, glowing with admiration.

'Now, Charlotte dear, while Ellen performs that operation, you will help me set up the photo-baromètres.'

Charlotte had never heard of such a contraption before and she could not wait to know more.

Out of her trunk Mrs Crowe lifted one of four small yet heavy mahogany boxes, about the size of a writing slope set on its end, but twice the thickness. Each of the boxes was hinged at the front to reveal a brass mechanism encased behind a narrow glass aperture.

'What are these devices?' Charlotte asked, intrigued, for she had never seen anything like them before.

'Quite a remarkable invention,' Mrs Crowe said. 'Made by the visionary in the field of electricity, Sir Francis Ronalds. His original device was installed at Kew, in 1845, and is designed to continuously record information about the natural world. With his permission, I commissioned miniature, portable versions for my field of research. Each photo-baromètre records a separate stream of information onto a roll of photosensitive paper as it passes very slowly over the aperture. It's driven by a clockwork engine and can record up to twelve hours of information. Each machine monitors atmospheric pressure, temperature, humidity, atmospheric electricity and geomagnetism, all of which I believe fluctuate intensely if a supernormal event is occurring.' Mrs Crowe disappeared under a cloak which she had thrown over the first machine. She beckoned for Charlotte to join her in the makeshift tent.'

'It is important to add the paper in the dark to avoid false positives,' Catherine told her.

'How does the information recorded help you?' Charlotte asked, rather thrilled to be enclosed in the small dark space with Catherine, with just a little light afforded through the weave of the cloak.

'Excellent question,' Mrs Crowe told her, making Charlotte burst with pride. 'For example, it is often reported during a suspected haunting or the like that the temperature may drop suddenly and drastically. Or that the atmosphere feels charged, as if a storm is building. These machines can prove incontrovertibly if there have been any such disturbances that align with these reports.' She snapped the lid closed on the last case and threw off the cloak.

'They are rather miraculous, don't you think?'

'I do,' Charlotte said enthusiastically. 'We are truly in an age where there is nothing that can't be engineered or built, it seems.'

'We are indeed, Charlotte,' Mrs Crowe said. 'We are indeed, which is why I feel certain that we are just years away from understanding the realms that so far have eluded us.'

'And what is this?' Ellen asked as she returned from coating the cobbles outside with flour. She brought out of the trunk what – for all the world – looked to Charlotte like a device to aid the deaf in hearing.

'That is a spirit trumpet,' Mrs Crowe told her. 'Our human ears are often too dull to hear the words of spirits, though they may be speaking to us all of the time. Such a device, installed, let us say, at the point where we believe the creature will halt her journey tonight, can serve to amplify her voice should she have a message for us. Of course, usually we would need a medium to offer up his or her body through which to channel the spirit voices, but on this occasion – as we believe we are dealing with a corporeal being – one should not be required. From time to time one might also find an *apport* produced from within the cone of the trumpet. That is, objects that are materialised out of thin air.'

'Goodness,' Ellen said. 'This is all rather a lot to take in. Do you mind if I ask, Mrs Crowe? What does the church think of your interests?'

Mrs Crowe blinked, and Charlotte thought she saw just a flash of irritation cross her face before her smile returned.

'Do we not each day prove our faith with our belief in the Holy Ghost?' Mrs Crowe said. 'Why, then, should it offend the church, or God himself, if we also seek to understand the other mysteries of His creations? He made us curious, Ellen. To follow that impulse is to serve Him.'

'Yes, I see what you mean,' Ellen said thoughtfully. 'Though I am quite certain that I do not wish to hear anything emit from that trumpet.'

'It is rather disturbing,' Mrs Crowe admitted.

'What is all of this, and who are you?' Mr Tolliver, Charlotte presumed, flung open the door of the cottage, his great bulk blotting out the daylight.

'Mr Tolliver, sir, delighted to make your acquaintance,' Mrs Crowe said, a study in feminine charm. 'I must thank you for your permission to make our study here tonight. I understand you witnessed the spectre yourself?'

Mr Tolliver was entirely wrongfooted, and somewhat flustered.

'I might have,' he said, still surly. 'I don't know, it seemed real then; but now, in the daylight, it feels like it was all a dream.'

'Indeed, indeed,' Mrs Crowe nodded. 'Yes, you do have remarkable insight, sir. And such courage to protect your wife and daughter against the unknown as you are. You do right to allow my research. I am sure we will have this matter resolved for you by morning, and that will be one thing less to worry about.'

'I . . . well. Thank you,' Mr Tolliver said.

'What other preparations must we make?' Charlotte asked, in wonder at how Mrs Crowe seemed to be able to bring anyone she encountered around to her way of thinking with just a few words and a delightful smile.

'Well, as long as Mrs Tolliver and her good husband will keep all out of the courtyard and the adjacent building, then for now we simply retire and wait for nightfall.'

Just at that moment, Mrs Tolliver returned with a tray of tea things. 'Mrs Tolliver, I ask that you, Rosalyn and your husband are all present and in our company tonight. And that you have a great many candles and lanterns available to us to make ready use of should we need to go to the source of any disturbance and ascertain its cause. Until then, my friends, we must open our hearts and our minds, and wait for all to be revealed. What mysteries await?'

TWENTY-ONE

Emily

Peter Wilson was exactly where his wife had said he would be, leaning heavily over a gate as a group of six beautiful, finely bred horses grazed contentedly in the pasture, their glossy coats shimmering in the sun. They looked well cared-for, and were perfectly at ease in his presence. Wilson himself was draped over the gate to the paddock, hanging down so loosely that he might be asleep. As they approached, however, it could be seen that Wilson was rocking the gate slightly with one foot. Never had Emily seen such a picture of pure despondency, which was quite something considering her family.

Wilson's gaze was directed so steadfastly at the dusty ground that he did not notice them until they were at his side.

'What's this?' he said, starting up and rocking back on his heels for a perilous moment before he found his feet. He was not drunk, Emily determined, for she knew that state intimately, but he had been quite recently. His skin was thick and ruddy, his eyes bloodshot and sunken. His expression was one of deep mistrust, almost obscured by a dazed and dreamy quality.

'Good day, sir,' Anne said, taking the lead as she was apt to do these days. Emily was happy to let her, for she had not fared well with the talking part of late. Anne was better with people than she was, while she preferred to observe. She was more suited to it than getting amongst people. Such involvement always clouded one's vision, she thought, and should be avoided in the case of the detector and the writer, both.

'We are Anne and Emily Brontë, from Haworth,' Anne went on, pleasantly, rather as if she were addressing a skittish horse herself. 'We are engaged in trying to help a young woman who has had her life ruined by a gentleman we believe you are acquainted with?'

'Lowood.' Mr Wilson spat the name as if he had just tasted poison. 'I wish him dead. That man can never stop taking from me. I swear, it's been a dozen years since he arrived – run out of Scarborough over something he'd done in those parts. Still, he steals away any moment of peace I have.'

'Indeed,' Anne nodded. 'And I truly beg your pardon for bringing his name to your ears once again, but you see, we are determined to find the evidence needed to prove his guilt in the murder.' Of course, they did not know what the evidence would tell them yet, if indeed they discovered any, but Anne clearly thought it best not to mention to Wilson the possibility that their detection might clear Lowood's name, a decision that Emily approved of.

Peter Wilson's face seemed to fold in upon itself, and Emily was surprised to find herself moved by his obvious pain at remembering what had befallen him. Why she was more able to care for this strange man's broken heart and ingrained disappointment than she was for her own brother, she did not know. But she made a note to try and be kinder to Branwell when she saw him next. To try once again to draw him out of his own tangle of misery.

'I don't know how I can help you, or the lass he ruined,' he shrugged. 'I knew him for a short span, years ago. He arrived, running from some scandal in Scarborough, travelled with a circus for a while, leaving ruin and misery in his wake, before he was obliged to depart even that life, and found work as a house painter. He laughed about all the ways he learned mesmerism off an old fortune-teller that travelled with them. How he was able to use cunning to talk anyone into doing anything he wanted. He tricked and hurt people left and right, conning money from the poor and honour from women. For a while I even admired him, how he lived a life pleasing no one but himself. I was young, and he was the sort of fellow that always had a crowd around him. But that was before he took everything I cared for from me, right out from under my nose, while I laughed at his jokes and thought him a fine fellow. Once he departed from the house, he departed from my life, and I have made it my business never to set eyes on him again.'

Anne glanced at Emily, as if urging her to take a turn in the conversation. Emily pretended she didn't notice for a moment or two, but Anne seemed determined that it was her time to speak.

'Lovely horses,' she said.

'Aye,' Wilson smiled for a moment. 'They are more family to me than humans, I often think.'

'I completely agree,' Emily said enthusiastically. 'I am certain that my dog, Keeper, understands the nature of my being far more than my own sister.'

Emily gestured at Anne who, she noticed, had pressed her lips into a thin line.

Well, Emily had been establishing a rapport with the fellow, as Charlotte did – surely Anne could see that? Besides, she would much rather talk about animals than the delicate subject with which – for some reason – Anne was entrusting her. But needs must.

Emily took a deep breath.

'We understand that you knew Barbara, Lowood's wife?' she asked apologetically. 'Did you make it your business never to see her again either?'

Wilson sucked in a sharp breath, as if he had just felt the cutting edge of a blade.

'I did,' he said stoutly. 'For it was the only way I could continue living myself. I was betrothed to her, you see. Till Lowood took a fancy to her, and little by little stole her away from me.'

'Were you . . . surprised when she eloped with Lowood?' Emily asked.

As she mentioned the fiend's name, a gust of hot wind ran over the grass, racing towards them, as if in warning of something dreadful approaching. The horses reared, snorting in fear, their eyes rolling white as they started in the opposite direction, galloping to the far side of the field. When Peter Wilson's gaze met her eye, Emily wasn't sure what she expected to see, but she wasn't prepared for tears – of grief, yes, but also fear.

'I don't like to speak his name,' he admitted. 'It seems to bring him, somehow; and if he wishes it so, he is a man that you can never be free of. Not while you are living, at least.'

Emily nodded, 'Then tell me about her. Tell me about Barbara.'

'Fair as a May morning, she was,' he said. 'I'd known her since we were both twelve. I grew up working for the family over at the old house, and she joined as a scullery maid.' A faint smile appeared through his unhappiness for a moment, as he recalled the girl he had known. 'You never seen anyone so pretty: pink cheeks and copper hair, eyes as blue as periwinkles.'

Emily tried to recall her last impression of Mrs Lowood, and remembered a scrawny, raw-faced woman with sharp features and a downturned mouth. It was true that great hate and unhappiness could worm itself into the very being of a soul, creating a monster within.

'I had never seen someone so perfect, and who was I, a boy who knew nothing of the world, nor how to speak to such a beauty? Still, by and by we came to know one another, slowly, a little at a time. My pa, and the old housekeeper, they kept a watch of us, but it weren't like that between us, you see.' Wilson reached a hand out towards one of the horses that had begun to cautiously walk back towards the man. 'It were gentle, it were pure. I thought of her like a flower, tender and fragile. We'd walk together in the garden on our afternoons off and, by the time we were sixteen, we came to the under-standing that we loved one another. It was true, I know it was. I loved her, but she loved me too. I saw it, I saw it in her face. She loved me too. That was until he came and turned her head.'

'And how did he do that?' Anne asked. 'I mean, no offence, it's just that Mr Lowood is not a pleasant man to talk to, or to look at now. I cannot imagine he was much more charming ten years ago. And he was so much older than Barbara. How could he have beguiled her so when she had a young man who cared for her?'

Wilson shook his head, kicked the heel of his boot into the dust.

'I ask myself the same question over and over again,' he said. 'What could I have done? How could I have saved her? He had a way, like a sorcerer. That's all I can think. Ugly as sin he was, but there was something. Something he said or did that seemed to set a fire in her and it stayed lit until she was burnt to ashes. I wanted to honour her. He wanted to drag her down to the gutter, and somehow he made her want that too. I don't know what he said to her, I don't want to know. But once she decided it was him she wanted, she couldn't see nothing else. Everything we'd had was gone. I knew the day they told me she'd run off with him, I knew he'd killed her that day. It was only a matter of time as to when her body would fall to the ground. I'm still waiting for my final breath.'

'It hurts to really love another,' Emily said, her eyes downcast. 'It's a wound that never heals.'

'Thank goodness you found happiness anew, with Mrs Wilson,' Anne added hastily.

'I don't love her and she knows it,' he said. 'And she hates me for it. We don't do nothing but hurt one another. I never loved another soul in my lifetime but Barbara. I only wished I'd done it sooner.'

Mr Wilson stopped abruptly. He pulled his cap low over his eyes.

'Done what sooner?' Emily asked.

'Had him put out of a job,' he said. 'I spoke to my master and he spoke to the parish. They agreed it wasn't proper after what he'd done, and they turned him out of the workhouse. Now, I beg you, leave me in peace, and perhaps I'll stop seeing her every night.'

'It is very hard to be tortured,' Emily said.

'Oh, I don't mean her memory, though it is always in my heart,' Peter Wilson said. 'I mean her. Since she died, I see her every dawn, grey and rotting like the corpse she is. And every time she appears, she draws a little closer.'

TWENTY-TWO

Anne

A very merry hour or two passed in the parsonage that evening, one that Anne thought she would never forget – not only for the warmth and love that filled every corner of their dining room, but for the turn of events that would change everything for the rest of their lives. In each instance, the catalyst was Mrs Crowe.

Ellen's arrival some days earlier had lifted their spirits, opening a door to the outside world that was all too easy to forget existed sometimes, when they were all cloistered together, needing nothing but one another. Yet it was Mrs Crowe's unexpected appearance that truly seemed to bring their shadowy little home back to life. Anne didn't think she could ever remember a time when an evening had been quite so gay.

While they had been making preparations for Catherine's investigation and speaking to Mr Wilson, Papa had instructed Tabby to prepare something special for their guest, and given her coin to go to the butcher's for a joint of beef. He'd also told Tabby to ready the best china and make sure the silver was polished, all in Mrs Crowe's honour. Naturally Tabby was terribly affronted at such last-minute alterations to her plans for the sake of some fancy woman, and though – by all accounts – she had not ceased mithering about it all day, she and Martha had indeed pulled off a glorious repast worthy of the finest country house.

Even more delightful than the glittering candlesticks, or the delicious food, was the good cheer of the company that was crammed around the dining table. Chairs had been procured from the kitchen and Papa's study and all were present, even Mr Nicholls and – more importantly – Branwell. If anyone could do Branwell good, Anne was sure that it would be Catherine Crowe and her irrepressible delight in almost everything she encountered.

'I must say, Mrs Crowe, your tales are fascinating,' Branwell said, his eyes alight with interest after Mrs Crowe finished telling them about her encounter with a ghoul. Only water was served at the table, and for once the charismatic pull of their literary guest outweighed Branwell's need to excuse himself in search of gin. Mrs Crowe's luminosity had seemed to reignite something similar in her brother, Anne noted with pleasure. He was interested, curious and alive. It was a joy to behold. 'Will you tell us why you came to be so interested in the unnatural, and how you have become so learned on the subject?'

'Not unnatural, sir,' Mrs Crowe told him. 'But *super*natural. Everything that exists in this universe is part of the great order of things. It is just that we children of God have yet to grasp its full magnitude. It is wondrous to think of it, is it not, Mr Brontë? I find that whenever I am brought low or find myself listless and uninterested, that the moment I return to my investigations, I am invigorated once again. For what is the purpose of Man, if not to study the marvels and miracles of this world, and seek enlightenment?' Mrs Crowe beamed. 'As for my own interest – well, it began with the death of my papa. I was very far from home, in Crete, when I woke in the heat of the night to see my own dear father standing at the foot of the bed. He smiled at me with such fond sadness. Of course, I called out to him, reached to embrace him. But, in an instant, he was gone, and the world seemed like an emptier place. I knew at once that he had passed into the Lord's embrace. A letter arrived some days later to confirm that it was so. You see, I do so fervently believe that there is a world open to us, if we could only understand it, that would grant us a great understanding of life and death, all that come after and our place in God's creation. I made up my mind at Papa's funeral that I would not rest until I had done all I could to discover more of the hidden realms. To study every branch of science and philosophy and religion so that I might approach my examinations with the power of education and the open mind of a curious soul.'

'You inspire me, Mrs Crowe,' Branwell said. 'Recently I have been guilty of allowing my sorrows to become my entire existence. Yet, my sisters are curious souls, and never cease to question the world in their search for truth. There was a time when I was the first quarter of our whole, and we'd explore endlessly every day; children, still capable of awe and hope.' He turned to Anne, taking her hand. 'Charlotte, Emily and Anne have never lost that quality. You make me wonder if it would be possible to recover it in myself once more at my age.'

'My dear young man,' Mrs Crowe said. 'Age is only a barrier to awe and hope if you allow it to be. Do you not agree, Reverend Brontë?'

'I do indeed, I do,' Papa said, brightly. 'A gentleman – or lady, for that matter, Mrs Crowe – must keep a steady head and a strong heart in this world. For we will face more sorrows than we can count in our mortal days, but the preservation of hope will always lead us to joy in the end. And, if we are good Christians, to love everlasting, Amen.'

'Amen indeed, Mr Brontë,' Mrs Crowe said, briefly bowing her head.

For a moment Anne allowed herself to entertain the notion that if her own dear mama had still been here, though she had no memory of her herself, she would have been exactly like Catherine. As full of energy and nurturing enthusiasm and quick wit. How lucky they had been to have Aunt Branwell to care for them in her stead, and Tabby to raise them at her knee. Yet how sweet it would have been to see her own mother's face, softened with age and made golden by lamplight, seated next to her papa.

Then Arthur Bell Nicholls broke the moment in two.

'I would add a note of caution to all of this talk of adventure and exploration, as if either endeavour came without risk,' Mr Nicholls said sternly, glancing at Charlotte, who studiously avoided eye contact. 'Curiosity can also bring the unwary and ill-prepared into dangerous circumstances. Think of the cat, after all.'

'I must say,' Ellen said into the awkward silence, 'that I rather think Mr Jonson was incorrect on that front, for I have never met a curious cat. Every cat I have ever known has preferred comfort and food over adventure.' Ellen laughed but the rest of the table remained silent.

Anne waited for Charlotte to rebut Mr Nicholls, but she only sipped from her glass, her eyes downcast, allowing the awkward moment to extend. Perhaps something she had eaten disagreed with her.

'I'm afraid I cannot agree with you, Mr Nicholls,' Anne said, instead. 'Would you caution my brother or my father so, or yourself indeed? Or is it only the fairer sex that you determine should remain forever closeted indoors, kept apart from the pleasure of making discoveries independently?'

'I do indeed believe that there are matters that are best left to men, Miss Brontë,' Mr Nicholls said, infuriatingly evenly. 'Mrs Crowe is clearly a very independent and determined woman of the world, and I have nothing but admiration for her. But not every lady can be Mrs Crowe. Particularly one who has never been married, and has no gentleman to guide and protect her.'

'Why not?' Anne replied at once, before Mrs Crowe could make her own answer. 'Why should not *any* person, regardless of their sex, make a life pursuing what they are good at?'

'I do not say that,' Arthur said. 'I meant only to say that if a lady overreaches herself, without the steady support of a gentleman to rely upon, she may find herself in difficulties as to her reputation, or – worse still – her safety.'

'Reputation,' Emily spluttered. 'Why should any person's value be made of some false ideal created a hundred years ago?'

'Because moral decency is a fine indicator as to the character of a person,' Mr Nicholls said. Anne's fury was made all the worse because he was being perfectly measured and logical. It was simply unbearable.

'Sir, you are quite correct of course,' Mrs Crowe said thoughtfully. 'For any woman to succeed in her chosen field or profession, she will have to work ten times as hard as a gentleman, *and* be ten times as brilliant. All the while safeguarding her honour against the inevitable rumours and scandal that always accompany such an endeavour, while ensuring that she meets the expectations of propriety along the way. You fear that an impulsive female might stray into danger unaware, Mr Nicholls. But sir, I assure you, any educated woman who strives to pursue a profession or interest on her own account is always keenly aware of each pitfall that might lay ahead; she must be, in order to survive.'

'I beg your pardon, madam,' Mr Nicholls's gaze returned to Charlotte again and again. And not once did her opinionated sister have a single thing to say on the matter. It was perplexing. 'I can see you are a remarkable person, but should you lead others who are less worldly and more fragile into danger behind you?'

'Do you mean us?' Emily snorted.

'I do not mean you,' Mr Nicholls replied quietly.

'Who do you mean?' Anne asked him.

'I mean no one in particular,' Mr Nicholls said.

'I do believe the storm cannot be far off now, don't you think?' Ellen said, bravely trying to smooth the troubled waters.

'He means me,' Charlotte said, speaking up at last. The table fell silent. Charlotte adjusted her position and raised her chin, before she went on. 'Mr Nicholls is afraid for me, because he saw me in conversation with Abner Lowood two evenings since. As any friend would, if seeing any one of us in conversation with a suspected murderer. His comments tonight are an attempt to warn me of a fatal misstep without making the incident public. I cannot find fault with him for that.'

'You let yourself be seen with Lowood?' Emily said. Anne's eyes were on her father.

'Charlotte, my dear,' Papa leaned towards her, 'what could have possessed you to speak to that man? Where did the encounter take place, and was it arranged?'

'It was not,' Charlotte said honestly, 'and it was just beyond in the graveyard. Lowood came to the house and I thought, rather than distressing others, I would deal with the matter myself.'

'Why did you not fetch me, or Mr Nicholls?' Papa asked Charlotte, not in fury but quiet regret.

Charlotte looked from Emily to Anne. Emily nodded.

'Because, Papa, Emily, Anne and I had become obliged to assist Mr Lowood as to the matter of his innocence in the case of the murder of his wife, and to discover who attempted to inflict the same harm upon him.'

'I beg your pardon?' Papa said. His light tone had vanished. His expression had become very grave, and Anne was reminded of the angry papa she had feared so deeply as a child. It was not that Papa was ever violent or cruel, but more that the weight of his fierce disappointment was almost unbearable to carry. It had been a long time since any of them had felt the threat of it. 'Daughters, explain yourselves at once.'

Mrs Crowe reached across the table and patted Anne's hand in encouragement. Emily slid lower and lower down in her chair, as if she might disappear under the table at any moment, which, when it came to Emily, was a distinct possibility.

'Papa,' Anne said steadily. 'From time to time, for the last two years or so, Charlotte, Emily, Branwell and I have taken it upon ourselves to venture into situations where we might be able to afford some help to the needy and the poorly treated and to redress the inequality that is so often suffered by certain sections of society.'

'Women and children,' Emily specified, her chin at table height. 'Those most at risk of being subjugated by men. We have helped women and children who had no one else to turn to.'

'Charitable works, then?' Papa said.

'Well, we certainly don't get paid for it,' Emily said. Now only her nose could be seen.

'We attempt to utilise all that you have taught us,' Anne went on, 'and our own intuitions and education to bring balance and justice where there is inequality and prejudice. Our "detections", as we call them, have taken us into places and situations where we have faced quite some peril. We have become accustomed to it.'

Patrick thought for a long moment as he attempted to absorb what Anne had just said. 'With your brother at your side, as your leader and protector?'

'Often,' Charlotte said, smiling at Branwell. 'Branwell has been with us and proved himself invaluable. But not always, Papa. Sometimes we have been quite alone. But we have never turned away from the dark, for you taught us that we must not.'

'Such inspirations,' Mrs Crowe said quietly.

'I can hardly believe what I am hearing,' Mr Nicholls said, stunned.

'We have done a great deal of good,' Emily said. 'We have unravelled mysteries and thwarted evil. It was our endeavours that discovered the truth about the vanished bride at Chester Grange.'

'And it was we who discovered the name of the poor child whose bones were found buried at Top Withens,' Charlotte said. 'It was because of us that a murderer was locked away where they could do no more harm.'

'Are you quite certain you are not speaking of one of your stories now?' Papa asked Charlotte very gravely. 'Your wild tales of Angria? For if what you say is true, then where is the law in these matters?'

'The law was inadequate on the first count and kept out of it on the second,' Charlotte said.

'And last summer, when we told you we were with Ellen, we were in London. All of us. We barely escaped the clutches of a most evil criminal who we then conspired to have brought to justice by . . .' Anne thought better of mentioning that particular personage. 'With the help of Mrs Crowe actually.'

Patrick looked from daughter to daughter to son, and then at Mrs Crowe, who regarded him with expectation. And then he burst into laughter.

'You see, madam,' he told Mrs Crowe. 'Since they were children, they have lived half in this world, and half in another of fantastical adventures and heroic deeds, each one blending into the other, so that I swear they don't know what is real and what is make-believe. They are singular persons, would you not agree?'

'I would agree, sir,' Mrs Crowe said. 'Quite remarkable young people. Which is why, my dear Reverend, you must believe them. For every word is true.'

TWENTY-THREE

Charlotte

'Well,' Charlotte said. 'It is done at least. We have told Papa about the detections and, though I cannot be sure how he yet feels, I for one feel lighter. Do you not, Anne?'

'I suppose that I do,' Anne said, slowly. 'Though, I feel dreadful for misleading Papa, I did not know that we were to confess to the curate also.'

'That matter was rather taken out of my hands when Arthur saw me with Lowood,' Charlotte said, though that was not strictly the entire truth. She had been glad to shift the weight of secrecy on this matter from her shoulders, but she had also been surprised and perhaps even a little moved by Arthur's determination to attempt to guide and protect her. Charlotte realised she wanted him to know the truth about their detections too.

As for their writing – well, that was another matter. That could remain between them for a little longer, at least until they knew if anything would come of it.

'I do not feel any better,' Emily said from underneath the table where she was ensconced with Keeper in a huddle, sulking. 'I am glad to tell Papa the truth, but I worry what price it will cost him, and us. One thing is certain, he will have thoughts on the matter. Once he has finished talking with Branwell and Mr Nicholls, he will have thoughts.

He might well prevent us from completing this detection entirely.'

'Well,' Charlotte said, thinking of her unfinished pages of *Jane Eyre* calling to her from within her writing slope. 'Perhaps we need not finish it now. After all, a sizeable reason as to why Lowood was able to oblige us to aid him has now been removed. With Papa's influence, I feel certain that he could limit the knowledge of our enterprise somehow.'

'After all, only half of Yorkshire knows about Branwell,' Anne said dryly.

'But we must finish this detection!' Emily said, her head and shoulders rising from beneath the tablecloth. 'Mrs Crowe is investigating tonight! I should hate to miss Mrs Crowe investigating!'

'As would we all,' Charlotte said. 'But if Papa asks us not to, Emily, then we must obey, both for the sake of his health and because he is our father.'

Emily sighed as she vanished out of sight once again.

'Are you quite all right, dear?' Ellen asked, crossing to join Charlotte from the sofa where she had been sitting ever since Papa, Branwell and Mrs Crowe had retired to Papa's study. 'You colour is high; you look rather agitated.'

'I suppose I am,' Charlotte confessed, lowering her voice. 'I have become rather good at keeping secrets over the last few years. To tell the truth and face the consequences seems somehow more terrifying than the possibility of facing an undead corpse risen from the grave!'

'I can't say that I agree with you,' Ellen said. 'And I can't say that I am not a little angry with you still, and a good deal hurt. Those secrets that you have kept, you kept from me as well. But I do think it was right to tell your papa what you have been about. After all, you are heroines, if the world but knew it.'

'The world must never know it,' Charlotte said, turning to her friend as she looked at the peaceful summer night. 'We have never sought recognition or thanks for our work; we only ever wished to help those who had no other means of it.'

Ellen nodded. 'I shall carry your secrets to the grave,' she said. 'I swear it.'

'And Ellen, dear,' Charlotte took her hand. 'I beg you, please don't be displeased with me for a moment longer. I only kept difficult things from you because you are my oasis and my serenity. Please accept my apology. I realise that half a friendship is hardly a friendship at all, but I do love you, Ellen. I sincerely do not know how I should manage without you.'

'Well, I suppose we have been together too long now for me to find a new friend,' Ellen said, with a faux sigh and a little smile. 'Imagine the bother of having to get so well acquainted with another at my age. I shall continue to tolerate you, if only for the sake of convenience.' She smiled, putting her arm around Charlotte's waist and hugging her briefly. 'But now we share all with one another, agreed?'

'Agreed,' Charlotte said, knowing that there were still some things – some thoughts and feelings – that she would never speak of to another human, not even her sisters.

'Then I suppose I ought to inform you of what you have not noticed in your distracted state,' Ellen said. She pointed to just the other side of the garden gate, where the figure of Mr Nicholls could be seen loitering. 'I rather believe he is hoping to speak with you.'

'I should go to him,' Charlotte said with a purposeful nod.

'No, you should not!' A voice came from under the table. 'Don't encourage him, Charlotte! His mooning around all over the place is insufferable as it is!'

'I shall do no such thing,' Charlotte said. 'I will only speak to him of what happened tonight.'

'Shall I come with you?' Anne asked her.

'I shall be just at the foot of the garden,' Charlotte said. 'You were less worried about me when I met with a suspected murderer.'

'We had no fear that Abner Lowood would try to marry you,' Emily said.

'Miss Brontë,' Mr Nicholls said, as Charlotte drew her light shawl around her shoulders and walked down to the foot of the garden. Between them was the gate to the graveyard, which she thought probably ought to remain firmly shut. Mr Nicholls stood two steps down on the other side of it, giving Charlotte some advantage of height. For the first time she found herself looking Arthur Bell Nicholls directly in the eyes. They were very dark behind his spectacles, and rather intense. The evening was laden with rain that even the drawing in of the night could not abate.

'Mr Nicholls,' Charlotte said, 'I ought to apologise.'

'No, no, indeed not,' he said anxiously. 'You have nothing to apologise for. Rather, forgive me, Charlotte. I should have found a time to speak to you alone about my fears for you. Not at a dinner, with strangers present. It was just that as I sat across the table from you, I could not contain my anxiety a moment longer. And as a result, I forced your confession to your father . . .'

'You did, sir,' Charlotte said plainly.

'I would never wish to cause you any discomfort or unhappiness, Charlotte, you must know that,' Mr Nicholls went on. 'It was just that ever since I saw you in close conversation with that man, I have been afire with an agony of worry, scarcely able to know what to do. I feared he may harm you or worse—'

'Worse?' Charlotte asked him, affronted. 'Do you think me so foolish and weak that I would let a wretch like that have any part of me?'

'I do not,' Mr Nicholls told her hastily. 'I only know that he is a monster and that you are . . . very dear to me.'

'Even after all you have heard tonight?' Charlotte found herself asking. 'You still think me dear, Arthur?'

'The choices you have made in these last months have been made rashly, and under great strain,' Arthur said. 'I cannot blame you for them, for you do not have the care and protection of a husband to guide you. Charlotte, if you would but allow it—'

'I do not allow it,' Charlotte said, collecting herself. 'I do not allow anything. Arthur, I thank you for your concern for me, I truly do. But you must know that I do not care for you romantically and, should I ever be married, it would not be to you. I would and could only marry for love.'

Arthur said nothing, but turned his face away from her into the shadows.

'Thank you for your clarity, Charlotte,' he said at length, his voice strained. 'I bid you a good night.'

'Arthur,' Charlotte spoke his name before she really knew what she wished to say, only that she didn't wish to leave him feeling so hurt. 'Perhaps you might like to join us tonight? For the investigation? It is sure to be fascinating, whatever is discovered.'

'I would not,' Arthur said. 'I have no need to know what lies beyond God's veil, or to wish into existence goblins and ghouls to thrill me. All in the world that interests me falls within the bounds of this village. Goodnight, Miss Brontë.'

Charlotte watched for a moment as he walked through the stones, and then turned back to her home where she found her father, Branwell and Mrs Crowe standing on the doorstep waiting for her.

'I have come to a decision,' Papa said, with great gravity.

'Yes, Papa,' Charlotte said demurely.

'I have decided I shall accompany you tonight on your investigations.'

Charlotte opened and closed her mouth, before making a small curtsey.

'Yes, Papa,' Charlotte said.

'Then gather your sisters, dear girl, and I will send for the coachman,' Mrs Crowe said with a double clap of her hands. 'There is much to prepare for a night such as the one that lies ahead – a night on which we venture into the unknown.'

TWENTY-FOUR

Emily

'Won't the very large quantity of people present for the investigation into the revenant disrupt the usual patterns of the occurrence?' Emily asked Mrs Crowe, as she followed her from one of her curious machines to the other like a child at her mother's skirts.

'Not at all in my experience,' Mrs Crowe said, as she double-checked the calibrations of the photo-baromètres. 'Indeed, the more observers there are, the better. For if anything does happen tonight, we have more than one witness. And that is extremely important when it comes to adding credibility to the sighting. That way the witness testimony we collect becomes objective, you see?'

'I see,' Emily said. 'And where shall we each be stationed?'

Mrs Crowe thought for a moment, turning in a slow circle as she observed the downstairs room of the cottage and its occupants. Her rotation ceased before Rosalyn Tolliver.

'Now Rosalyn, you always see the revenant at three of the morning?'

'Yes ma'am,' Rosalyn said, her gaze very solemn and serious, and she pointed to the swinging pendulum of the longcase clock before clapping her hands together. 'It always chimes three times just before she appears.' Rosalyn turned to Emily, her face white with terror. 'I believe they say it's the hour of the devil.'

'It *is* the hour of the devil,' Emily replied with enthusiasm. 'I have read that is so.'

'Some say that,' Mrs Crowe smiled reassuringly. 'And, Anne, you said Mr Wilson claimed to see the same vision just before the dawn?'

'Yes,' Anne said, 'he was convinced poor Mrs Lowood was coming for him.'

'Identical visions hours and miles apart offer fascinating potential for study,' Mrs Crowe mused. 'And the Wilson fellow resides about five miles away as the crow flies.' She thought for a moment, one finger resting against her lips. 'It would not be impossible for a person, either living or dead, to travel that distance in the given time.'

'Strange to think,' Branwell said, 'that a dead woman might have a diary of engagements she must keep.'

'It's often thought that what motivates us in life is also what drives the dead,' Mrs Crowe smiled. 'Revenge, envy, regret, guilt. The mortal impulses that can drag us so low in life can propel us even beyond death.'

'Your ghost will always be in the pub, Branwell,' Emily said.

'And yours up on the moor, singing with the wind,' Branwell said, fondly.

'Charlotte will be ordering everyone around, absolutely furious that no one is paying her any attention,' Emily added. 'And Anne will just be Anne, a light for others always.'

'Well, if none of us could die this eve that would be preferable,' Charlotte said. 'I much prefer issuing orders to the living.'

'Now, Rosalyn, and Mr and Mrs Tolliver,' Mrs Crowe recommended her directions. 'Please go about your business as you ordinarily would: go to bed at the same time and try to sleep. Anne, I would like you to sit in Rosalyn's room and observe from there if you would.'

'Certainly,' Anne said. 'Come now, Rosalyn, let me put you to bed.'

'There will be many long hours of waiting, I'm afraid,' Mrs Crowe told her, 'and no certainty of action, but there is no way around it. The nature of researching this subject is one of absolute patience for no promise of reward.'

Anne nodded, retiring up the stone steps with Rosalyn to her bedroom.

'Mr Tolliver, opposite is the dead house and the laundry, both situated in the old buildings from the original farmhouse. Am I correct?'

'Yes ma'am,' Mr Tolliver said. 'The dead house and the laundry across the way. The bakery and the grain store adjacent to this cottage. All built more than three hundred years since, by all accounts.'

'And are there any occupants in the dead house tonight?' Mrs Crowe asked him.

'There are not, ma'am,' Mr Tolliver said. 'Been a slow week.'

'Young Mr Brontë,' Mrs Crowe turned to Branwell. 'If you are willing, would you position yourself inside the dead house so that we may have an observation from the rear? It is certainly not a job for the faint-hearted.'

'Then I am the man for it,' Branwell said at once, straightening his shoulders. 'I have no fear of the dead or their places.'

'Excellent.'

Branwell went to his post, and Emily waited for Mrs Crowe to turn to her, but it was her sister who was next to receive orders.

'Charlotte, you will watch the photo-baromètres for any readings that coincide with our perceived experiences of changes in the atmosphere, temperature, et cetera – and if you could make a note of any sudden changes in readings, that would be wonderful.'

'I understand perfectly,' Charlotte said.

'Reverend Brontë, my dear sir.' Mrs Crowe took Papa's hand, smiling into his eyes. 'If you would be so kind as to station yourself at the ground-floor window, sir, you will offer yet another perspective of observation. I see there is a quite comfortable armchair there that will assist you perfectly.'

'At your service, madam,' Papa said with a small bow. Emily could wait no longer.

'And what of me?' she asked Mrs Crowe eagerly. 'What shall be my duty?'

Mrs Crowe was thoughtful as she observed Emily.

'You are familiar with the spirits, are you not, Emily?' she asked.

'Not intimately,' Emily said with half a laugh, although suddenly the atmosphere had become very still, almost as if the air itself were listening.

'You are one of those rare beings who is able to walk between worlds, I think,' Mrs Crowe said. 'I feel it whenever we meet. Not in body, but in mind. Your spirit is able to detach itself from your physical being and cross into other realms; in your dreams, in your imagination, sometimes in your waking hours. It is a remarkable talent.'

'We call it laziness,' Charlotte laughed nervously.

'I have never considered dreaming a talent,' Emily said. 'Once or twice I have felt that I might have encountered a ghost here and there. But no more than that, half a thought in the dead of night, all washed away by the sunrise. In this one instance, I believe Charlotte is right that I am just exceptionally prone to telling stories to myself.'

'We will see,' Catherine said. 'You wait here with us. I believe your role will become clear as the night unfolds.'

'Oh,' Emily said, disappointed. 'I have no other duty?'

'You need no other duty; your presence itself is like a magnet. You need simply to be.'

'Some sustenance,' Mrs Tolliver said, appearing with a large plate of buttered bread and a pot of tea. 'Before Mr Tolliver and I withdraw to bed.'

'I'll pour the tea then,' Emily sulked, taking a bite from a slice of bread. Just simply be, she thought to herself miserably, as if such a thing was ever possible.

Time passed slowly, dragging heavily. Emily sat at the kitchen table, while Charlotte and Mrs Crowe held a murmured conversation by the fire, their voices low and confidential. Papa had settled in the armchair by the window and soon nodded off, his chin vanishing into his muffler.

Gradually the sounds of the people of the cottage retiring to bed receded and were replaced by the ticking of the clock, the quiet motions of her companions, and the cry of a barn owl hunting somewhere in the fields beyond. Emily was drowsy with food, and the voluptuous heat of the day still lingered in her bones. She leant her head on the heel of her hand. Little by little her head grew heavier and she could feel her lids sinking shut. She snapped them open with a start. Emily knew that if she stayed still a moment longer, she would fall asleep at the table and that would never do. Standing up abruptly, she went over to where Charlotte and Mrs Crowe whispered to one another.

'I believe I will go out and take a walk about the vicinity,' she said. 'To see how Branwell is and to check for any ne'er-do-wells who might seek to trick us.'

'I'm not sure that you should—' Charlotte began, but Mrs Crowe cut across her.

'That is a splendid idea, Emily,' she said. 'Follow your instinct and see where it leads you, though let me take a measurement of your boots before you depart, so that we may recognise their imprint in the flour.'

'It is ten minutes until three?' Charlotte questioned, with some anxiety. 'Emily should not be outside at the allotted hour. We know not what danger might manifest.'

'You will not dally, will you, Emily?' Mrs Crowe asked, unconcerned.

'I will not,' Emily said. 'I had not much desire to meet Mrs Lowood when she was alive, never mind several weeks after her death.'

The night outside the darkened cottage was still and warm, the air full of moisture. Above, gathering clouds had all but obliterated the stars, covering and uncovering the full moon from moment to moment. And yet whatever wind moved the heavens, not a whisper of it was to be felt on the ground. In the silence, Emily thought she could hear a distant roar of thunder. How she longed for the wind and rain of a storm to wash away the heat and discomfort they had all suffered for so long. But there was something else that Emily thought she could detect in the air that night, a sense of expectation, as if all things living and dead were alert to all possibility.

As promised, she made a circuit of the courtyard taking careful deliberate steps over the flour-coated cobbles; it appeared to be entirely empty of life. Not even a scurrying fieldmouse or a wayward cat was to be found lurking in the shadows, never mind a villain intent on trickery or a recently risen rotting corpse. Guessing she still had a moment or two before she was required back inside, Emily went to the dead house window to see if Branwell were still sober, because she absolutely would not put it past her brother to find a way to get drunk in a mortuary.

As she peered in through the small dirty window, the atmosphere around her shifted and changed into a living thing. At once she felt as if there were something lurking at her back. Turning sharply, she heard her own gasp of half-fear, half-relief at the sight of nothing at all.

'Stop telling yourself stories, Emily Jane,' she muttered to herself. 'You'll make yourself a fool if you're not careful.'

Emily went back to the window, searching for Branwell in the shadowy room that was lit only by fluctuating moonlight. What she saw made her blood chill in her veins. For there was Branwell, lying on one of the mortuary tables, still and white. His eyes were open and unblinking, staring at whatever waited in the shadows. Emily knew with a cold rush of dread that her brother had died, that he was a corpse.

'No, Branwell!' Emily gasped, running to the door that would not open. She shook it again and again, but it seemed to be bolted shut from within. Racing back to the window, she beat her fists against the glass. Still Branwell rested, as if laid out for his shroud, his pallid skin glowing in the dark. Worse still, now Emily could see that three other tables in the dead house were also occupied. Three bodies lay side by side, each one covered by a sheet, one small bare foot appearing blueish under the sheet. But Mr Tolliver had told them the mortuary was empty! Why would he lie? Did he mean them harm? Had he killed her brother?

With fear gripping her chest in its clenched fist, Emily pounded on the door of the dead house, doing her best to wake the dead.

'Branwell, Branwell!' she sobbed, suddenly afraid that the other shrouded figures were dear to her too. 'It cannot be, it cannot be!'

And then the door she beat upon opened suddenly, and she tumbled into the chill dank room, and into Branwell's arms. Into her living, breathing brother's arms.

'Emily, whatever is the matter?' he asked her. 'Did you see the revenant? I think I must have drifted off sitting on that old stool over there.'

Emily looked from the stool, where Branwell's coat was crumpled as a makeshift cushion, to the vacant stone table where she had been certain she had seen him, dead.

'I-I . . . are you well?' Emily pressed her hands over his shoulders and torso, shaking her head in disbelief and muttering in confusion. 'I saw you, you were as white as marble . . . Are you well, Branwell?'

'What is well, if you really think about it . . .?' Branwell began.

'You are alive!' Emily half sobbed in relief, dragging him into a tight embrace. As she looked over his shoulder and around the room, she saw that the other tables were indeed empty. Everything she had seen, or thought she had seen, had vanished.

'What happened to upset you so?' Branwell asked her, his thumb and forefinger under her chin. I do not believe I have ever seen Emily Brontë so frightened.'

'I am not frightened,' Emily said at once, sucking in a shuddering breath.

Just then the clock struck three.

'Come,' Branwell beckoned Emily to his side and they both stood at the window, waiting, Branwell with a keen eagerness, and Emily still half submerged in the dreadful nightmare from which she had only just awoken. Seconds ticked by one by one and they saw nothing. Until Rosalyn appeared at the window of her bedroom, looking down. A second later Anne was at her side, both of them gazing down at the cobbled yard. Rosalyn pointed down with one hand, the other flying to cover her horrified mouth. Her scream could be heard quite clearly, as could the door to the cottage swinging open of its own volition.

Emily saw Anne support a hysterical Rosalyn, taking her away from the window.

'But there is nothing there,' Branwell said, perplexed.

'No, there must be something!' Emily ran out into the courtyard and utter quiet. Every tiny creature of the night, every bird and mammal had fallen silent, and there was not a whisper of wind. Then it came upon her like a physical blow. A feeling of such rage, such fury that she could not help but lift up her head to the moon and scream for vengeance. Emily had a dim impression of her brother at her side, and her sisters close behind.

From somewhere, perhaps inside the cottage, she heard a rasping voice boom.

'*Beware her vengeance!*'

In the very next moment, she fell to the cobbles, a dead weight.

TWENTY-FIVE

Anne

As Anne had watched her sister collapse to the floor, it had seemed to her that time had become so heavy with the weight of the events that it had slowed almost to a standstill.

One moment Rosalyn had been screaming and pointing at an entirely vacant courtyard, adamant that she could see the decaying figure of Barbara Lowood lurching towards her very own front door. The next Emily appeared as if from nowhere and seemed to be occupying that very place that Rosalyn insisted was occupied by a walking corpse. In the bright moonlight, Emily's eyes had made contact with Anne's, every vestige of colour had drained from her face and Anne experienced a rush of fear, not of a revenant or a ghost, but of the expression of utter sorrow that was wrought on Emily's face. There was something else too, something Anne could not make sense of. For a fleeting glimpse she thought she could see two realities at once. Where Emily stood, she also saw a darkness that surrounded her sister but was not cast by her. Something less than a solid form, but more than a shadow. There had been the terrible disembodied voice, which sounded as if it were made from gravel and phlegm, booming from the spirit trumpet, its message clear: '*Beware her vengeance!*' Then Emily had crumpled to the floor, her head hitting the cobbles, and time rushed on at speed.

'Bring her in,' Mrs Crowe directed, as Branwell, rushing to Emily's side, lifted her in his arms, though she was both taller and stronger than he. Purposefully, he brought her into the cottage, his face alert and full of concern. Her brother was still present, Anne realised, suppressing the sob of relief that threatened at the sight of him.

'Lay her on the sofa, support her head,' Mrs Crowe told Branwell, pointing at a pillow for Charlotte to place under Emily. 'Mrs Tolliver, make tea. Anne, bank the fire.'

After all these tasks were completed, Anne and Charlotte knelt at Emily's side, Papa sitting at her head, resting his big hand on her forehead as he murmured a prayer. Taking Emily's icy hand, Anne studied her sister's face for any sign of consciousness. Her eyelids fluttered, her shallow breaths came rapidly as she muttered something unintelligible, though Anne thought she heard her own name amongst the fevered whispering.

As they gathered around Emily, Rosalyn and Mr Tolliver came slowly down the stone steps, as if they too were in some kind of trance, not yet fully awakened from the terrors they had seen, Anne supposed. The room felt thick and heavy with fear of the unknown, and Anne felt it too. How would she continue to live without Emily? Without any of her dear siblings? The thought was too frightful to countenance.

'We must try and rouse her,' Mrs Crowe said. 'Charlotte, see if your voice will rouse her.'

'Come now, Emily Jane,' Charlotte said gently, her tearful tone at odds with her commanding words. 'You are to stop this at once. Wake up – enough of this nonsense, you frightful, dear, dear girl.'

'Emily, wake up,' Anne added, firmly patting Emily's hand. 'You will worry Papa if you do not wake up now.'

The message seemed to have the desired effect.

'Anne?' Emily's eyes fluttered open, taking a moment to focus on her face. And then dear Emily smiled, her other hand reaching to touch Anne's face. 'You are here, you are quite well? You are certain?'

'Am I certain that *I* am quite well?' Anne half laughed, half sobbed as she caught Emily's hand to her cheek and kissed it. 'Are *you* well, sister?'

'And Charlotte?' Emily raised herself up and, upon seeing her sister, dragged her into an embrace. Papa stood up, nodding and blowing his nose on his handkerchief.

'Quite so, quite so,' he said faintly under his breath.

'I am here and I am also quite well,' Branwell said from behind. 'All things considered.'

'Come here at once,' Emily demanded of him. 'I need to feel my brother and my sisters alive in my arms. To feel your hearts beating against mine. Come hither at once!'

For a good minute, Anne found herself in a tangle of arms, noses and stifled laughter as Emily did her best to embrace them all simultaneously, and they embraced one another in return.

'What happened?' Anne asked.

'I do not know,' Emily said. 'I was coming to you and then nothing. Nothing until just now, when I came to my senses with a terrible feeling of dread that harm had come to you. To all of you.'

'This is most interesting,' Mrs Crowe said, taking a seat as Mrs Tolliver handed Emily a cup of tea. Rosalyn was also given tea, where she sat wrapped tightly in a shawl, her eyes huge and haunted.

'I don't know about interesting,' Mrs Tolliver said. 'I don't know that being terrified out of one's wits is interesting, exactly. Nor the voice that came out of that thing.' She gestured at the spirit trumpet which sat benignly atop Mrs Crowe's trunk. 'What did it mean, beware her vengeance? Beware Barbara's vengeance, I suppose. She is set upon murdering us all!'

'We must not let the unexplained frighten us, Mrs Tolliver,' Mrs Crowe said firmly. 'We must face it, study it, understand it. Only then will it lose its power over us, do you see? Rosalyn, you saw the same vision of the revenant, at the same allotted hour?' Mrs Crowe asked the trembling girl, who nodded.

'You *must* believe me, she came to the house and opened the door,' Rosalyn whispered, gripping hold of Mrs Crowe's wrist. 'Tomorrow she will come to claim me, I know it to be true.'

'The door,' Emily started at the word, speaking quickly and without much sense. 'The door did seem to blow open. It is possible that I didn't properly secure it when I went out, I suppose, but I do remember it slamming open! The last thing I remember is the door, which was shut, opened suddenly inwards, and there was no visible explanation as to why, which is interesting, is it not, Anne?'

'Be still, Emily,' Anne said softly. 'Calm your nerves, dear.'

'But you saw no walking corpse, Emily?' Mrs Crowe asked Emily.

'No,' Emily frowned, as if trying to recall something, and then shook her head firmly. 'No. I did not see that.'

'Nor did I,' Branwell interjected. 'I confess I nodded off in my chair at my station, but Emily woke me, and a moment afterwards we saw Rosalyn and Anne at the window. Emily ran out, not quite herself, even then. I witnessed the door opening, and then my sister fainted.'

'I saw the creature,' Mrs Tolliver said stoutly. 'I don't care what you might have seen, but I saw her with my own eyes and it was a fearful sight. One I will not recount, but I saw her clear as day, standing there outside the door. Then gone.'

'And I,' Mr Tolliver added, with the distinct intonation meant that he would not be drawn into elaborating further. 'Just like she said.'

'And I,' Papa said, making them all turn their heads towards him. Anne gasped.

'Papa, are you sure?'

'Quite sure,' Papa said gravely. 'Yet, when I try to recollect exactly, the memory is just out of reach, as if it were a dream. Only I am certain it was not. I saw her. I smelled her. And I believe we should end this night with our prayers and ask the Lord for his protection.'

'And we shall,' Mrs Crowe reassured him. 'As soon as this perplexing investigation is concluded. Anne, you were standing with Rosalyn as she sighted the vision. Did you see it?'

'I did not,' Anne said, wondering if she were being entirely truthful. It was as Papa said, she thought she'd seen *something*. But not a person risen from the grave. That she had not seen.

'Nor I,' Charlotte said, rising to her feet and going to her papa. 'Though I did see the door fly open as others did, and felt no gust of wind that might have dislodged it. I've checked the photo-baromètres too. All the readings were consistent, except that there was a drop in temperature just as the clock struck three, which rose quickly again within the minute. And I too heard the voice.'

'We all heard the voice,' Emily said.

'What do you make of it all, Mrs Crowe?' Anne asked the older woman as she paced the stone floor, her skirts swishing at every turn.

'Emily's footsteps are quite clear in the flour, and Branwell's as he ran to her, but I see no other disturbances. It is most intriguing,' Mrs Crowe said thoughtfully. 'One could have concluded family hysteria, which would hardly have been surprising given what these good people have suffered of late, if it were not for Reverend Brontë's experience. Perhaps, as a man of God, the good gentleman is more in tune with the spiritual realm, more open to possibility . . .' Her sentence trailed off as her eyes fell on the tray of refreshments that Mrs Tolliver had brought out for them last night before the investigation began.

'It seems as if most of the bread that Mrs Tolliver brought out was left untouched,' Mrs Crowe said. 'Who partook of the meal?'

'I took a bite,' Emily said. 'And also the tea . . .'

'I had a little bread and butter,' Papa said. 'I thought it would do me good and help sustain me through my vigil.'

'Do you suspect that someone has got poison into the house, and the food? And that is causing the sighting and disturbances, Mrs Crowe?' Anne asked, leaving Emily's side as she crossed the room.

Mrs Crowe did not reply. Instead, she marched purposefully outside the cottage and into the centre of the courtyard, turning slowly on her heel as she regarded each building in turn. With a nod of her head, she marched off towards the grain store, picking up a lantern as she went, for though the sun threatened, the pre-dawn light was still grey and full of mist.

'A-ha,' she said, as Anne and the others caught up with her, and then, 'Such a disappointment.' Mrs Crowe turned to face her audience. 'Well, here's at least one part of your mystery solved, I believe.'

'What's that?' Anne asked her, stepping into the grain store. Mrs Crowe held up her lamp to show the ancient wall of the store, thick with black mould and glistening with damp.

'Go out of this place and I will explain fully,' Mrs Crowe said, ushering them out and closing the grain-store door behind her. 'It is as well you are present, Reverend Brontë, for you will need to speak to the parish at once as to this matter.'

'What is the matter in question?' Emily asked, frustrated, Branwell supporting her under her arm.

'What we have here is not a paranormal occurrence, but a case of St Anthony's Fire,' Mrs Crowe told them, 'or rather ergot poisoning. It's a tiny mould that grows on wheat in damp and waterlogged environments. It's not visible to the naked eye, and can be ground into flour without altering the flavour. However, when ingested even in small amounts, it causes strange behaviours and terrifying visions within a few hours. If you partook of some bread at supper, for example, you would begin to feel the effects at . . .' Mrs Crowe calculated. 'Around three in the morning. Rosalyn, you aren't being stalked by the undead. You were experiencing the nasty effects of a poison.'

'No, ma'am,' Rosalyn darted forward, grabbing Mrs Crowe, 'that isn't it, that isn't it at all! She is real, you must believe me, she is real, I tell you true!'

'No, my dear,' Mrs Crowe said, gently disentangling the young woman's fingers from her forearm. 'If there had been an apparition, we would all have seen it.'

'We did all hear the voice, though,' Emily said. 'You heard the voice, did you not?'

'I did,' Mrs Crowe said. 'It could have been a spirit communication, but not from any revenant. This cottage is centuries old; it might simply have been an echo of the past, brought to our attention through last night's experiments. I cannot rule out that it was a sudden strong gust that both opened the cottage door and sounded the trumpet. Or that our heightened minds converted the noise into a phrase that made sense; I've heard my German colleagues call it auditory hallucination.'

'Oh,' Emily said. 'How disappointing.'

'Not at all,' Mrs Crowe said. 'We have an explanation, Emily. And it is a good deal easier to put right infested grain than to banish a revenant back to their grave. All the grain and all flour milled from it must be destroyed at once,' Mrs Crowe told the Tollivers. 'And it must not be stored in that outhouse any more. My suspicion is that the already damp and old structure, in close proximity to the humidity of the laundry and the atmospheres of the dead house, created the perfect breeding ground for the ergot to take hold. The family have been partaking of it regularly, allowing a sense of unease and fear to grow and to sicken them almost to madness.' She turned to Patrick, 'For you, Reverend Brontë, and for Emily, it was as a fleeting nightmare, thank goodness, and will do you no further harm.'

'I shall call upon the parish today to ensure that new measures are implemented at once, and ensure that grain is brought in from elsewhere until new storage arrangements can be made,' Papa said.

'Wonderful.' Mrs Crowe went to where Rosalyn sat flanked by her parents, shaking her head.

'No, no, you are wrong, she is coming, you must believe me,' the girl said, holding tight onto her parents' hands. 'What I've told you is the truth.'

'It was the truth as your mind understood it. Do you see, Rosalyn?' Mrs Crowe told her kindly. 'You are not being plagued by a vengeful being. You have been a victim of an illness, and the symptoms will pass now you know what caused it. You need not be afraid any more.'

Rosalyn only continued to shake her head, almost as if she were angry with Mrs Crowe rather than relieved.

'Mrs Crowe,' Anne asked as she worked through the implications of what had been discovered. 'We were told by an eminent medical person that the presence of arsenic in the deceased does not conclusively mean they were deliberately poisoned. Could it have been this ergot poisoning that killed Mrs Lowood?'

'She was seeing things before she died,' Mrs Tolliver said. 'The bodies attacking in the dead house, for one.'

'In rare cases it can be fatal,' Mrs Crowe said thoughtfully. 'But though it could account for Mrs Lowood's unhappy visions, I do not believe it would have resulted in her death. Mr Tolliver said that deaths had been below average at the workhouse of late. Perhaps their meagre rations served them well for once. And while there are records of ergot poisoning taking over whole villages, leading to an epidemic of madness, we have not seen that here, thankfully. In short, no, I do not believe that St Anthony's Fire was the culprit in that poor lady's demise.'

'Thank you, madam,' Mrs Tolliver took her hand. 'I can't thank you enough for easing our minds. I'm sure our Rosalyn will come to see the truth of it before long, once her mind is settled and clear.'

'My dear lady,' Mrs Crowe said. 'It is altogether my pleasure. Now I suggest a hearty breakfast of eggs and bacon, and nothing made with wheat. Mrs Tolliver, I shall provide the funds to make sure each inmate here receives the same today and for the rest of the week, if you will procure it?'

'I will, ma'am,' Mrs Tolliver nodded. 'I will.'

'Ah well,' Mrs Crowe said, as she packed up the last of her equipment. 'One can't expect a ghost waiting to be discovered around every corner, I suppose.'

'I'm so sorry for wasting your time,' Charlotte said.

'Wasted it? Not at all. For I have spent time with your dear family, and saved another from the grave consequences of an invisible poison. Not a moment has been wasted, Charlotte. Perhaps I will have more luck in my next investigation at the Covent Garden Theatre.'

It was some time later, as Anne, her papa and her sisters stood out on the lane to wave Mrs Crowe off back on her travels, that a troubling thought came to Anne.

Ergot poisoning might explain what had happened at the workhouse. Except that Anne had seen something, and she had not eaten any of the infected wheat.

And it did not explain Mr Wilson's sighting of Barbara Lowood. It did not account for the fact that he and he alone saw his dead lost love searching for him every waking dawn.

It did not explain that at all.

CHAPTER

TWENTY-SIX

Charlotte

At last Charlotte had secured some time to write. Mrs Crowe had departed, seemingly requiring precisely no sleep, and Anne and Emily had retired to bed for an hour or two to refresh their minds, fevered from a night of strange happenings. Emily seemed fully recovered from her faint, and decidedly averse to being fussed over. Branwell announced he was going for a walk, and Papa had closed himself in his study.

'I have thoughts about your recent disclosures,' he had told them just before they went their separate ways. 'They require some development and further elaboration, but the matter is not closed.'

Only Ellen remained to occupy her.

'I have made us some tea,' Ellen said when Charlotte came into the dining room. Charlotte feared her expression must have betrayed her very strong desire to be alone, for Ellen's face fell in response. 'You must be tired.'

'I am a very poor friend indeed,' Charlotte said. 'Neglectful and forgetful. I should not have invited you to come to visit, had I known what disruption and misery awaited you. Can you forgive me?'

'It is a positive pleasure to be disrupted from my usual business,' Ellen told her. 'And I do not feel neglected, Charlotte. Why, I have met a great deal of interesting people since

I arrived, and moreover I am party to a mystery. That's more adventure than I can recall in all my life,' Ellen smiled. 'I do confess I look forward to your company, and it stings rather to see how much you crave solitude, but you should know by now that in seeking your companionship, I do not require you to entertain me. You wish for time to write. And I wish for time to sit and sew, and let the stitching calm and regulate my mind after all I have seen and heard these last few days. Shall we not partake in our easement side by side, if not exactly together?'

'We shall,' Charlotte said. 'You are a tonic, Ellen. You pour your gentle balm onto my brow and I find peace again. Yet I know you have your own troubles and unhappiness. How do you always manage to make a haven for others without attending to yourself?'

'Well, Charlotte, dear,' Ellen said as she settled on the sofa. 'I have you for that. You are marvellously distracting, you know.'

Once everyone but Ellen had taken themselves away, Charlotte had gone directly to her writing box, and begun to write without even a moment's hesitation.

Though she was exhausted, the strange events of the night seemed unreal now in the bright light of day, as if they had been fragments of a dream. The sense of unease seemed to weave in and out of her words in a repeated pattern; her hand would not be still. In every quiet moment, even in the midst of their present detection, Ellen's visit and Mrs Crowe's appearance, Jane Eyre had been ever-present. Growing word by word in her mind and heart; a building pressure that she could not wait one more moment to release onto the page.

As Ellen sewed, focused, neat and methodical, Charlotte wrote, lost in a frenzy of creation.

She wrote until her vision blurred, her fingers cramped and her wrist ached, but still she could not stop. She wrote into being Edward Rochester, lingering at the foot of the stairs, delaying Miss Eyre for just a little longer because he could not bear to let her go. She lived the surge of hope and desperation in Jane's heart as she struggled to understand that the possibility of love could really be hers. As she wrote, her pen travelling across the page almost by its own volition, Charlotte was unaware of anything but the vision in her mind made real. Not of the tick of the clock in the hallway, the sound of Ellen's silk pulling through cotton, nor the tears that silently tracked their way down her cheeks. Not even the ever more tightly compressed atmosphere, where trapped heat fought against low, glowering skies.

That was until the dining-room door opened and Emily, refreshed after a few hours' sleep, crashed in, like the human version of her dog.

'Sister, what has happened?' Emily asked, at the sight of Charlotte.

'What? What has happened?' Charlotte sat up, dragging herself out of the orchard at Thornfield and into the dining room, very much against her will. There were no declarations of love here, no promise of an impossible future with a man who could not bear to live without her. Charlotte took in her worried sister's face, and drew in a deep, steadying breath as she touched a fingertip to her cheek. 'Oh this, this is nothing, just writing, that's all.'

'It must be very good to inspire such emotions in you,' Emily said, turning her head as she attempted to read the latest page upside down.

'I do believe it is good,' Charlotte said, snatching the page away and tucking it with the others in her writing slope. 'And you shall not read it until it is done.'

'I wish I were able to write as freely as you, Charlotte,' Ellen said. 'I can write a letter, of course, but to conjure worlds and beings out of your mind is a wondrous ability.'

'It is indeed,' Emily said as Anne joined them. 'It's rather like witchery.'

'Don't let Tabby hear you say that,' Anne said, as she sat at the table. 'She will send us across the border to Lancashire before we know it.' Anne looked from Charlotte to Emily to Ellen. 'Sisters, are we done with this detection?'

Ellen put away her sewing and joined them at the table as they reflected on what had transpired.

'Mrs Crowe presented a compelling case that seemed to conclusively disprove the revenants,' Emily said, regretfully.

'Only at the workhouse, though,' Anne replied. 'Don't forget, Mr Wilson had visions too. That they should both see the same creature, and for it to have the same cause, would be quite a coincidence.'

'The workhouse sells some of their grain to local millers. It is possible that some of the infected stuff found its way to Harrowings, I suppose,' Charlotte said.

'But then why is not the whole town in the grip of dancing fever?' Emily asked.

Charlotte frowned at her.

'I was unable to sleep so I studied Papa's medical books,' Emily said. 'I discovered that a hundred years ago an entire village became overwhelmed with madness and dancing fever, dancing until they dropped dead in many cases. We have no mass hallucinations in the area. Just a handful of people, one of whom lives five miles away, experiencing the same sighting. It is not impossible that a man in as much mental distress as Mr Wilson, and with his predilection for alcohol, might somehow see the same visions as Rosalyn without the need for poison.'

'Unless Mr Wilson went to the workhouse, and partook of some food there,' Anne said. 'If he has indeed been to that establishment, but neglected to mention it to us, that could be troubling. After all, he had a motive for revenge on Lowood that still burns very brightly in his mind and heart.'

'He did not seem like a man minded to murder,' Emily said. 'He loves the horses he cares for and he told us that he made it his business never to set eyes on the Lowoods.'

'Well, I suppose he would say that, if he was hiding a motive for murder,' Ellen said mildly.

'Evil can be very adept at hiding in plain sight,' Charlotte agreed. 'And even the friends of animals can be enemies of humanity. If we can prove that Wilson was at the workhouse, then his sighting of revenants might lead to his downfall. Our best chance of discovering if he was telling the truth about avoiding Lowood is to try and ascertain if he was ever seen at the workhouse. We should return there this afternoon.'

'Must we proceed?' Emily asked her. 'Lowood has very little to blackmail us with now. If another attempt were made on his life, would there be anyone in the world who would weep for him, save his living victim? The law made no progress at resolving this matter. Perhaps for once we could just accept that this is not our business, and we could cease the detection.'

'Don't be ridiculous,' Charlotte said indignantly.

'Somehow I anticipated that answer,' Emily smiled. 'Let me see whether or not I can intuit what you are about to say now.' Emily raised her forefinger to her temple, as Charlotte's mouth fell open.

'For even a wretch such as Lowood,' Emily said, doing a passable imitation of her sister, 'deserves a true and thorough discharging of justice. If there is a guilty party, we must do our best to establish their identity, no matter who they are. Even if we prove the beast Lowood innocent.' Emily smiled mischievously at Charlotte. 'Fear not, I know that we three will not stop until we have discovered all. Nor would I wish to.'

Charlotte slowly closed her writing desk.

'Ellen, will you accompany us to the workhouse?'

'Are you sure you should make another journey today?' Ellen asked Charlotte. 'You have not had one wink of sleep.'

'I would not rest, Ellen,' Charlotte said. 'A ruffled mind makes a restless pillow. It would be better to press on, and finish this final detection before it finishes us.'

'There *is* one other thing I have noted.' Ellen started to speak and then closed her mouth again.

'Do you have a thought, Ellen?' Charlotte asked her.

'I do not wish to say anything foolish,' Ellen said.

'Please Ellen, go on,' Charlotte said, sending Emily a look. 'You are amongst friends here, and whatever you have to say will be helpful in some way.'

'Well, it's just that – as you were talking – I recalled something that might be of interest. I went to check over the notes I have been making whenever you three meet to share information, and yes, there it is. When Anne and Emily were telling us of their first visit to Mr Wilson, Anne mentioned that he told them that when Lowood first arrived at Harrowings as a house painter, he let slip that he'd not long left Scarborough, in an attempt to escape some kind of trouble there. Perhaps there could be some evidence in that town – a witness, even – who might reveal more of Lowood than he would wish us to know.'

'Why Ellen, that is entirely brilliant!' Charlotte said. Ellen blushed with pleasure.

'Mr Wilson can wait for another day or two. We must go to Scarborough, as soon as we are able to make arrangements, and search out those who knew Lowood,' Anne said enthusiastically. 'His past is bound to hold the key.'

'But where would we begin?' Charlotte asked. 'Scarborough grows in size by the hour, and people come and go from there often. How should we begin to find a trace of him?'

'In the churches,' Papa said as he entered the room. 'Not Methodist or Baptist or Catholic, Mr Lowood is none of those; he told me once that he had no truck with that nonsense and preferred a good English church with a good English God. But if he had relations of the same name or was baptised or married in Scarborough, there will be a record of him. That is, if he did not change his name when he left; though even if he did, he is a distinctive-looking man. Otherwise, he would not have had the nerve to manipulate my daughters into serving him. So, I believe that if you visit the churches, you will find a record of him, and the names and addresses of those who are related to him.'

'Papa, do you wish us to stop?' Anne asked her father as he came in and took a seat at the table.

'I do,' he said. Anne's head dropped in shame.

'We are sorry, Papa,' Charlotte said. 'To deceive you, to go behind your back, it was wrong. You are undeserving of such contemptuous treatment from your children.'

'It is and I am,' Papa agreed, his tone very grave as he took a moment to look into the faces of each of his daughters. 'Since we came to this house, I have buried my beloved wife, your mama. And my two dear daughters, Elizabeth and Maria, your sisters. Your aunt Branwell also passed beneath this roof. Every day I fear for the fate of my only son.' He held out his two hands. Charlotte took one and Anne the other, Emily wrapping her arms around his shoulder.

'My daughters are my treasures,' Papa told them. 'You are my hope. To lose you would finish me. And so yes, I wish you to stop any endeavour that could cause you to come to harm. I wish with all my heart that I could know that you will each be safe and secure for the rest of your lives, even when I am no longer here to provide for you. But God does not afford us such comfort, it is not his design for us. Just as I do not have it within my power to give you an income that will secure your futures, neither do I have the right to tell you to stop, not even as your father. You choose to seek out danger and darkness because you believe there is right and wrong, truth and injustice. You have chosen to help those without money or influence. I cannot ask you to cease being champions of the weak and needy, I have no right to. So, I ask you only to let me aid you where I may and protect you as much as I am able. I have given your brother a great deal of money these last few months, but I have a little in reserve that you may use to travel to Scarborough. And, my dearest daughters, I beg you, *come to no harm.*'

'Papa,' Charlotte was the first to speak, kissing the back of his hand.

'Your mama would have approved of your revolution,' he said, rising a little stiffly. 'Arthur will not, of course, so we shall tell him the matter is closed, you are forbidden from making any further detections, and keep all else away from him, otherwise I shall never hear the end of his concerns.'

'Papa!' Emily laughed. 'Is Arthur not worthy of the truth?'

'Of course he is,' Papa said. 'As long as it is the sort of truth that will not trouble him to excess verbosity. So, you shall leave for Scarborough tomorrow?'

'I should enjoy a trip to see the sea, and I have enough to pay my own way,' Ellen said.

'That has proved to be invaluable,' Charlotte said. 'I will write to the boarding house, secure a room for us at once, and post the request on my way to the workhouse.'

'Are we working for Lowood or for ourselves now?' Emily asked.

'We are working for truth,' Anne said. 'For where it thrives, evil withers away.'

I should come a trip to see the sea, and have enough in
Two, my children, Here said.
That has no end to it, my child, Challupe said. I will
write in the boardinghouse, to us a room to us at on a
and an hour at a time, as it is in two months.
About every night I dreamed of the people where we lived
back.
Well, it makes no difference, but that's for when it comes,
comes there away.

Emily

'I could not find a single soul who had had any dealings with the groom from Harrowings Hall,' Charlotte reported when she returned in the early evening, utterly exhausted. 'Mr Tolliver said he knew of that man, but that he never visited the workhouse. Rosalyn had no idea who he was. We spoke to all the staff and a few of the inmates, but though some were familiar with his name, not a one had ever seen him set foot on the premises. It doesn't mean he hasn't found a covert way to pay a visit, of course, but for now we can neither rule him in nor out as a suspect.'

'I should have gone in your stead,' Emily had said, wrapping a shawl around Charlotte, who was too tired even to eat. 'You must go to bed now, and recover your strength.'

And so, Charlotte and Ellen had retired to bed early, and Anne followed them soon after, meaning that Emily found herself alone in the late evening, reading as the last light of the dour day faded, still as yet to be refreshed by rainfall. The novel was only passably entertaining, and she found her mind wandering again and again back to the previous night, which seemed to have taken place an age and yet a moment ago, simultaneously.

Emily had determined not to think about her strange, nightmarish vision at the workhouse at all, to block it out and cast it into the darker recesses of her mind, where she sent every thought or memory that did her harm. But the nightmare would not be silenced. Worms of insistent queries wriggled their way into her mind, despite her best attempts to squash them. Why, she questioned, should she have been subject to a ghastly hallucination of her very own, when she had not taken any of the infected foods that her father and the Tollivers had?

Though she could not answer the question, Emily could not bring herself to discuss what she had seen with her sisters, for fear that somehow her telling them might make it more real. When she had witnessed those four corpses laid out in the dead house, she knew that she was one of them. More than that, she felt the chill of death spread through her bones, her fingers stiffen and her sight dim. That it was her two sisters and her brother at her side, was also certain. Every time the image returned to her unbidden, Emily felt a thrill of fear like an electrical surge, and she was sickened with worry. No matter how hard she tried, she could not shake off the feeling that she had been shown a portent of disaster that would befall them all.

This would not do. Shutting her book with a loud enough snap to make Keeper leap to his feet, Emily found her way to the kitchen, where Tabby was preparing for the morning.

'Oh aye, what's this then?' Tabby asked her as she entered the room, without turning around.

'What do you mean, Tabby?' Emily asked her, scuffing her toe in the sawdust that coated the stone tiles.

'You in here, at this time of night.' Tabby turned towards her as she undid her apron. 'It must mean you've something weighing on your mind you need to discuss. Been the same since you were a girl, you have.'

'Oh,' Emily said. 'And here I was thinking I was mysterious and aloof, not a book open for any passing fool to read.'

'Are you calling me a fool?' Tabby asked, mock-menacing her with a wooden spoon. 'Out with it then, lass, for I am old and tired and I need my sleep, what with you all gallivanting and unexpected visitors, and your papa getting all riled up like a cockerel in the spring.'

'There's no need for that,' Emily said, cringing. She paused for a moment, struggling to find the right words.

'It is nothing,' she said, turning to leave.

'You stop right there, lass, and speak, or I *shall* tan your hide with this spoon.' Tabby pointed the spoon at a stool by the range, and Emily took a seat.

'It is impossible to resist such lovingkindness,' Emily said wryly, sitting down at the table. 'Tabby, do you put stock in bad omens?'

'I do,' Tabby said, sitting herself with a low groan of pain in the old armchair she kept by the range.

'Which omens do you place particular stock in?' Emily asked, her hand resting on Keeper's head for reassurance.

'Well now, let's see. Crows mean death,' Tabby said.

'There are trees full of crows outside,' Emily laughed.

'And a graveyard full of dead folk,' Tabby nodded, as if her point was proved. It was hard to argue otherwise.

'What else?' Emily asked, unwilling to confess her fear outright.

'A bat in the house means a death,' Tabby said. 'Lean a broom against a bed, death. Follow a corpse candle, death.'

'You mean a will-o'-the-wisp?'

'Death,' Tabby reiterated, nodding at the candle on the table. 'If that there flame flickers and turns blue, death,' she added. 'Drop a loaf fresh from the oven, death. Fold a tablecloth backwards, death. Plant parsley amongst other herbs, death. Dream of a wedding, death.'

'A dream of a wedding is an omen of death?' Emily asked her.

'Oh aye, dreams are sent from the fairy realm, you see, and show you your fortune backwards to what they mean to human folk. A wedding means death, a funeral good luck.'

'Makes perfect sense,' Emily said. 'What about a sort of waking dream, a kind of vision, would that – could that – be taken as an omen?'

Tabby nodded as she realised what Emily was trying to ask her without actually posing the question.

'You speak of what went on at the workhouse with that Mrs Crowe woman leading you all on a merry dance and getting your father all hot under the collar? Did you see the revenant too then?'

'No,' Emily said, uncomfortably. 'I saw . . . I saw death. My death, and Branwell's and Charlotte's and Anne's. I saw our bodies laid out side by side. And I didn't even put a pair of new boots on the table.'

'Well, that means now't, you foolish child,' Tabby said, blowing a raspberry of derision at the very idea. 'You pay too much mind to this old lady, prattling on about death and ghosts. You should know by now, Emily Jane, I don't mean half of what I say. A vision of death is no omen! Go on to bed with you and stop your mithering. You always were too much in your own mind, which would not be a concern if it were not for the fact that your mind is a haunted forest.'

'Wait one moment!' Emily was not about to pretend that Tabby's response was not entirely comforting; even so, she felt she deserved a little clarification. Folding a tablecloth backwards meant death, but having a waking vison in which you see the bodies of the people you love the most laid out on slabs does not? 'How does that make sense?' Emily asked her.

'Sense is as sense does,' Tabby said, infuriatingly. 'What you saw last night, in the middle of all that talk of ghosts and revenants, came from up here.' She tapped Emily's temple quite hard. 'It's as clear as day, if you think about it, which you were. You were het up, and half asleep. What you saw was not a warning. That's your thoughts and worries all in a muddle. You are unsettled, Emily Jane, what with all this coming and going, and packages arriving and letters being sent.' Emily raised her eyebrows. 'You think I haven't noticed all the whispering and sideways glances? You may have confessed one of your secrets to your father, but you've more besides to spare, have you not?' Emily pressed her lips together. 'In any case, you are unsettled, my dear, and it does not suit you. You are a girl who needs peace and quiet. All this adventuring, it has disturbed you. If you'd pay mind to old Tabby, and I know you will not, you would stop it at once and get back to how you used to be. Quiet and no bother. Except for always bringing half-dead animals home.'

'I do miss those days,' Emily said. 'For all the excitement and intrigue.'

'Well, there's your answer then,' Tabby said, leaning forward to plant a kiss on Emily's forehead. 'Also bringing in a branch of flowering hawthorn.'

'What about it?' Emily asked her.

'Death,' Tabby said.

Just as Emily was about to mount the stairs, Keeper went to the front door and whimpered, pawing to be out.

'Now?' Emily asked him. 'You are so contrary you would make an excellent cat.'

As she pushed open the front door, Keeper barged past her, snaking out through the gap as soon as he deemed it wide enough, which was half an inch too soon, and shooting off into the long grass of the graveyard in search of sport.

'I hear there's been a séance at the workhouse,' Abner Lowood said, stepping out of the shadows, the embers of his pipe glowing faintly in the lilac light. 'I heard you were up there, dancing round the fire like a coven of witches, trying to summon my Barbara's ghost. And what I want to know, Miss Brontë, is how does that help me?'

'Not at all,' Emily said, whistling to Keeper, who – just when she needed him to look fierce and threatening – was nowhere to be seen. 'Mr Lowood, do you see the trail of destruction you leave behind you? Apart from stealing your late wife away from her betrothed only to give her a life of misery and violence, you have ruined Rosalyn in body and mind. Do you care not one whit for how your actions harm others?'

'I do not,' Lowood said, with a tilt of his head. Twin moons glittered in his dark eyes. 'It took me some years to learn that no one cared for me and, once I knew that to be true, I decided I should not waste my time with guilt or sorrow. Life is short, and it is brutal. What else may a man do for himself other than take as much pleasure from it as he can? And as for Rosalyn, she came to me only too willing. Is still willing, by all accounts, not that I'd want her now.'

That this man had not one ounce of care for others, Emily had already known. It was only in this moment, as she stood alone with him in the dark, that she had an all too real sense of just how dangerous he was. Emily had no doubt that he would break her neck in a moment if he was certain he would not be caught.

'Well,' she said archly, determined not to reveal a single ounce of fear. 'You are incorrect. We were not summoning the ghost of your dead wife. We were attempting to meet with her revenant. After all, if Barbara herself could tell us how she died, that would save us all a great deal of effort, would it not?'

Lowood's eyes widened for a second.

Once more she whistled for Keeper, slapping her thigh to summon him. Where was the useless hound when she needed him?

'And did you?' he asked.

'We did not,' Emily said. 'What would she have told us if we had?'

'That's for you to find out,' Lowood said. 'You are supposed to be clearing my name and finding the scoundrel that tried to end me. Time is running out for you and your lot to please me. Any further delays and I will be forced to—'

'Do not threaten me or my family.' Emily took two sudden steps towards him, pleased to see him give half an inch of ground. 'That we continue to examine your sordid life is for our own account and no one else's. It is you who should be careful, sir.'

For a moment Lowood was still, and Emily thought she had succeeded in quelling him, but then he burst into harsh laughter.

'I have never been careful one moment in my life,' he told her. 'I take no care, not with my life nor anyone else's. I do as I please, and here I am, still standing, still a free man. I will not take care, Miss Brontë, that is why you should fear me. I will never take care.'

'What's this then?' Branwell stumbled into the yard, Keeper at his side, leaning into his thigh in what seemed like a concerted effort to keep the drunk upright. 'Abner, my good fellow! 'Tis I, Branwell Brontë! Why, it's been an age since we last shared good cheer, has it not? Come in, come in my dear fellow, and let us lift a glass in the spirit of reunion, come in, come in . . .'

'Branwell, *no*.' Emily stood in front of her brother. 'That man will not enter our home. This is Abner Lowood, the suspected murderer. He means us – *all* of us – harm. And you, you share your secrets with this stranger as if he is your boon companion.' Emily shoved Branwell away from her. 'When will you grow up and become a man?'

'I have no need to, when we have you,' Branwell replied, leaning heavily against the doorframe. 'You are the son Papa always hoped for, Emily. Abner here is a fine fellow. Something of a poet, actually. At least an appreciator of poetry. I read him some of mine and . . .'

Lowood laughed at the sight of Branwell stumbling down the step and rolling onto his back at Emily's feet. At once Keeper licked his face all over, prodding at Branwell with his paw to try and get him up.

'Oh, I am certain you are familiar with him,' Emily said, sickened by the sight of her brother, brought so low. 'That you are pathetic enough to be fooled by his tricks into betraying your own sisters to him! That you saw fit to tell a man who has shown nothing but cruelty and violence to others exactly how to hold a knife to our throats!'

'I did not,' Branwell insisted, pushing Keeper off him. 'I did no such thing. I never speak of you at all, Emily, for you are terribly dull.'

'Tell him,' Emily gestured to Lowood, who shook his head.

'A gentleman never betrays a gentleman,' he said with a smirk. 'I will see you again, Miss Brontë.'

An owl called and Lowood made a dart towards her, as if he meant to take hold of her. But this time Keeper was exactly where he needed to be, leaping in front of his mistress. Four paws set wide apart, he bared his teeth at Lowood.

'I'd say our friendly arrangement is at an end, Miss Brontë,' Lowood said. 'I'd say we are enemies now and there's a new game at play. You'd better find what you need to put me away, and quick. Before I find what I need to put you, all of you, in the ground.'

Anne

Anne had slept the moment her head hit the pillow, the excesses of the previous night still taking their toll on her fraught mind and exhausted body. And so it was slowly, very slowly and with great difficulty, that she dragged herself out of the depths of slumber, summoned by a distant commotion and the acrid scent of something unpleasant and dangerous.

'Wake up!' Emily's call jolted her out of the last vestiges of sleep, and all at once Anne found herself in the midst of a disaster. It took a moment for her to understand what was happening.

'Fire!' Emily shouted. 'There's a fire in Branwell's room.' She grabbed two pitchers of water from the dressing table and left. Anne stumbled out into the hallway to see the billow of smoke float across the ceiling. Her brother sat on the floor, all but incoherent, his head tipped back against the wall, his mouth hanging open.

'Who did this?' Anne gasped. 'Did Lowood find his way inside?'

'Branwell did this,' Emily said. 'Get everyone outside at once!'

'Charlotte, get Ellen outside. Make sure Martha and Tabby are safe,' Anne told her sister, who threw a shawl around her friend and guided her to the stairs as the smoke poured out of Branwell's bedroom, quickly filling the air.

'Papa, what can I do?' Anne asked as Emily fetched another pitcher from Tabby and Martha's room and poured it onto an already soaked counterpane.

'Have no fear, Anne,' her father said, pulling his nightshirt over his mouth and nose. 'Rouse your brother and get him outside if you can. If you cannot, then leave him. Emily and I will put out the fire.'

Despite her father's orders, Anne found herself fixed to the spot, watching as Emily and Papa drenched yet more blankets in the water before her father used them to beat down the flames that engulfed Branwell's bed. Finally it was reduced to smouldering embers. An inward breath filled her lungs with smoke, and she bent double, coughing and unable to catch her breath.

'Go outside, Anne,' Emily told her impatiently. 'You are getting in the way here.'

'I want to help,' Anne gasped.

'Help by going outside; you will do us no good if we must carry you out dead. And take that fool with you.'

'I believe the danger has passed,' Papa said, wiping his cuff across his sweaty brow. 'Emily, go to the well and draw more water to soak blankets, so we may ensure there will be no reignition. I must open all the windows, and clear the air.

Emily nodded and, collecting up jugs by the handles, headed downstairs without looking at Anne or her brother. Hearing herself wheeze and feeling the squeeze on her chest, Anne admitted defeat. She could be of no use here.

'Come now.' Anne slid her arm under her brother's and attempted to drag his dead weight upwards. 'Branwell, get up. Get up, for God's sake. You could have killed yourself tonight. You could have killed us all.'

Branwell stirred, regarding her through half-closed lids, 'What?'

'Get up, before I throw you down the stairs,' Anne threatened, though in truth she was on the verge of weeping in despair.

Perhaps it was that that brought Branwell to, more or less. For, grabbing onto her arm, he dragged himself up, leaning heavily on her as he staggered to the top of the stairs. The staircase was too narrow for them to descend side by side, however, and before Anne could make a strategy, Branwell's dead weight and the effect of gravity conspired against her to peel him from her grip. Horrified, Anne watched him tumble down the first flight, folding to a stop at the foot of the long-case clock.

'Why are you always in the way?' Emily asked, on her way back up carrying two brimming buckets. As she stepped over him, she allowed a good slosh of ice-cold water to douse his head, causing him to splutter and moan.

'I will have no more to do with him,' she told Anne as she pushed by, going into Branwell's room where she and Papa worked side by side to ensure the danger was entirely passed. Despite her burning lungs urging her to find fresh air, Anne's trembling legs wanted only to sink onto the top stair, lean her head against the banister and begin weeping. For this was too much. It was all too much to bear.

There was no time for self-pity, or to wallow in wishes that her life had turned out differently at every fork in the path. There was only now, her sisters and friend standing outside in their nightgowns and bare feet, Emily rising to meet calamity alongside the cool calm head of their papa, while Branwell, broken and crumpled, was on the half-landing, where he could not stay. Straightening her shoulders, Anne shoved him, feet first, juddering down the stairs.

'Get outside, out the back door where the others are spending their night,' she told him. 'Perhaps the air will do you some good.'

Charlotte waited beside Ellen, her shawl wrapped around her shoulders, her plaited hair falling over one shoulder. Her small face was pinched with worry and upset, her eyes seeking out Anne's, as Branwell sank down onto the back step, his head clutched in his hands.

'Anne, you are as white as a sheet. Take a deep breath, dear.'

Anne complied and immediately convulsed into a fit of coughing.

'Sit down on the step,' Charlotte told her, shoving Branwell along to make space for Anne, as she knelt before her. 'Some of the smoke must have penetrated your lungs. Just breathe slowly and deeply; replace the filthy air with clean.'

Anne nodded, holding Charlotte's hand as her breathing evened out and the coughing subsided, though her throat still felt hot and raw.

'Thank you,' Anne said. 'I am a little better now. I should have come out at once, and left Papa and Emily to their work. I thought I could be of service.'

'I do not doubt evacuating Branwell slowed you down much more than was good for your chest,' Charlotte said tightly, unable to look at Branwell. 'Is the fire out at least?'

'Emily and Papa have put it out,' Anne nodded, taking the cup of water that Martha had brought her. 'They are just dousing the room once more to ensure there will be no reoccurrence.'

'How did the fire start, Branwell?' Charlotte asked, her worried gaze still fixed on Anne.

'I do not recall,' Branwell said, blinking in bemusement. 'A fire, you say? A fire? Was that now? I dreamt that I awoke with the curtains around my bed engulfed in flame. Is that what you mean? I thought at last I would be free of this puny prison.' He beat his chest with a closed fist. 'But then I awoke and the dream had come to pass.'

'It was a dream that could have killed us all.' Emily forced her way between Branwell and Anne, clutching a blackened pewter candlestick in her fist. She shoved it into his face. 'This was on your bed, Branwell. I can only surmise that you lit a candle, took it into your bed and then . . .' Emily dropped the item onto the cobbles with a clang. 'You let it fall.'

Emily kicked the offending item hard against the wall.

'I thought you had found a purpose again,' she said. 'That perhaps Mrs Crowe had inspired you to a better path. Time and time again we think there is hope for you, but there never is, is there? Your good intentions do not last beyond you making promises that you will never keep, do they?'

'Emily, not now,' Anne said. 'He is in no fit state—'

'He is never in a fit state,' Emily said, turning to her brother. 'You are weak, Branwell. You are pathetic. Our father has afforded you every advantage. Every time he ploughed money and time into you, you threw it back in his face. And then, when Anne finds you a position at her place of work you . . . you *defile* it with your selfishness.'

'I fell in love!' Suddenly Branwell surged up, roaring at her. 'My love has been rejected, trampled upon and rebuffed again and again! How I am to bear such indignity when my heart – my very soul – is on fire with grief?'

'Bear it like a woman,' Emily spat at him, giving him a hard shove so he staggered back onto the step. When Emily truly lost her temper, it was near impossible to calm her before her storm blew itself out.

'Emily, please,' Anne begged her, but Emily was deaf to her.

'Bear it like Charlotte bore it when she was sent away by her professor. Do you think that she does not feel just as much as you? That her pain and misery is less than yours because she does not declare it across the world for all to know? Or bear it like Anne bore it when William Weightman, a good, kind man, was taken to his grave. Do you believe that her hopes for the future, her dreams of what might have been mean nothing compared to yours? Do you think your sisters to be unfeeling automata who have never loved, or lost? That you amongst us are the only one ever to suffer pain and disappointment?'

Anne tried again, 'Emily stop, I beg you.'

'Bear it like I have . . .' Emily faltered, tears streaming down her face as she jabbed her finger at Branwell. 'I, who have seen the only soul I could ever have cared for die in my arms.' Anne gasped as Emily slapped her brother smartly around the face. 'Do you see your sisters abandon themselves to such wallowing? Do you see us grasping at every drink or drug to dull our pain? You do not! Because we fight, we stand strong, we feel our agonies, but we do not let them rule us.'

'Well, of course you have done everything right.' Branwell rubbed at his cheek as Papa came to the doorway. He stood up once again, lunging towards Emily until they stood nose to nose. 'Have you any idea what it is like to be me? To bear the weight of responsibility for the care of this entire family on my shoulders? Have I not always been told that I am the one to lead the way, to support my sisters, to ensure your security? All my life I was trained for greatness and, when it came to it . . .' He stopped, his face crumpling, his body doubling over. 'When it came to it, it was not me who was great. It was you, and her, and her.' He gestured at Emily and Anne in turn. 'At least with her I mattered, at least with her I was a man for a while. I felt glorious in her arms, and now that one joy is barred to me, I am nothing. What use has nothing with living?'

'Branwell,' Anne went to her brother, pulling at his arm to guide him away from Emily whose eyes still sparked with lightning. 'Don't speak so. You are unwell. You don't know what you say.'

'Come in, my son,' Papa intervened, taking Branwell's hand and leading him away from Emily, as if his son was a little child again. 'Come in all, we must restore order to this night and go back to our beds. From now on, Branwell will sleep with me.'

As Papa shut his door, the women gathered in Charlotte's bedroom. The walls in the hallway were blackened, and the stink of smoke could still be tasted in the air, even with all the windows open.

'Perhaps an asylum,' Ellen suggested. 'The one where George is housed is very good, I think. Not unkind, at least.'

'We have no money for an asylum,' Charlotte said. 'And I have no energy to think of him another moment. We have to fend for ourselves, sisters, we have known this a long time. Nothing has changed, except that we have to fend for Branwell now, too. We carry on as we planned. We make our way in the world on our own account.'

'He is our brother,' Anne nodded. 'We can never abandon him.'

'We have never abandoned him, Anne,' Emily said. 'He deserted us long ago, when he chose her and the bottle. The brother we love will never return. I know that now. All hope is lost.'

'I cannot accept that,' Anne said. 'I will never stop hoping for him until he draws his last breath.'

'Then you will be forever disappointed,' Emily said.

TWENTY-NINE

Charlotte

It was all Anne could do not to run down to the seafront, Charlotte noticed. The moment they had arrived at Wood's Lodgings, which comprised a row of four pretty white cottages attached to a larger Georgian house right on the sea-front, Anne had all but galloped to their attic room to gaze out of the window. The room was really too small for four ladies, and it would be a hot and uncomfortable night that lay ahead, but it had a view of the sea, and Anne was enchanted. Charlotte could see her delight at the great expanse of the sea light up her younger sister's face, and for a moment at least all the troubles they had left behind were forgotten.

'We may go down to sea first, may we not?' Anne turned to her, eyes shining. 'The tide is fully out, Charlotte, just acres of gold – now is surely the perfect time, and it would be such a shame not to go and say hello to the sea.'

'Of course we may,' Charlotte said. 'We likely have more than a dozen churches to visit while we are here, and I believe it would be advisable to try and narrow down our search list as much as possible by employing some local expertise.'

'You mean we have to talk to people,' Emily huffed. The sight of the sea had not enlivened Emily nearly as much as it had Anne. In fact, it had taken some persuading to get Emily to accompany them on the excursion at all.

Long after Branwell had retired to bed with her poor exhausted papa, Emily's fury remained unabated. Charlotte had lain awake, the sharp scent of smoke still thickening the air, listening to Emily pace the floor of her small bedroom, back and forth, back and forth, almost until the break of dawn.

That is why it came as no surprise when, at breakfast, Emily declared that she was in no mood for travelling and elected to stay at home. Charlotte considered this to be unwise. If Emily remained, there would only be another confrontation with Branwell, who very likely would not recall a great deal of what he had said and done the previous night. The likelihood of great injury, both personal and psychological, being done to all parties, including Papa, was unacceptably high. So, Charlotte had devised a plan to prevent Emily getting her own way, without her realising that she had been thus cajoled.

'Emily, you must come,' Charlotte had said, adding quickly, 'we simply cannot manage this part of the detection without your specific talents.'

'My specific talents?' Emily had frowned. 'Am I the only one who can trudge from street to street in this cursed heat, or read a parish register? That is no speciality amongst such sturdy and learned woman. And when it comes to making conversation with people we have never met and eliciting information from them, I am happy to admit that I am the very least good at that among us. I do not see what advantages my accompanying you brings to the detection, and besides, the floor needs a fresh layer of sawdust and I have a mind to bake.'

'You must come because only you can intuit a pattern, rhyme and reason from the disparate facts that we have collected,' Charlotte pressed on, looking at Anne for assistance.

'Only your superior imagination is capable of drawing together fragments into a whole picture. Anne and I have no such talent.'

'That is true,' Emily acknowledged.

'And Emily, I do so wish you to come for my own selfish sake,' Anne said, sweetly. 'I want to visit the sea and sky with *you*, and run up the steep hill to the castle with *you*, and make believe we are pirates mounting an assault on the navy, in search of treasure!'

Emily was packed within the hour, kissing Keeper smartly on the nose and patting him firmly on the head before leaving him and a thoroughly fussed Flossy tangled up in Tabby's skirts at the door.

The journey had been long and arduous. They had passed a few, sleepless night-time hours in York on the way, during every minute of which Charlotte found her thoughts circling between anger and impatience. Anger at the injustice of what men like Lowood and her brother got away with, and impatience both to be in Scarborough and yet also to be back at her desk with Jane.

This was not the life she wanted for herself. Not even this, watching Anne and Emily's fast walk down the steep pathways, which finally broke into a giddy trot and then, as they reached the edge of the sands, a full skirt-hitching bonnet-holding race towards the distant surf. Ordinarily Charlotte might have called to them to slow down, or pleaded with them to think of propriety; but not today. Today, she wanted to see her sisters laughing in delight. To witness Anne flinging open her arms to the wide horizon in an ecstatic embrace and Emily following, trailing her hems in rock pools as she filled her pockets with pebbles and shells.

If there was one overarching lesson that writing *Jane Eyre* had taught her, it was that Charlotte could wait no longer for the freedom to be true to herself. That the time had come to hold fast to her talent, her ambition, and her desire to be seen by the world entire, and to make it a reality. She realised that if she reached the end of her life without having fought tooth and nail for the recognition she knew she deserved, then she would not have considered her life worth living. And if she sought her own freedom to be happy, then she could hardly deny her sisters the same for a glorious hour or two.

'They are removing their boots and stockings!' Ellen cautioned Charlotte, glancing around the few holidaymakers, holding picnics, working on paintings, or simply strolling on the beach. Though the tide was out, the sun was high and hot and fortunately the beach was sparsely populated.

'I shouldn't think anyone is close enough to notice their ankles besides an anemone or two,' Charlotte said indulgently, lifting her hand to shade her eyes as she made out her sister in the haze of the afternoon. 'Oh, look, Ellen, they are like their little selves again! To see them laugh and play is worth the risk of a little disapproval, don't you agree?'

'I believe I do,' Ellen said, as if she were surprised by the notion. 'Although I shall not be removing my own stockings.'

'Goodness no,' Charlotte said. 'We are not savages.'

It was a little later – with their skirt bottoms sodden, and their hair releasing itself from under their bonnets in unruly tendrils – that the group reconvened further along the bay, where the harbour ended with the exclamation mark of the lighthouse. It was along this cob that fishwives sold the day's catch in the early morning and peddled what other livings they could make in the afternoons, presenting an array of fruit and vegetables, mending and lace-making. An abundance of pretty things displayed before a community of hard-faced women, who enjoyed none of the luxuries they peddled to make ends meet.

'We must make a start searching for traces of Lowood,' Charlotte said, looking up at the church that sat just beneath the castle. 'I suppose up there is as good as anywhere.'

'Why not question these women?' Anne suggested, nodding at the fishwives. 'Between them they must know a good deal of the history of this town, particularly in the last few years. It is not as if Lowood is a man of a subtle nature. I would venture that wherever he has been, he has left infamy in his wake.'

'I believe that is an excellent idea,' Emily said. 'Talk to them, Charlotte.'

Charlotte gave Ellen a long-suffering sideways glance and did as she was instructed.

'Good afternoon.' After something of a nervous appraisal of the women who hawked their wares as loudly as a Covent Garden trader, Charlotte lighted upon a youngish-looking woman on the basis of her clear complexion and trim waist. Such a female, who had not yet borne a child, Charlotte reasoned, might be a little freer with local intelligence than her older, more careworn counterparts. For those were the faces of women who did not trust strangers, and for good reasons.

'Afternoon, miss,' the girl had replied cheerfully. 'Apples, refreshing and sweet?'

'Four please,' Charlotte said, holding out a ha'penny. 'I wonder if you could help me, I am looking for a local family, of a friend I used to attend school with. The Lowoods – would you know them?'

'I don't, miss,' the young woman said as she handed each of them an apple. 'That's not a name I've ever heard, and I've grown up my whole life here.'

'That's no Scarborough name,' the next woman along said. At first glance Charlotte saw a coarse, thickset woman, but then she saw she was working on an intricate beaded lariat to accompany the several already set out on her stall, made with turquoise beads and tiny seashells that must have come from other, more exotic shores, her nimble fingers threading and knotting her line into an ornate pattern. It closely resembled Anne's treasured turquoise and shell necklace, and could even be by the same maker.

'Where did you hear that name, for that's not one of us folk,' the woman asked, regarding Charlotte as if she might be from the moon and not just further south in Yorkshire. 'Where have you heard that's a Scarborough name?'

Charlotte discovered she did not have a sufficiently good answer to this question.

'The truth,' Emily said, 'is that we are seeking the man who ruined our cousin in order to make him marry her. We were trying to be discreet. The name he gave her was Abner Lowood.'

'Hmm,' the woman huffed as she threaded another bead. 'There's more than one that would fit the bill in this town.'

'This gentleman left Scarborough going on a dozen years since,' Anne added, picking up a bracelet that would suit her necklace perfectly. 'He told a fellow he had been a druggist, and moved on to escape some kind of trouble, though we know not what trouble exactly.'

'Carus Reaper,' the woman said.

'Is that a name?' Anne said, a little taken aback by the woman's swift certainty.

'What else would it be? Reaper is a local family. Carus Reaper his name is, or was when he lived in these parts. Eldest son of a fishing family, him and his brother orphaned young. He worked in the Appleby apothecary as an apprentice, and married Appleby's daughter – Grace, her name was. Never much to look at, but when he set his mind on a woman, he had a way of making them believe he was the finest prince to ever walk this earth. They had four bairns, all died before they were ten. Grace died before she was thirty. And it came out after that he had a mistress, and she was with child. Questions were asked and that's when Reaper vanished. None ever heard of him since. Could it be him you are after?'

'That does sound like him,' Charlotte said. 'But how can we be certain?'

'Were there any distinguishing physical features you could describe?' Ellen asked, her pencil poised.

'Aye, when he were a boy he lost a hand working in the shipyard and nearly died. I don't suppose it grew back.'

The women exchanged a look.

'Thank you,' Charlotte said. 'I believe that is the gentleman we are referring to. Anne, you were right.'

'It is hard to hide your past when you are a man as distinctive as Mr Lowood, or Reaper,' Anne said.

Now all that remained was to connect the name to a church and request access to the parish register, in order to locate the addresses of those who would have known him, and who might hold some valuable information as to his guilt. For one dead wife might be considered unfortunate, but two seemed much more likely to be by design. 'Do you happen to know which church the Reaper family attended?'

'St Mary's, like all us seafaring folk,' the woman told them. 'But if you want to find out more about Reaper, then you might as well talk to her. She'll tell you what you want to know for a penny.' She nodded across the harbour to where a woman of indiscriminate age, wearing a bonnet trimmed with bright pink ribbons and a skirt that matched, seemed to be waiting for someone.

'Who is that?' Charlotte asked.

'That's the girl he left in the lurch,' the fishwife said with a disapproving sniff. 'You only have to look at her to see how low he brought her.

Emily

'I have a previous engagement, I'm afraid,' the young woman told them in a practised, well-spoken tone, when Anne asked if they might have a moment of her time. 'I am waiting for my friend.'

She was a very pretty young woman indeed, plump with a creamy complexion, and dark blue eyes fringed with long lashes. From beneath her bonnet, golden curls escaped, giving an overall effect of a kind of wholesome girlish charm. This was only amplified by her choice of dress, a brightly coloured turquoise and coral ensemble, beautifully tailored from heavy silk that communicated a certain level of wealth.

'Would you just give us a moment of your time, while you are waiting?' Anne pressed her, as Charlotte hung back a little with Ellen, who was slowly coming to the realisation about how the young lady afforded such fine clothes at a pace that was a little slower than her sisters.

'Your friend is rather late,' Emily pointed out. 'You have been standing in the sun now for at least a quarter-hour. We could take you into the tearoom and have a glass of cold water brought to refresh you.'

'I am not permitted in that tearoom,' the young woman told them, lifting her chin and dropping her refined tone to reveal a broad Yorkshire accent in the same moment. 'They know who I am and how I make my living, and my very presence brings shame upon their overpriced, tough-as-old-boots cakes and establishment.' The last part of her sentence had been delivered in rather raised, robust terms, directed over her shoulder and towards the open door of the tearoom. A moment later the door was firmly closed.

'You look like vicars' daughters,' the woman said, looking them over with a critical eye. 'Spinsters too. Plain mended clothes, but with a little independence. Old enough and unattractive enough to be allowed to come to Scarborough unaccompanied by a brother or a papa. In any case, you probably shouldn't want to be seen with me either, if you know what's good for you.'

Emily could feel her older sister bristle at the remarks, though they were entirely accurate. Poor Charlotte did so mind about not being beautiful, whereas Emily had made it her business not to care one jot what people thought of her person. For this reason, she quickly decided that she liked this particular fallen woman, who showed no shame or inclination to hide who she was, even from a gaggle of parson's elderly daughters.

'Well, we are rather disinclined to take much notice of what other people think is good for us,' Emily said. 'In fact, we make a speciality of doing the opposite.'

Emily would have thought that after their time in the cursed city of London, during which Charlotte struck up a friendship with an opera girl who was not so very different from the young lady they stood before now, that her sister might be less skittish about encountering people who made a profit from others' desires. She could see, however, from Charlotte's small, pinched face that she had found Emily's comment rather close to the bone. Nevertheless, Emily had succeeded in putting the girl, who smiled with something like relief, at ease. It was clear she didn't often find friendship or courtesy from other women. And she wasn't so very different from Rosalyn Tolliver, after all.

'We are Charlotte, Emily and Anne Brontë,' Charlotte said a little stiffly, 'and this is our dear friend Ellen N—' Catching Ellen's look of alarm, Charlotte did not complete her surname.

'I am Miss Annabelle Merryweather.' Annabelle curtsied, nodding at Emily. 'I like you, so you may call me Bella. Now, what can you possibly want from me?'

'We are seeking information on a gentleman we believe you have had an association with,' Anne said carefully, thinking of how fragile Rosalyn had become after Lowood had dispensed with her, and how she didn't want to rekindle any such painful sensation for this bright young creature.

'Are you wives, mothers or sisters?' Bella asked. 'For I take no responsibility for the transgressions of my gentleman friends. They choose the path they set out on. I tempt no one to my door; they arrive there deliberately.'

'No, we seek the truth about a gentleman who may be guilty of a very heinous crime, but there is no evidence to secure his conviction, at least not any that he hasn't managed to somehow buy his way out of. We believe you might have had an association with him and that – if you can stand to speak of him again – you might help us find something with which to damn him.'

'Carus,' Bella said, her pretty face draining of colour just as a cloud passed over the sun, giving the impression that Lowood's evil eye followed them everywhere. 'He is not in Scarborough, is he?'

'No, he is far away,' Emily told her at once. 'You are quite safe.'

'Oh, I'm not afraid of him,' Bella told her. 'If I ever saw him again, I'd gut him with a fish-hook.'

'My dear Miss Merryweather.' A very young, flush-faced young gentleman of eighteen or so only just brought himself to a stop before careering into their party. 'Please do forgive my lateness. I was kept at home by Mama—'

'I do not forgive lateness, sir,' Bella told him, her refined accent returning. 'You may return to your mama and consider how you are to atone for your transgression. Come and see me in the morning at nine and, if you are one minute late, I shall be done with you.' She turned back to their group. 'Perhaps you would like to accompany me home, and I will give you refreshment. I know I will need some if I am to speak of that man.'

'That would be marvellous,' Emily said, before Charlotte or Ellen could voice any concerns about visiting the home of such a woman. 'Unless you are too . . . tired, Charlotte? Ellen?'

'We are not tired, are we, Ellen?' Charlotte said at once, rankling at the suggestion that she did not have the stomach to converse with the woman.

'I am rather tired,' Ellen said anxiously.

'No, you are not,' Charlotte told her, and that was how the four of them found themselves following Bella, like four very serious pigeons in the wake of a parakeet.

'What a charming home,' Anne said the moment they stopped at the white-painted Georgian terrace, which was small but perfectly proportioned, and with an abundance of pink roses climbing all around the door. They entered into a clean and fresh-scented hallway, which led into the shadowy depths of the house. Bella led them into her bright parlour, gesturing at two emerald green, plumply upholstered sofas for them to sit upon. Emily was a little surprised when Bella rang a bell, and a young maid appeared to take their bonnets and shawls from them, as well as an order for refreshment.

'You have staff?' Charlotte asked her, rather impressed, as if dearest Tabby and dawdling Martha didn't count as the same thing, which Emily supposed they did not.

'Oh yes, only a maid and a governess,' Bella told them.

'A governess?' Charlotte asked, rather taken aback.

'Yes, for my Thomas. He's such a bright boy, you see. I shall see him to university, and he will go on to make great things of his life. I would have engaged a male tutor, but I had no end of trouble with young gentlemen thinking I required them to rescue me with offers of marriage.'

'We have had similar trouble,' Emily said. 'Our brother being one of the enthusiastic young gentlemen you refer to.'

'My sympathies,' Bella said. 'So many men are unable to accept that a woman does not require them beyond . . . what is necessary. Not my Thomas, though. He has been raised to treat everyone with respect, and honour.' Her smile of maternal pride was very affecting, particularly as this had to be Lowood's son – the only one of his children to live past eight years old – of whom she was speaking so fondly.

'About Lowood – Carus Reaper, as you knew him,' Emily began.

'I was his mistress,' Bella nodded bluntly. 'Though a mistress is the name given to a superior and I was not that. He saw a child, with not one notion of how dangerous a place the world can be, and he caught me on his line, and reeled me in, inch by inch, until I was willingly dishing myself up on a plate for him to devour.'

'Goodness,' Ellen muttered.

'Goodness had very little to do with it,' Bella observed. 'That man was a monster, but he did teach me about pleasure.'

Ellen went quite pink.

'Carus,' Bella said, her hands folded in her lap, 'for all that he was an ugly brute, and I'm sure would have done for me too if he'd stayed much longer, he had a way about him that made me feel like I was made of spun gold. He fed me his beautiful lies, and I followed his trail of pretty words to my ruin. Or at least, it was supposed to be my ruin, when he left me and vanished. I decided it would be the making of me instead.'

'You mentioned that you thought he would have "done for you too", had he stayed in Scarborough after his first wife died. Do you believe that he might have killed Grace Appleby, perhaps even his own children?' Emily asked.

Bella was about to answer when the maid came in with a silver tray, laden with neatly cut sandwiches, a pot of tea, and glasses of water flavoured with lemon, the kind of luxury that Emily had barely ever seen in the highest of drawing rooms. There was clearly money to be made if one was willing to make oneself a commodity, and Bella was the first person Emily had met who did so as captain of her own destiny, providing the life she desired for herself and her son. Though the idea of such a thing was deeply unpalatable to her, and entirely at odds with what she believed to be morally right, she could not help but respect this singular woman.

'Sarah, will you bring the medical books, please?' Bella asked the girl. 'And make sure that Miss Ellis and Thomas take lunch in the school room today, please.'

The girl bobbed a curtsey, returning a moment later with a pile of intriguing-looking books that she placed on the arm of Bella's sofa.

'I do not believe that Carus murdered Grace,' Bella said the moment the maid closed the parlour door. 'I *know* he did. And what's more, he annotated the margins of this book with how to gradually poison a person, and how much dosage to administer, depending on their weight and age.'

Anne opened the book and gave it to Emily. Sure enough, there were the notations and calculations just as she had described them.

'This is excellent,' Emily said. 'If only he had written somewhere that he planned to use these calculations for murder.'

'Oh, but he did,' Bella said. 'Just before he vanished, he wrote a confession and gave it to me to give to his brother. So that his brother at least would pray for his soul.'

'And did you?' Emily asked.

'I did, I'm afraid,' Bella said. 'It was as if I were in a dream. I knew what he was, and yet I still loved him. I would have followed him off the castle ramparts. It was only when he had gone that I came back to myself.'

Once again, Emily thought of the way Rosalyn seemed to be somehow mesmerised by Lowood, as if he had devised a way to control her mind from afar.

'And do you know where his brother is now?' Emily asked.

'I do,' Bella said. 'But I can promise you he will never betray his brother, no matter who he is.'

'Why does it matter who he is?' Anne asked.

'Because he's the curate at St Mary's, the church at the top of Paradise.'

CHAPTER

THIRTY-ONE

Anne

Despite the dark events that had propelled their party towards an unexpected visit to Scarborough, not to mention the arduous journey, Anne felt invigorated the moment she caught sight of the sea.

Here on the coast, the heat of the summer was tempered by the cool breezes borne on distant horizons, which – when conditions were right – created a fret; a cool sea mist that rolled in over the coast, as if the heavens had come down from above to pay a visit.

The billowing vapour swept inwards, enveloping the long golden beaches and softening the rocky cliffs, to shroud them in a wonderfully refreshing cloud that fell like dew on every hot cheek and tight-ringed hand, made swollen by the heat. Anne removed her bonnet as they walked from Bella's cottage, just one street back from the south bay, and up the steep cobbled lanes towards ancient St Mary's. Above it all, the castle seemed to float on its very own skyborne island, a place where a thousand years of war and treachery raged on in ghostly silence.

The final steps brought them up into the area that was known as Paradise, and for good reason, for it afforded a far-reaching view of the town and the rolling moorland beyond. On the one side of the town stood everything Anne had ever known and ever done, bar Brussels. On the other, beyond the blue horizon, lay everything that might and could yet be. The very thought of such promise of the unknown thrilled her to her core. It gave her purpose and direction always to strive for that which she knew was within reach, even if she could not see it with her own eyes. Anne would not falter in her resolve.

The ancient church of St Mary's was in the process of being restored, and not for the first time. As they set foot in the graveyard that skirted the church, the fret dropped away, and Anne found her face bathed in sunlight, her eyes dazzled by the sparkling sapphire-blue sea, feeling a great swell of affection for the little town, its buildings strung out along the bay like a row of irregular pearls.

For a moment, as the others hurried towards a sizable cedar tree in search of a moment of shade and to catch their breath, Anne remained, her gaze fixed on the view. For a few indulgent moments she allowed herself to picture a time, after *Agnes Grey* had been published, and of course well received by all, when she and her sisters would be making their own livings. And, just perhaps, if God was kind, she would be able to afford to take a little cottage here, big enough for the three of them, though Emily would never leave Papa. Even so, Anne envisaged a life where she could greet the sea each morning, listen to its whispered secrets every evening, and paint the ever-changing sky each hour both in words and in pigment. From this viewpoint, anything seemed possible.

'Come now, Anne.' Emily came out from under the tree to fetch her, hooking an arm around her waist. 'Put on your bonnet and let us go and find this curate. If we are lucky there might perhaps be time enough to visit the sea again.'

The rectory was just across the lane from the church, but the sisters had decided that they would try to avoid calling there if possible. The chances were that they'd be greeted by the lady of the house, be she a wife, daughter or sister, and required to take tea. They did not want the few hours they had left in the town to be occupied by tiresome niceties, as Emily put it. In all honestly Ellen, who looked a little wan, seemed in favour of spending a few hours in a shady sitting room, but neither Anne nor her sisters could stand to waste a moment more than they must.

As Anne pressed her palm against the great ancient door of the Norman church, she felt a frisson, a kind of shudder that ran through her whole frame. It felt somehow like a homecoming. The church interior was simple, the half that had already been restored painted white, the other half showing its still beating heart amongst the cracks and crumbling stone. Nevertheless it was cool in the church, and silent, save for the sound of rather melodic humming coming from somewhere beyond the altar.

Charlotte issued forth several polite coughs as they approached, but the young man that they happened upon was so caught up in his singing that he failed to be alerted. The four of them stood just within the doorway, uncertain of what to do next as the fellow in question half hummed, half sang the words of a hymn as he returned prayer books to a bookcase, entirely oblivious of their presence. In truth he had such a sweet melodic voice that Anne found herself loath to interrupt him.

Charlotte had no such hesitation though.

'Good day to you, sir,' Charlotte said, causing the fellow to start and whirl round, sending one of the books flying more or less directly at Emily's head. Fortunately, she deflected it with her forearm, using the fast reflexes that made her such a good shot.

'I do beg your pardon,' the curate said, immediately dropping the remaining books as he brought his hands to his cheeks. 'You all took me rather by surprise!'

'Evidently,' Charlotte said, with a raised brow.

'Are you in the search of the reverend?' he asked, 'Or . . . or perhaps some spiritual guidance of some sort? I can . . . I can attempt to provide you with some sort of comfort?' He scooped up a book and proffered it to them. 'Perhaps a psalm?'

Anne suppressed her smile, turning her face away for a moment so that her bonnet shielded her urge to laugh.

'We are in search of a Mr Stephen Reaper.'

'Are you really?' The young gentleman was quite taken aback. 'Well, that would be me, I suppose, though I am quite certain you cannot really wish to see me? I truly am a person of no great consequence.'

It was quite remarkable how the young curate looked so much like his older brother but also nothing like him at all. Both had the dark hooded eyes, the thick dark hair and the long face. But Lowood's skin had been made thick and ruddy by years of drinking, and this young gentleman's complexion was not only fair and smooth, but untroubled by whiskers even at his age, which must be around thirty. The aquiline nose followed the same strong path, and even the mouth bore a strong resemblance, though Lowood's had been bent and made somehow ugly by years of spewing hate and threats, whereas Mr Reaper's seemed to reflect his tuneful voice and gentle tone. In short, they were certainly related in body, but thankfully their spirits seemed to inhabit an entirely different realm.

'It is with regard to your brother, Carus,' Anne said. Mr Reaper's eyes immediately filled with tears.

'Have you come to tell me of his death?' he asked her, his voice trembling. Slowly Anne realised that such strength of emotion was not brought about by fear or loathing, but love. Mr Reaper feared that his brother was dead, because he loved him. How was it that such a man could still command such devotion?

'Sir, your brother is alive and though not exactly well, is still standing after an eventful period,' Anne said, glancing at Charlotte for some kind of guidance. Her sister indicated that she had no better plan of advancing the conversation with a small shrug. It seemed that it was to be Anne's duty to reveal the awful truth. 'He goes by the name Abner Lowood now, and has recently been acquitted of the murder of his wife. His second wife. The deaths of his five children are also under suspicion.'

Poor Mr Reaper suddenly took on a greyish countenance, and sat down on one of the narrow benches that lined the room. It was as if all the energy had been sapped from his person in the space of one breath.

'But you say he was acquitted?' he asked, turning his head towards Anne. 'That he was found innocent?'

'It seems that – for reasons that are not entirely clear – all the evidence that was brought against him was withdrawn or altered to be less damning. Perhaps under some duress . . . Mr Reaper, we know your brother. We know he is no stranger to blackmail. We cannot rest until we are sure that his acquittal is just. For what if he marries another unsuspecting young woman? What if he fathers more children who never reach the age of eight?'

The curate did not move, except to slightly and repeatedly shake his head in a muted denial.

'We came to Scarborough to find out more about his past. And found out about Grace and her children. We also discovered the fate of Miss Merryweather, and that he was . . . in contact with you before he vanished.'

Mr Reaper said nothing as he bent to pick up another fallen prayer book; his expression was very solemn.

'Will you tell me where he is that I might apply for leave to see him?' he asked Anne, the longing in his voice taking her off-guard. Even after all she had told him, all he wanted to do was to see his brother. Would Lowood feel the same way about this boy, she wondered?'

'Miss Merryweather told us your brother confided in you,' Anne said. 'Until we met, I had not realised that he must be more than fifteen years older than you. You must have been very young when he abandoned you.'

'Oh no, he didn't abandon me,' Mr Reaper shook his head. 'You have that wrong about Carus. He protected me.'

'It seems hard to believe that the man we have encountered would protect anyone beyond himself,' Charlotte said.

'From the beginning we only had each other,' Mr Reaper told them. 'My mother died giving life to me, the four siblings between were taken to the Lord young. And when I was three, and Carus about eighteen, my father drowned at sea. Carus was there, he tried to save him, but the sea was stronger than his one good arm.'

'Your brother was present when your father died?' Anne questioned.

'Our childhoods were unkind. There was no mother to love us, our father barely fed, and always beat us.' The young gentleman's eyes were cast down. 'But Carus had it far worse than I. That I lived was a miracle, but at least I was only starved and neglected. My father worked him like a dog. Beat him like a dog. When Carus lost his hand in the rigging, the infected wound nearly killed him, and our father didn't lift a finger to try and save him from death. Though I was only small, I recall sitting at my brother's bedside night and day while the fever raged on, and how he told me he would live because without him I would be killed. When our father drowned, he did his best to better us. He became an apprentice druggist and found a kind woman to take me in and send me to school, though he paid all my expenses.' His face fell into his upturned palms. 'I cannot imagine what happened to him to alter him from the good, kind brother I knew. But I cannot believe him a soulless man, for I owe him all that I am. He always said he hoped that helping me to become a good man was his earthly atonement. I pray for him every day, morning, noon and night.'

'You are not your brother's keeper,' Anne said. 'I regret to say it, but I do not think knowing that you are living a life beyond reproach would be much comfort to his second dead wife, or the five dead children he has left in his wake.'

There was the sound of talking in the church, and someone called Mr Reaper's name.

'Mr Reaper, is there a place elsewhere where we can talk uninterrupted?'

Stephen nodded, picking up the last fallen prayer book and returning it to the shelf. As they were about to leave, he turned to Anne.

'How many souls,' he asked her, 'do you think my brother has taken?'

'It could be at least ten,' Anne said.

Head bowed, Stephen led them out of the church, around to the side where the remains of the medieval ruins still stood. It was quiet here, and sheltered. To a passer-by it might look as if the young man were giving them comfort at a time of loss.

'Did he write to you a confession to murdering Grace and his young children?' Anne asked, regretful of the pain she was causing.

'No!' Stephen protested. 'No of course not . . .' Then his expression fell and his shoulders slumped. 'He wrote me a letter, sealed with wax. He told me to open it upon news of his death and pray for his soul.'

'You have not read it, though he's been gone twelve years?' Emily asked.

'I thought him dead, but did not wish it to be true,' Stephen told them. 'I have hoped for his return every day of my life since I last saw him. You have to understand, he is my brother. He is my family. I love him.'

'Mr Reaper,' Anne said, 'I believe you know that you have a duty to open and read that letter now.'

'Even if I am condemning him to the rope by doing so?' Stephen asked her desperately.

'Sir, if you find evidence of murder within the letter then, yes, he will face the law. It is only when he is repentant and asks forgiveness of Our Lord that he will be given a seat in heaven. You may not save him on this earth, but you could save his soul from hellfire.'

'We depart on the evening train,' Charlotte told him. 'Bring us the letter there. Whatever it contains, we will tell you your brother's name and location. Good day to you, Mr Reaper.'

As the others began the steep walk back down to the guesthouse, Anne tarried a little while for one more word with the young curate.

'I am very pleased to meet you, sir,' Anne said. 'You show me the miracle of God's love in your integrity and stead-fast love for your brother. I hope you understand that we mean you no ill will. You wish to protect your brother, or at least your memory of him. We wish to protect those he has harmed, beyond repair, both living and dead, and those he has not yet met who might fall victim to his hatred if he is allowed to go unchecked. You are a good man, I can see that. And you are partly who you are because of him. But sir, you are not enough to redeem him. Only God can do that. You, above all else, know that to be true.'

THIRTY-TWO

Charlotte

Stephen Reaper did not come to meet them at the station.

Anne had insisted that they wait in the ticket hall until the very last moment possible and they had, until there really was no more time and they had been forced to depart on the long journey home.

Perhaps it had been madness after all to take such an exhausting journey for the sake of one night in the town that Anne loved, despite all they had uncovered. Charlotte watched her sister as she stared out of the window, lost to her own thoughts, and feared for the toll this exertion had taken on her spirit, if not her mind. Anne believed in the inherent goodness in all people, even in people who had fallen as low as Abner Lowood. She believed that every soul could be redeemed and there was never a moment in one's earthly life when it was too late to seek forgiveness. Charlotte knew that Anne's drive to discover the truth, no matter the cost to her, was partly driven by her desire to save even the most despicable from hell, if she could. That was why she had delayed so long in the hope of seeing young Mr Reaper. That the gentleman, a man of God, no less, had chosen to protect his brother rather than to unequivocally bring his sins to light had clearly distressed her.

Charlotte watched the blue, greys and greens pass by at speed, reflected in Anne's eyes, all meaningful conversation dulled by the noise of the train. How she wished she could always protect her baby sister from harm or hurt. Anne had already had too much of it in her life. Of course, Charlotte had experienced the same losses and heartbreaks herself, but she could bear it. Though her frame was small, and her health often fragile, she felt that she had been made to bear sorrow. Over recent years Anne had asserted her own personality, rising up against the way her family cast her as gentle and mild, and though Charlotte had been pleased to see that, it frightened her too. She worried that Anne's body was too fragile to carry such a fierce soul and that the latter would scorch the former from the inside out. And Anne was determined to live without compromise; she had become so independent of late and Charlotte could not prevent that, no matter how she might wish to.

They were all exhausted when they finally arrived at the parsonage door, having opted not to spend another night in York but to pay a coachman an exorbitant fee to bring them directly home, despite their weariness. Which was why they were surprised to find their papa opening the door as their bags were loaded out of the coach.

Once the bags were brought in and Keeper and Flossy were more or less done with greeting their owners in ecstatic delight, Patrick invited them all into his study, where the fire burned low, and a half-written sermon still waited to be finished.

'Papa, is all well?' Charlotte asked, taking his hand in hers as he led them into his study.

'Peter Wilson is dead,' Papa told them.

'Dead? But how?' Charlotte asked him.

'He was a drinking man, but not so lost to it that you might think it would end him,' Emily said.

'He was troubled though,' Anne added. 'And he reported visions. Was it . . . by his own hand, Papa?'

'No,' Papa pushed his spectacles up his nose, and coughed. A sure sign that he felt uncomfortable about what he was about to say. 'A fatal wound was inflicted to his neck and the loss of blood was too great for him to be saved.'

'His throat was cut,' Emily said. 'No poison. This is new.'

'It could be that the murder is not linked to Lowood and his crimes,' Anne observed. 'Where was poor Mr Wilson found?'

'In the fields of Harrowings,' Papa told them gravely. 'The Justice believes it was mostly likely horse thieves. A search of the county is in progress. Yet none of the horses were taken. It occurred in the morning, as he always takes the horses out of the stable at five, and a young maid found him by eleven.'

'That poor child,' Anne said, picturing the girl who had been polishing silver.

'It is possible that the crime is not linked,' Charlotte said, thoughtfully. 'After all, beyond his beloved leaving him for Lowood, what did Wilson have to do with any of it?'

'True,' Emily said. 'Yet, in my experience, it is always the connection that we have yet to see that is both the strangest and most unexpected, and also the arrow that goes straight to the heart of the matter. We know that Mr Wilson felt a great animosity toward Lowood. Perhaps they had an interaction, and Lowood took his own kind of revenge?'

'It would more likely have been Mr Wilson attacking Mr Lowood,' Anne said. 'I believe we should return to see Mrs Wilson again, and also visit the Tollivers. This news will have unsettled them. It might be that Lowood is clearing up all the loose ends of his misdemeanours here before moving on once again and inventing himself anew. Which would mean they are all in danger.'

'But not today, I beg you!' Ellen said, 'I may be a Brontë in spirit, but not in physique. I know you will all think me very weak, but I for one need a day of nothing at all.'

'Weak is the very last thing you are, Ellen dear,' Charlotte leaned towards her. 'You have proven yourself an excellent detector and I think we all need to take a little rest or collapse!'

'I am weary of it too, Ellen,' Emily said. 'I prefer the dark tales of my own design, stories that I can end exactly as I wish.'

'Go up to bed, Ellen,' Anne told her. 'You have been of great assistance to us in this matter. Not one of us thought of taking notes!'

'It has been exciting and terrifying, but I confess I do not have the heart for detection,' Ellen said, as she went to the door. 'Even so, you know that I will always be present to assist any one of you to the end of my days.'

Charlotte supposed that Anne too sensed that Papa had something else to say, something that was for their ears only.

Once Ellen had retired, Charlotte turned to their papa as he sank exhausted into his chair. Somehow his long and angular frame seemed to wither and crumble before her eyes and for the first time Charlotte realised her papa was an old man now.

'Is it Branwell, Papa?' Charlotte asked at once. 'Have there been more events while we were absent?'

'I fear he is lost to us,' Papa observed them each in turn, shaking his head slowly. 'The night after the fire he remembered nothing of what had gone on. I showed him the wreck of his bed, and he had no recollection at all of what had happened.' He looked at Emily. 'Or what was said. That same evening, he left the house in the afternoon for a walk to clear his head and order his thoughts, he said. I was obliged to collect him from a ditch two miles towards Stanbury early this morning after a shepherd found him. The poor lad thought he had happened upon a corpse.' His expression became very grave, and he closed in on himself, as if unwilling to go on.

'Dear Papa,' Charlotte sat at his feet, taking his hand. 'Tell us the worst. Let us share your burden with you.'

'I have prayed, and worked, and hoped to save my son,' Papa said. 'But this morning when I found him, unconscious in the muddy ditchwater, only saved from drowning by the fortunate placing of a hawthorn tree, I realised that it is in the Lord's hands now. Daughters, your brother will die from his affliction. I cannot see a cure for him any more, he is too far gone in his frenzy. We must accept that it is time to simply do our best to limit the harm he does to himself and others. I have failed him.'

'You have not, Papa,' Emily said. 'He has failed you. You have given Branwell every chance for greatness, and he has squandered them all! You care for him as a mother does for her newborn, and he flings it back in your face. He has failed you; he has failed all of us.'

'Not I,' Anne muttered quietly.

'Your mama would have found a way, I'm sure,' Papa said, resting the reassuring weight of the palm of his hand on Charlotte's head. 'Your Aunt Branwell always knew how to get through to the boy. But he is a boy no more. He is a man grown and I believe that he has travelled too far towards death. We will never retrieve him from the precipice that he will one day plummet from, and – for our own sakes, for your sakes – we must stop trying to.'

'I am in complete agreement with you, Papa,' Emily said.

'No'. Anne shook her head. 'No, Papa, there is still a way to reach him, I am certain of it.'

'I wish it were true, my child,' Papa said. 'What consumes him now is more than the need to dull his pain. He cannot exist without the relief his vices give him. He has become reliant on them entirely. We must think of him as dying from an incurable condition. Do our best to protect and comfort him, but expect no miracle.'

'I will never do that,' Anne said, looking to Charlotte. 'I will always expect a miracle. It is hope, faith and expectation that bring such wonders into being.'

'Papa is right, Anne,' Charlotte said gently, turning to lean her back against Papa's chair. 'I love my brother dearly, but we cannot go on as we have been. Our hopes rising and plummeting again. Papa having to find the funds to please his debtors. We must ensure that his downfall is not also ours – not only for our sake, but for Papa's. And even for Branwell, who – if he were at all like himself, the brave, bold boy he used to be – would not wish this upon us.'

'I will not stop trying to bring him back to health,' Anne said as she stood up. 'Papa, I love and respect you, but I will not leave my brother to die while there is breath in his body. And I hope that any one of you would do the same for me! Shame on each of you!'

After Anne whirled out of the room, slamming the door to, Charlotte, Emily and their father sat in silence as the fire burned down in the grate, each one of them grieving for the man Branwell could have been, if he had only had the courage.

'Anne is made of hope,' Emily said after a short while. 'She would give up her whole self in the service of a brother who has long since stopped caring about what he does to us.'

'Anne is the best of us,' Charlotte said, rubbing at her temples. 'She is right, and Papa is right. We cannot abandon Branwell to his fate, but we cannot pretend that he will make a recovery any longer. We must do all we can to protect them both, though they may hate us for it.'

'There is one more thing,' Papa said. 'Another trouble that weighs heavily on me that I must discuss with you.'

'Yes, Papa?' Emily said.

'This killing, and your plans to investigate it further,' Papa said. 'It troubles me that my daughters intend to walk straight into the heart of this heinous crime and start searching for answers. When you told me of your detections, I confess I rather enjoyed the idea of mystery and adventure. And of course, the entertaining Mrs Crowe brought an element of theatre to it. Now I see that it is a very real risk to your lives. And now, more than ever, I must say how precious you are to me. God has seen fit to take your mother and sisters from me. And soon enough, I fear, he will enfold your brother to his bosom. You three girls are my heart, and I do not wish to lose you, any of you. You must stay safe, and this must be your last such detection.'

Emily and Charlotte exchanged looks.

'If we are your heart, Papa, then you are our soul,' Charlotte told him. 'We must continue to the end of this detection, for the sake of all those already harmed and for those yet to be. Do not fear for us. We are strong and clever. We must uncover the truth of Abner Lowood, because we are your daughters. But this will be our last such excursion, we swear it.'

'You are each a miracle,' Papa told them. 'Whatever woe this life has brought me, I must thank God that he gifted me with each of my daughters. But I beg you, release Ellen from your circle until this matter is done. I do not believe she is made of such stern stuff as you.'

Charlotte nodded; with regret she had to acknowledge that Papa was correct.

'We will give Ellen leave to depart,' she said. 'For not all the world can be a Brontë, Papa.'

THIRTY-THREE

Emily

The following day they gathered on the lane to say farewell to Ellen as it seemed that at last the threatening storm was about to break. A brisk wind had picked up during the night, and the oppressive sky that had kept a lid on the humid heat had broken up into mountainous clouds. The distant sound of thunder rumbled ever closer over the hills.

'I am so sorry we did not give you the rest and respite that I promised you,' Charlotte said, taking both of Ellen's hands in hers, as she kissed her on each cheek. 'Oh, my dear friend, I fear that you will never think the same of me ever again. Even so, I shall sleep a little easier knowing that you are far away from danger.'

'Do not be sorry,' Ellen said. 'I am sorry to be leaving you before we have resolved the matter. Of course, you and your papa are concerned for my safety, as I am too. But what kind of sister am I to leave you three still facing the utmost danger? While I scurry off to safety? I admit to being both relieved and disappointed in myself.'

'You have aided us so much more than you can imagine,' Emily said, as she kissed Ellen goodbye. 'I have been reading your notes this morning, and they are invaluable. A person thinks she can keep every detail in her head, but there are annotations in this little book that even I had not retained. You have brought us order, Ellen.'

'I have brought you book-keeping,' Ellen said. 'Still, records are vital, if not thrilling.'

'I hope your journey home is short and gentle,' Anne said, stepping forward to kiss their friend. 'I will miss your steadfast loyalty, Ellen. It is such a rare commodity in this ever-darkening land.'

Anne's remark did not pass unnoticed. She had arisen as usual, and went about her morning practices just as she always did. No mention was made of the conversation they had had last night in Papa's study. Yet both Emily and Charlotte could sense her disappointment and hurt in every look, every word and every gesture.

'Ellen, dear,' Charlotte leant close into her friend as she stepped into the carriage that had been sent to fetch her. 'I shall never write to you about that which occurred this week, and I beg that you will also keep your counsel. We shall take the secret of our detections to our grave. As this is to be our last, we should hate for even a trace of our adventures to remain anywhere beyond our own memories and imaginations.'

'Of course,' Ellen said. 'There is no need to ask, it is a given. Besides, I believe you have even greater gifts to give the world, and it will be those that you are famed for.'

'You are too kind,' Charlotte blushed, and Emily could feel how much her sister wanted that to be true. There was even a part of her that wanted it to be true too. To be remembered for her words, burning eternally in the ether.

But for now, it was back to the very dreadful business of murder.

Mrs Wilson sat in her housekeeper's parlour, already dressed in black crêpe, her face sallow and drawn, her expression one of a woman whose mind had gone elsewhere in order to spare her any further pain. Emily noticed how the woman simply stared, frowning deeply at the palms of her upturned hands in her lap as if they were unfamiliar objects.

'She ain't well,' the young undermaid told them anxiously, rubbing her palms on her apron. 'The mistress has the under-cook at the old house coming over to take on her duties for a short while, but I fear for Mrs Wilson. A new groom is likely to come with a new wife, and then where will she be with no position, no husband and no child to care for her? And she ain't . . .' The girl faltered. 'She's not herself, miss. She's . . . I'm afraid for her. And . . .'

'Tell me, child,' Emily said, bending at the waist to bring them face to face. 'It were me that found him,' Helen told her, tears standing in her eyes. 'Mrs Wilson sent me out with a packet of bread and cheese for him. I found him there, it were . . .' She shook her head.

'Did you see anything other than poor Mr Wilson at the scene?' Emily asked her. 'Anything at all. It does not matter if it seems unimportant. You can tell me, and it may prove vital.'

'Mrs Wilson sent me out with his food,' Helen said. 'The horses were on t'other side of the pasture, making a racket they were. And he lay in the long grass.' She lowered her voice. 'He drinks, miss, so I thought he'd been at it again. Mrs Wilson always told me to kick him in the ribs if I find him like that. I never do, of course. But I went over to rouse him and I saw the grass all around him was sticky and black, and covered in flies. I still didn't understand until I rolled him over . . .' She paused. 'It was the worst thing I ever saw.' She shook her head as if trying to dislodge the memory. 'But there was one thing more that seemed strange to me. Because Mrs Wilson is never wrong, she never makes a mistake and is never in a muddle.'

'What do you mean, child?' Emily asked her.

'Well, under Mr Wilson there was a packet, just like the one I'd been sent to give him. Somebody had already brought him his bread and cheese, though he never had the chance to eat it.'

'I see,' Emily said thoughtfully.

'Will Mrs Wilson be right again?' the girl asked her. 'I want her to be right, miss.'

'Try not to worry,' Emily said. 'Mrs Wilson has received a hard and sudden blow. She is stunned, but she will return to herself. You and I have both seen at her fiercest. Once her mind has made sense of it all, she will come back to life, I promise you.'

'My ma died,' the girl said absently. 'She was ill for most of the year, so it weren't no surprise. But still, it did feel strange to be in the world without my ma. Me without a ma, and Mrs Wilson without a child, we sort of leaned on one another, if you take my meaning. She is strict and many fear her, but to me she is a friend.'

'I understand,' Emily nodded, giving the child an encouraging smile despite the troubling information the girl had given her.

Emily had insisted on coming alone to visit Mrs Wilson.

Charlotte had not been in favour of it, but Emily decided that if those who had done for Mr Wilson were horse thieves then they would pay her no mind, and if it was somehow connected to Lowood, then he had done his business at Harrowings and would be unlikely to return.

'It is you and Anne who have more to fear visiting Rosalyn,' she had told them out of earshot of their father. You must be vigilant, and take this with you.'

Emily had handed Charlotte her pistol. 'It is loaded, so take great care with it. If you find that you must discharge it, simply take aim, pull back the hammer and depress the trigger. You might not aim true, but even so my hope is that the noise and commotion would give you a moment more to escape danger.'

Charlotte had taken the weapon gingerly. As she was not in possession of pockets, which she considered to be altogether inflammatory, she did not precisely know what to do with the loaded weapon. After a moment, she had buttoned it securely into her sleeve, which Emily thought was as good a place as any for it.

'This seems excessive,' Charlotte had said.

'There cannot be an excess of caution when it comes to Abner Lowood,' Emily replied.

Emily knocked on the open parlour door three times, and then three more. When the second knock elicited no response, she entered the small room, and took a chair opposite the widow. Mrs Wilson did not acknowledge her presence in any way.

'Mrs Wilson,' she said in firm, clear tones. 'I require your attention, madam. It is a matter of great importance. For I am certain that between us we can discern the identity of the man who murdered your husband.'

There was a moment when nothing happened, except for the ticking of the clock and the distant clanking of pans in the kitchen, and then Mrs Wilson raised her eyes to meet Emily's.

'There is no need,' she said.

'What can you mean?' Emily asked her.

'I believe I know who murdered my husband,' Mrs Wilson said. 'Though I do not understand how it can be.'

'Who do you accuse?' Emily asked her intently.

'Myself,' Mrs Wilson said, reaching for an object that sat wrapped in a cloth on the table next to her. Unfolding the material, she revealed a bloody knife. 'It must have been me that killed my husband, though I have no recollection of it.'

Emily went to the parlour door and closed it.

'Start at the beginning,' she said.

'There had been a change in him,' Mrs Wilson said. 'It was since you came to visit him. He seemed lighter somehow, happier. Like the world was a bright place again.' She touched her fingers lightly to her lips. 'He was kind to me; loving. As he has never been, not in all the years we've been married. He told me that life would be better now, that we, that I, had much to look forward to. He hadn't touched a drop of alcohol since he met you. I thought that perhaps somehow your visit had reformed him.'

'And you cannot ascribe this change in mood and person to anything other than my sister Anne and me paying him a visit?' Emily asked, eyeing the knife that sat on the table, sticky with blackened blood.

'No, only that the evening you saw him he was light of mood and seemed as if a burden of unhappiness had been lifted from his shoulders. I saw a glimpse of the man he could have been if he had not let his disappointment overtake him. I felt hopeful.'

Emily thought back to the meeting they had had with Wilson. There was nothing that she could remember that would indicate this change in him. There was only one event that they had not managed to resolve with Mr Wilson.

'Madam,' Emily began slowly. 'Did your husband mention any sightings he'd had?'

'Sightings?' Mrs Wilson frowned. 'Sightings of what nature?'

'The last thing he told us when we went to visit him was that he had begun to see an . . . apparition.' Emily collected herself. She must be blunt with Mrs Wilson; the woman deserved the truth. 'A revenant, a person risen from the grave.'

'He did?' Mrs Wilson eyes widened. 'No, he never mentioned that to me, and he never came home afeared or pale. If anything, he was up and out of bed in good time before the dawn every day, singing like a lark.'

Wilson had told them he had seen the revenant of Barbara Lowood drawing a step closer every dawn. Whereas Rosalyn had thought that her vision of Barbara was coming to wreak her revenge. Perhaps Wilson had seen her more as a siren, a vision of his long-lost love come back from the grave to claim him at last. If he had died by his own hand, she would have been satisfied with that explanation. But he did not. With regret she pushed on.

'He told us that he saw Barbara Lowood, every dawn. And each day she would draw a little nearer to him,' Emily said.

Mrs Wilson sat back in her chair, thought for a moment and nodded once.

'That's why he was happy,' she said. 'Why he told me life would get better now. He did not mean for us, he meant for him. He must have lost his mind. Thought he was about to run off with the love of his life, though she's dead and rotting. That must have been why I killed him.'

'Yet you have no recollection of the event,' Emily said.

'Nothing,' Mrs Wilson said. 'No, nor most of the day before. It's as gone as if it were somehow cut out of my mind. Perhaps, perhaps the horror of what took place is too great for me to recall, though I know it must have been terrible. For it made me commit the gravest sin. All I recall is the hour I packed Peter's food up for him and sent it off with my girl. Then she ran back screaming. I fainted. When I woke up, I was in my chamber and it was night. I got up like there was something very important I had forgotten. I went to my washstand and there, in the bowl, was this knife. At first, I thought the murderer had come for me, I was so afraid. But then I saw a bundle under the bed, my marriage bed. It was my dress and apron.' Mrs Wilson looked up at Emily in confusion. 'Covered in my husband's blood. So, it must have been me, you see? You must call the constable, Miss Brontë. Have them take me away. And if you would be so kind, take care of my girl. She's a good girl.'

Emily thought for a moment. Even with the evidence pointing firmly in one direction, it simply did not feel right. It was as if the world of nightmares had seeped into waking hours, and was infecting every corner without any pattern or sense. This had to be something to do with Lowood, with the power he seemed to have to charm and influence people. Perhaps it was connected to Mrs Crowe's theory of ergot poisoning. Someone, somehow, was altering reality for no discernible cause; at least none, it seemed, except pure malice.

'Mrs Wilson, you need do nothing. I will take care of the matter further. Just stay here in your parlour and talk to no one for the time being. I will return as soon as I'm able.'

The child waited for her outside, her hands twisted in knots, her eyes huge with fear.

'Did a gentleman come to call on Mrs Wilson in the last day or so?' Emily asked her. 'You would know him: tall and gaunt with only one hand.'

'No such gentleman came,' the girl said. 'There were no strange visitors. We bought some ribbons from a pedlar woman, and the grocery boy came. Those are both commonplace things, though, miss? Is that bad?'

'Not at all,' Emily told her reassuringly, though she was deeply perplexed. 'Take good care of Mrs Wilson. If you can prevent her from speaking to anyone at least for the rest of the day. I will do my best to help her.'

For, despite all signs to the contrary, Emily was convinced Mrs Wilson was innocent.

THIRTY-FOUR

Anne

By the time Charlotte and Anne arrived at the workhouse, heavy drops of rain had begun to fall intermittently from the sky, plopping audibly onto the road and canopy of leaves, as well as the rims of their bonnets. Anne turned her face up to the rain for a moment, grateful for its cool refreshment as drops ran over the contours of her face and down her neck. Perhaps the rain would wash away all the strangeness and discomfort the last few days had brought once and for all. For it seemed to Anne that it wasn't just the grain store at the workhouse that was infected with rot. Everything and all around her were tainted too.

The scene they came upon when they entered the workhouse gates was one of upheaval and disarray. The inmates were not working, only watching the chaos unfold, even as the rain began to soak them through. It seemed to Anne as if the crowd that had gathered was captured in some kind of trance, as if they could not look away. No one attempted to admonish or direct them. The starved and the poor lined the courtyard like a host of revenants, caught in confusion. The only difference being that they had not yet deigned to die. The sight they were all fixed upon was almost as strange, if not unexpected.

For the Tollivers had brought a cart onto the cobbles, into which they were hastily tossing what seemed like all their possessions from the cottage, without a care of order or safety. It seemed that they were intent on taking flight, as if it were possible to escape the devil himself.

'Mrs Tolliver?' Anne attempted to attract the woman's attention several times. 'Mrs Tolliver? Please stop a moment.' At last Mrs Tolliver looked up.

'Are you departing?' Anne asked.

'Yes, Miss Brontë,' she replied as she loaded a chest that seemed to be filled with loosely cracking crockery onto the cart. 'And right away, too. We cannot stay here while that creature is stalking the streets, murdering anyone who has crossed him. We must get our Rosalyn to safety at once, for she is sure to be the next victim.' She stopped and looked at Charlotte and Anne, as if she had only now truly realised they were there. 'And you Misses Brontë, you must not be here. You are not safe. You must run home at once.'

'But who will take care of the poor?' Charlotte asked nervously, as the crowd of spectators grew with every passing second: silent, staring, pressing forward. Anne could feel a slowly rising tide of anger that she feared might spark the poor folk into action at any moment. And who could blame them? There was no escape from their fears, no cart to come and carry them away. Only the ever-increasing grind of utter poverty robbing them of even their humanity.

'That is for the parish to decide,' Mrs Tolliver said, returning to the cottage to fetch more items. 'I did my best for them, but now I must take care of my own. I am quite sure they can manage themselves for a bit.'

'Is there food? Is there fuel?' Charlotte asked, following Mrs Tolliver as she hurried back and forth. 'They must be cared for, Mrs Tolliver.'

'Then they should have had a care not to end up in the workhouse,' Mrs Tolliver snapped. A murmur of dissent ran through the crowd as a low rumble echoed at once in the heavens.

'Mrs Tolliver, pause for a moment and think, I beg you.' Anne followed her to the door, away from the dozens of pairs of eyes that followed her every moment through the driving rain. 'We cannot be sure that what happened to Mr Wilson was anything to do with Mr Lowood. It hardly seems prudent to give up all you have fought so hard for until you know more.'

'We know enough,' Mr Tolliver spoke for the first time, loading a mattress into the cart. 'I have seen enough with my own eyes. Your Mrs Crowe said we had eaten bad flour and that's what caused our visions. But there has been no bad flour consumed in this place since that day, and yet still I see her, still I hear her, still I *smell* her! She comes in the house now, Miss Brontë, she is at the foot of our stairs. It's Mrs Lowood who killed her old lover. Don't you see? She's come back for us all and if she don't, he will. This is a cursed place. Our only chance is to escape it.'

At that moment, the clouds lit from within with a flash of lightning, and a loud crash of thunder boomed overhead. It felt as if the storm was almost above them now. This was hardly the time for a family to be leaving the shelter of their home without knowing where they were headed.

'But where will you go?' Charlotte asked as the rain began to truly drill down upon them. 'If you are able to wait a little longer, I am sure we could help you find a new situation.'

'We do not know where we go,' Mrs Tolliver said. 'Nor do I care to, for it would only give the monster a trail to follow. We shall travel and trust in the Lord. As long as it is not this place then I shall be glad, for it is cursed. Everything rots here, everything is tainted. From the grain in the store to a person's mind. If I stay here a moment longer, I shall go mad, I know that I shall.'

'But where is Rosalyn?' Anne asked, looking about her. She was concerned by Mrs Tolliver's frenetic anxiety. Had she lost sight of her daughter in such dangerous times?

'In the house,' Mr Tolliver said. Glancing at Charlotte, Anne headed into the cottage to search for the girl, but she was nowhere to be found.

'She is not in the house,' Anne told Rosalyn's mother.

'What? Where is Rosalyn?' Mrs Tolliver said, turning this way and that. 'Dear God, James, where is our daughter? She's not in the house!'

'She must be, I told her not to move a step,' Mr Tolliver said, running back into the cottage with Mrs Tolliver at his back.

Anne hurried towards the empty master's house.

'Perhaps in there,' she said to Charlotte. 'Where she visited with Lowood.'

'Be done with your idleness and go and search for Miss Tolliver!' The girl's father began to shout and shove at some of the men in the crowd.

'I fear this place is a powder keg,' Charlotte whispered. 'The best we can do is remove the family before they become the spark that lights the fuse. Go look for Rosalyn, I will do my best to calm matters here.'

'You, Charlotte?' Anne asked her. 'Alone?'

'Go,' Charlotte said. 'I will join you when I can.'

Anne hesitated by the door to the master's house as she watched the tiny figure of her sister march up to the bulk of Mr Tolliver and pull him back from the brink of confrontation.

'Good people,' Charlotte raised her voice and her palms. 'I see your distress and anger, and I know you have a right to it. You who have been punished and neglected through no fault of your own. My father will not let this place fall to ruin, or any of you go hungry or cold. You know that to be true. These good people will soon be gone and my family will ensure you receive the aid you need to return to your lives and dignity. I beg you now, disperse. Search for Rosalyn. Let us bring an end to this time of fear and uncertainty.'

A few of the crowd had begun to call to one another to start the search as Anne opened the door to the master's house.

At once she was assaulted by the terrible scent. It seemed to rush at her as she opened the door; the smell of sickness and death, along with rot and decay. The house was shuttered and dark, full of shadows. Bread had crumbled to mould on the kitchen table, which crawled with flies, seemingly attracted by something darkly sticky that pooled around the long blade of a knife.

'Rosalyn?' Anne called out, finding her voice was only a whisper. Her fear was irrational, she knew that. And yet she feared that if she called too loudly, she would wake the dead.

'Rosalyn, it's Anne.' She called again, louder, venturing a little further into the room. Above her head she heard the creak of a floorboard, and what sounded like one, two, three footsteps. Outside Anne could still dimly hear her sister's voice continuing to talk to the gathered. If Charlotte could muster such courage, then so could she.

'Rosalyn?' She called up the steep stone steps. 'Are you there?'

Anne cocked her head, as she heard a shuffle and a long sigh that rattled with pain. Anne feared for the girl.

'It's time to come down now, my friend,' Anne said. 'Your mama is worried for you. Come down and let me help you.'

'None can help me now,' came the reply, hoarse and full of sorrow. The poor girl must have wept until her throat grew raw. 'None can help you now, neither.'

'Rosa—'

There was a hammering at the door.

'Anne,' Charlotte called urgently, opening the door to a rush of cool air and heavy rain. 'One of the children told me that she has seen Rosalyn in the orchard – with a man. It can only be Lowood. We must go to her at once, and before Mr Tolliver hears the whisper, or there will be murders this very hour, I'm sure of it.'

'But . . .' Anne looked up the shadowy staircase, and heard the creak of the boards and another footstep drawing something ever closer to coming into view; she ran to her sister at once. Whatever waited for them in the storm could not frighten her more than the nameless sense of dread she had felt, rooted to the spot at the bottom of those stairs, while something that should not be lurched ever closer.

'The orchard,' Charlotte said, grabbing Anne's hand, 'at once.'

After days of oppressive heat, the sisters now found themselves unprepared for the heavy downpour and whipping wind. As they hurried to the orchard, neither one of them meeting eyes with the silent crowd that lined their way, their skirts grew heavy, sodden with rain. Their light boots were soaked through and sticky with mud. Their heads were bent against the torrent until they were almost upon the great oak tree. Which was why it caught them by surprise to discover that Rosalyn was not alone. Seated beside her on the bench beneath the huge tree was none other than Abner Lowood.

Anne came to an abrupt halt a few steps away from them, Charlotte almost walking into the back of her. Her sister's hand went at once to the subtle profile of the pistol secured behind the buttons of her sleeve. Anne moved so as to shield Charlotte from Lowood's view as she loosened two buttons on her cuff, securing the weapon in her grip. Rosalyn leaned close into Lowood and whispered something in his ear.

'Ladies,' Abner Lowood said, leaning back against the bark of the tree, blowing smoke from his pipe into its verdant branches, which danced and flinched in the wind. 'You catch us in a lover's tryst.'

'Rosalyn,' Charlotte said, raising her voice to be heard over the driving rain. 'Your mama requires you at once. Come with us, please. At once, if you would not mind.'

'I shall not come now,' Rosalyn said in a dreamy singsong voice. 'I cannot possibly come now.'

There was something very wrong with her, Anne knew. She had the same countenance that she had worn on the night she claimed to have seen the revenant of Barbara Lowood, as if all reason had vacated her mind. Could it be that the grain store had not been cleared after all, or was it possible that Lowood had found a way to dose her, her family, perhaps the whole workhouse? In any event, the girl was quite out of her mind.

'I could not leave without bidding farewell to my dear Abner,' Rosalyn said, as if they were at a genial picnic on a pleasant afternoon, not sitting in the driving rain with lightning flashing in the heart of the heavy clouds that thundered overhead. 'For, believe me, he has been such a very good friend of mine. Are you not my friend, Abner? Are you not my dearest love, and I your very own heart?'

'You would not begrudge us a final parting, would you, Misses Brontë?' Lowood said, drawing his knife out of his belt, and rubbing the blade, first one side and then the other, on the leg of his britches. It left a rusty smear of something in its wake.

'You have said your goodbyes,' Anne said, taking a step forward to hold her hand out to Rosalyn. The rain was now so heavy it obscured her view, and she could not fight the nagging fear that the awful 'something' that had lingered in the master's cottage was watching them from somewhere she could not identify. Even in the fresh rain there was a stench of death rising from the earth. 'Now you may take your leave.'

To Anne's horror, Rosalyn turned her face to Lowood's and kissed him fully on the mouth, their lips parting as the embrace lingered.

'That's quite enough,' Charlotte said, her voice shrill and high. 'Now, Miss Tolliver, if you please.'

'I will never forget you, Abner,' Rosalyn said, as if in a trance. 'Time to say goodbye to the Misses Brontë now, like a good fellow.'

Abner stood up as Rosalyn did, watching her as she walked over to the sisters. Anne took her hand at once.

'Are you quite well, Rosalyn?' she asked her.

'Quite well,' Rosalyn said serenely, looking at Anne. 'Are you, Miss Brontë? Why, you look like you've seen a ghost!'

At that moment Abner started racing towards them, wielding the knife to strike.

For a crucial second Anne was frozen to the spot in fear and disbelief and then Charlotte fired the pistol into the air, the recoil making her stumble back and drop the weapon in the long grass. Abner stopped abruptly, looking around, confused, just long enough for Anne to turn on her, tighten her grasp on Rosalyn's wrist, and drag her after them. Turning on their heels the three women ran, sliding and stumbling on the rain-slicked grass, Rosalyn laughing, as if they were playing a childhood game and not running for their lives. Anne tried to see their way through the driving rain, but it fell in sheets of water now. Was it a trick of her mind in the flashing light of the storm that made her think she saw a figure standing motionless in the long grass? All Anne knew was that they had to find a way to safety, somehow. Lowood had lost what was left of his mind, and now all his intent was to do them harm.

A howl of animal rage coincided with a boom of thunder, as Lowood gave chase once again. Leading the way, Anne wove in and out of the stunted apple trees, slipping on the long grass, unable to make out the gate that led to the cottage and at least some semblance of safety. Weighed down by her heavy skirts, and dragging a half-hysterical girl behind her, Anne realised too late that they had run the wrong way in their panicked bid to escape Lowood. All that was ahead of them now was a low knot of stunted hawthorn trees and gorse, and beyond that the open peat bogs of the moors, where they would find the going even slower and no shelter for miles around.

'In here,' Anne hissed to Charlotte as she dived into a thorny thicket of gorse, obliged to secure Rosalyn in her arm while Charlotte covered the girl's mouth with a firmly clamped hand. The barbs bit into their arms and caught at their skirts as they scrambled as deep into the undergrowth as they could.

Lowood stopped in the grass a few feet from them, his head lifted into the breeze as if he might sniff them out. The long blade of his knife flashed as a bolt of lightning threaded through the sky, striking a lone tree, but fifty or so yards away.

'Return to me!' he howled into the storm, the wind whipping his hair back from his wild features. 'Return to me and let me rest, I beg you!'

Was Lowood also talking about his dead wife? Anne caught her breath as he seemed to turn towards where they were hiding. If he found them there would be no escape. Charlotte had already discharged the gun, and dropped it. They would not be able to scramble out of the thicket quickly enough. Not for all of them to escape the sharp edge of that blade.

For a moment Anne was certain that his gaze had locked onto her, his dark eyes burning like the coals of hellfire. And then a dazzling bright whip of lightning lashed at the trees that sheltered them and caught fire, driving down into the earth, leaving a lingering scent of burning in the air. That could have killed them.

'We must run,' Anne told Charlotte and Rosalyn, whose expression had grown suddenly serious. 'We must throw our skirts over our shoulders and run in the direction of the workhouse. It cannot be far. Run as fast as you are able and do not look back. If one of us falls, the others must . . .' Anne faltered for a moment. 'Must keep running. Keep running and fetch help. Do not turn back, for you will surely be injured.'

'I cannot,' Charlotte said, shaking her head. 'I cannot keep up with you, or ahead of him, Anne.'

'Take courage, Charlotte,' Anne said. 'For we must run *now.*'

They scrambled out of the overgrowth on the opposite side of where Lowood had stood, hoping to secure a moment when his attention was diverted elsewhere; at least that had been Anne's plan, but as she crawled through the sucking peat to peer around the edges of the thicket, Lowood was nowhere to be seen. Anne wiped the rain from her eyes, as she searched for any sign of him, but he was gone. Cautiously she stood up, searching as far through the curtains of rain as she could. There was no sign of him at all. Then she saw it, a figure or something very like one, pale against the sunburnt grass, standing perfectly still in the heart of the tumult.

'That is the way back,' Anne told the others, pointing to where the figure had appeared moments before. 'That way to safety.'

THIRTY-FIVE

Charlotte

'Then the lightning struck and it was as if he were commanded to hell. He vanished almost before our eyes,' Charlotte told Emily, her voice still trembling as she reached for Emily and squeezed her arm. 'In truth I am half afraid that we are still trapped there, with the killer just inches away from discovering us and that this warm kitchen, and you and Tabby, are just visions of my fearful mind.'

'Be calm,' Emily said. 'You are here, you are safe. You escaped.'

The three sisters had arrived back at the parsonage within minutes of each other, all of them soaked through to the skin. Emily had seemed lost in her own thoughts as her sisters careered into her, out of breath and shivering. Emily had snapped into action, bundling them inside at once and bolting the door. Horrified by the state of them, Tabby had herded them all into her kitchen, where she banked the fire in the kitchen range, and bade them remove their damp garments at once. Martha was dispatched to fetch blankets and dry clothes, which they were struggling into in the tiny kitchen space, made all the more difficult by the enforced proximity of their dogs, who would not leave their sides.

'That is the absolute last of you going out,' Tabby said unhappily as she picked up their sodden and filthy clothes, skirts torn and hems rent asunder, and dropped them into a basket. 'If you do not wish to kill me, you shall remain within these four walls until I give you leave to do otherwise. You three will be the death of me, you will. I told you not to consort with murderers, as if any sane person should need to be given such advice, and yet here we are! Soaked through and as likely to die of fever as a knifeman.' Tabby gestured towards the heavens. 'What have I done to deserve such worry? I must have sinned very gravely for the Lord to punish me so with loving these children!'

Still the thunder grumbled on in reply, the rain battering at the glass with every gust of wind. Still Charlotte could not control the shudders that wracked her small frame. She had fired the gun, felt its shot reverberate through the bones of her arm, and all that followed had been a blur of survival. It felt as if part of her was still hiding in that orchard, certain that the very next moment would be her last. She leaned into Emily, who wrapped a rough blanket around both of them, cradling her head against her shoulder.

'We are sorry,' Anne said, similarly cocooned. 'We had no thought that Lowood might be lying in wait at the workhouse. The whole scene was so peculiar.' Anne seemed to remember something else, as her whole body convulsed in shudders. 'I do confess, I was more afraid for my life then than I have ever been.'

'Thank goodness you got away in time,' Emily said, not for the first time since Anne and Charlotte had related what had happened. 'What of Rosalyn?'

'Her parents dragged her onto the waiting cart,' Charlotte said, 'and left at speed, with the cottage door still standing open and no one at the helm at the workhouse.'

Charlotte thought back to the scene as she and Anne had hurried out of the courtyard. Those left behind had jeered and called obscenities after the cart as it rattled down the lane. She could feel the anger and resentment crackling in the air, even as the worst of the storm passed. For a moment it had seemed likely that the abandoned souls of the workhouse would turn their frustration on to Anne and her. The crowd had pressed around them, almost engulfing them, until Charlotte realised they had been shepherded out of the gate which was closed firmly behind them. 'In actual fact, I should think it would be better for them to be left to themselves, at least tonight.'

'Do you know where the Tollivers have gone?' Emily asked.

'No, Mrs Tolliver told us she did not know where they would go and that she did not care to. Just that she wanted to be as far away from danger as quickly as she possibly could.' Charlotte looked at Emily. 'I find I am obliged to you for lending me your weapon. I am afraid that I left it on the mud, in the orchard. It went all too quickly for me to be able to retrieve it.'

'Well, I would rather have my sisters than my pistol,' Emily told her, 'though Lowood is still loose, and I suppose he could come to find us here.'

'I've bolted all the doors,' Tabby said. 'Mr Brontë is in his study, his pistol loaded at his bedside. One great dog, and one silly one here to guard you. We are not unprotected.'

'Not while we have you, Tabby,' Charlotte said.

'And you, Emily?' Anne asked. 'How was it with Mrs Wilson?'

'Mrs Wilson is convinced she is a murderer,' Emily said, and she told them the events of her afternoon.

'I told her to say nothing, to do nothing, until we had had a chance to make sense of it. Fortunately, Mrs Wilson is still half stupefied, so I think we have a little time to discover the truth before she turns herself in.'

'But if she is guilty, should she not do exactly that?' Anne asked.

'Though the evidence seems conclusive, I feel that it can't be true,' Emily said, rubbing at her temples. 'There is a piece missing from it all. The piece that makes a fractured picture whole. And there has been from the very beginning. One singular part of the puzzle we have not yet discovered that will surely tell us the why. For once we have the why, then we have the who.'

'We already have the who, do we not?' Anne said as she pulled on fresh stockings that Tabby had warmed before the grate. 'Lowood came after us with a knife! We saw his murderous intent with our own eyes. We know, without a doubt, exactly what he is capable of. We must go to the Justice and ask for him to be arrested at once before more harm can be done.'

'I agree,' Charlotte said. 'I will see if there is anyone in the village who might drive us to Keighley.'

'You are not leaving this house,' Tabby told her. 'If anyone is to go anywhere, we will send Mr Nicholls.'

Charlotte sat down by the range, frowning deeply.

'Something is not right,' Emily said, poring over Ellen's notebooks, which she had collected the moment she had arrived home. 'It must be something we have seen but not yet recognised.'

'I agree that this all feels like a play, like theatre,' Charlotte said, letting her hair loose to dry before the fire. 'Nothing we seem to know feels true. As if we are still under the influence of ergot. I wonder if—'

Before Charlotte could say more, there was a knock at the front door. Charlotte rose and went to peer through a slender gap in the kitchen doorway to see Martha opening the parsonage door to young Mr Reaper, whom she abandoned in the hallway as she made her way to find them.

'There's a Mr Reaper,' Martha confirmed when she came into the kitchen a few minutes later. 'Wet as an old dog, he is.'

'Are old dogs especially wet?' Emily wondered.

'I've left him in the hall. He's soaked through to the skin,' Martha persisted.

'Fetch him a sheet to dry himself, please,' Charlotte told the girl, 'and then put him in front of the fire in the dining room. Tell him we will be with him shortly and then come back to the kitchen and make him some tea.'

Martha turned to trudge off to do as she was bid, and was met by Mr Nicholls.

'Who is the gentleman you just admitted, Martha?' Charlotte heard him ask the girl.

'A Mr Reaper,' Martha said uncertainly. 'Like the grim one, sir. Miss Charlotte sent me to get him a sheet to dry himself with while she put on her clothes in the kitchen.'

Mr Nicholls looked at the door that Charlotte closed hastily.

'I will speak to the gentleman,' Charlotte heard him say. Her heart sank. Arthur would come and try to take control of the situation, with all his masculine pride, just at the moment all was so finely balanced.

'It seems that Mr Reaper has had a change of heart,' Anne said. 'This will be all we need to secure Lowood's capture, I am certain of it. He will have brought the confession with him.'

'Perhaps,' Charlotte said. 'If Arthur doesn't frighten him away first. Or perhaps he has come to beg us to help find his beloved brother once again. Either way, as we speak, Mr Nicholls is being apprised of much more than we would wish him to know.'

'I've come to make tea like you said,' Martha said, re-entering the tiny kitchen. 'Mr Nicholls asked if there was cake.'

'We will go to the dining room now,' Charlotte told Martha. 'Bring the tea soon, and if you can find a way to get Mr Nicholls to leave the room, that would be most beneficial. Perhaps attempt to lure him with cake.'

'Like a rat into a trap?' Martha asked.

'Quite so,' Charlotte said.

She stopped her sisters at the foot of the stairs. 'Remember, Mr Reaper is young, and kind. If we treat him gently, he will tell us more. Let us not berate and frighten him.'

'I don't know why you are looking at me,' Emily said.

Charlotte raised her eyebrows.

Emily returned the poker to the kitchen grate.

'Ah,' Mr Nicholls and Mr Reaper stood as the ladies entered the room. 'Misses Brontë, allow me to introduce you to Mr Reaper, a curate out of Scarborough. He has come to Haworth in search of a lost relative, and came to call on the parsonage in the hope that we may assist him.'

Charlotte breathed a sigh of relief. It seemed that Mr Reaper had not said anything to Mr Nicholls about Lowood, their visit, or his brother's sealed confession. Indeed, as Charlotte met his eye, he inclined his head slightly, as if indicating precisely that.

Martha entered with tea, which she set down upon the table.

'Mr Nicholls, there is cake in the kitchen,' she said with some ceremony and a theatrical flourish of her hand.

'I beg your pardon?' Mr Nicholls said, rather astounded. 'Why don't you fetch the cake here, miss?'

'Because Miss Charlotte said I was to make you leave at the first opportunity,' Martha said. 'And you said you wanted cake, so I am luring you away.'

Charlotte sank down into a chair and poured the tea.

'Never mind, Martha,' Charlotte said, mildly. 'Not to worry.'

'You would send me away so you can converse with this stranger alone?' Mr Nicholls asked Charlotte sternly.

'Mr Reaper is no stranger to us,' Charlotte said. 'In fact, it is us he has come to see, Arthur, on a matter of some urgency. Your presence is not required.'

'I believe it is my duty to stay and know all,' Mr Nicholls said stiffly. 'Someone must keep check of your more impulsive traits, Charlotte.'

Emily sighed as she took a seat next to Anne. Charlotte only bowed her head and pressed her indignation silently inward.

'This will take twice as long as it should now there are men involved,' Emily said.

THIRTY-SIX

Emily

'May I ask how you came to find us, sir?' Emily asked a few moments later when their guest had been somewhat warmed by the fire and a cup of strong tea. Thanks to Martha's attempt to help them, they had been obliged to explain all that had taken place in Scarborough to Mr Nicholls, who stood by the mantel, his arms crossed and his expression one of a very disappointed headmaster. It was only Charlotte's pleading that had convinced him not to call for their papa. Emily had watched his chest puff up with every quiet word Charlotte spoke, revelling in her need for his complicity. What very foolish, simple creatures most men were, Emily thought, and Mr Nicholls was no exception.

'I had your names from when you came to visit me in Scarborough,' Mr Reaper said. 'I asked the reverend if he knew the name and he told me of the Brontës at Haworth. And then I thought of Mrs Martin, and I knew this is where my brother would be.'

'Mrs Martin?' Emily asked. 'Mary Martin?'

'Indeed, you know her name?' Mr Reaper asked Emily. 'Mrs Martin was the good lady that took me in after our father died. When she passed, she asked to be buried with her people in Haworth. It made sense that Carus would come here, to begin again somehow. It was far enough away from the troubles he left, but there was still a thread connected to his family. To me.'

Emily leaned her chin into her hand as she observed Mr Reaper. That such a decent and gentle young man could still feel so kindly about the brute they were now so terrifyingly familiar with seemed impossible. What had happened, between the Carus whom Mr Reaper knew leaving Scarborough, and the vile creature who had attempted to kill her sisters today? They had yet to tell Mr Reaper of the attack that Anne and Charlotte had only barely escaped from, hoping to keep that at least from Mr Nicholls, but if they were forced to confront the young man with that information, would he believe it had been the same man as his brother who had hunted them with a knife?

'Have you read the letter your brother left with you?' Emily asked him. 'I cannot impress upon you how vital it is that you share the contents and help to bring your brother to justice before any more are hurt or killed.'

'I have,' Mr Reaper said, unhappily. 'Though it breaks my heart, I was compelled by duty to bring it you. For it is a confession to murder.'

Mr Reaper passed the letter across the table to Emily, who digested the words in a few moments before reading it aloud.

Dear Stephen,

If you are reading this then I have finally met my end, and you should not grieve for me, for I will have deserved it. I wish I could have escaped an eternity of damnation, but I was condemned to hell before I were a full-grown man, and have known there was no redemption for me my whole life long.

I killed our father. I had not set out with him that morning to do him harm, though I wished it for every moment I can remember being alive. I endured him for you, to protect you. When he told me he was sending you away to a Mr Myers, who *had a particular fondness for boy servants, all my efforts at being good gave way. I will not tell you the details of his murder, only that I pushed his body into the sea and told all it was an accident. I expected to feel wracked with guilt, Stephen. But was our life not so much better without his shadow hanging over us? Some men are meant for good, and you are one of those. Some are meant for evil, and that is I.*

After, I thought, perhaps, I might be happy with Grace. But I never could refrain from ruining what was pure and good. From taking all that was kind and gentle, and twisting and twisting it until I tore it limb from limb. Grace did not die directly at my hands, no matter what they say. But I did kill her nonetheless, though not the children, who never thrived. There's a cruelty in me, Stephen. Handed down to me from our father. I will always be its servant; I know that now. And so all I can do is to go away, far from you, and await retribution. I can only hope it comes quickly.

Pray for me, brother, that I may find myself a quiet corner of hell. If it were not for you, then I would not have known what it is to love another soul.

Your brother, Carus

'He was already a killer before he even met Grace,' Emily said, lifting her eyes from the letter and looking around at the company.

Mr Reaper bowed his head, 'He sinned to save me. And then lived as long as he could with the guilt, trying to lead a respectable life. But he could not; he did not believe he deserved happiness. He married young, thinking that the best way to secure his position with the pharmacist was to marry his daughter. So, he courted Grace. Every child they bore was lost to them before the age of eight. Grace couldn't stand these losses, she prayed to the Lord to forgive her and bless them, but it was always the same. A healthy child would fall suddenly ill, there would be a fever and breathlessness and then inevitably death.'

'The symptoms of poisoning,' Emily said, grimly.

'But they were not poisoned,' Mr Reaper said. 'Grace was desperately unhappy, and Carus knew it was because of him. Instead of easing her unhappiness, he only made her suffer more. It was like a sickness in him. In a strange way, I think he went to Miss Merryweather to ease Grace's anguish.'

'Poor Miss Merryweather, she will ever pay the price for his "kindness",' Anne said, bitterly.

'I paid a visit to her, before I came here,' Mr Reaper told them. 'She is rightly very angry, and I am rightly very ashamed that I never tried to visit her previously. We have made amends. I hope she will allow me to help her from her current situation, if she wishes it.'

'Miss Merryweather chooses to rely on no one but herself,' Emily muttered quietly.

'It was while Carus was with Miss Merryweather that Grace herself fell ill. Her father was in York on business, and Carus left his wife to cope with her pain on her own. She went to her father's medicine cabinet, and took a deal of morphine. A deal too much. Enough to stop her heart and end her life.'

'She died by accident?' Emily asked, feeling a distinct sense of unease rising in her stomach. What was the hidden part of this mystery that remained so stubbornly out of focus? The part that swam and swayed out of view every time she turned towards it.

'His life was ruined, so he determined to ruin as many others as he could?' Charlotte asked, incredulous.

'I do believe that guilt and bitterness ate him alive,' Mr Reaper said. 'Before my father was drowned, Carus always bore the brunt of his cruelty, and was judged because of it. Folk recoiled from him because of his scars, his disfigurements. I believe my brother became the man that others saw, to save himself from further painful rejection. He became his scars. And though he committed the most grievous sin, I still pray for a chance to see him. To save his soul, if not his body. I beg you to help me in my cause.'

'I fear he is far too dangerous, now,' Charlotte said. 'Sir, your brother attempted to kill us only hours ago. We are fortunate to be alive.'

'Madam, I—'

'Mr Nicholls,' Charlotte cut across him. 'You must take this letter and ride to the Justice in Bradford at once. Tell him they must send men, as many as he can to secure Lowood.' She turned to Mr Reaper. 'Once he is secured in prison, perhaps then you may save him.'

'I am pleased at last to take this matter into my own hands,' Mr Nicholls said, taking the letter and departing at once. He was so very easily distracted, Emily thought; the man would never make a detector.

'There is one thing more,' Mr Reaper said, once they were alone and Mr Nicholls had ridden off into the afternoon to summon help. 'I realised it when I read this letter, and put together all that I know of my family with what you have told me of Carus's other lost children. I began to see a terrible pattern. Our father was the only surviving son of eleven children. Four of my brothers and sisters died, and, you say, all but one of Carus's offspring. I have read on the matter only a little, but I believe there is perhaps a fault of the heart that has been passed on in every generation. A fault that only becomes apparent when a child reaches the age of greatest activity and that organ begins to fail. If that can be proven by some means, then it would show that my brother, for all his sins, did not kill his own children at least. That they were born with a defect they would never have been able to survive.'

'It's possible, I suppose,' Emily said.

'Once this . . . if this is ever over,' Mr Reaper said, gravely, 'then I must endeavour to find out if my theory is true. For I should hate to bring my own children into the world only to condemn them by their very birth.'

'We know of an excellent medic and his equally skilled wife in Bradford,' Anne told him. 'I'm sure they will be able to determine if your story is true, sir.'

Mr Reaper dipped his head as he thought for a moment.

'You hate and fear my brother, and indeed he is a man steeped in evil,' he said gently. 'But as his brother I beg you to think of that terrified child who never knew love, or safety. Only abuse and violence. Think of him when my brother is brought to justice. Pray for that frightened boy who gave the last of his humanity to protect mine.'

'A frightened boy,' Emily mused to herself, sensing something coming into focus. 'He tries to better himself and his brother, but sees that he is punished at every turn for his efforts and turns against God as his children die, his wife dies. A man as repugnant as he is charming, who is as vulnerable as he is dangerous.' Emily reached for Ellen's notebooks, and began thumbing through them, stopping every now and then. Then suddenly she clasped the open book to her breast.'

'There, yes, and there and there, how could we not have seen it before? It's all in Ellen's notes. All the proof we need.'

'Proof of what?' Charlotte asked her, standing up as Emily did. 'What have you seen, Emily?'

But before she could reply there was a frightful commotion at the front door, and suddenly Benjamin Cross, the driver of

Ellen's carriage, burst into the room, soaking wet and white as a sheet.

'They took us,' he gasped, grabbing on to the back of a chair for support. 'They took us both, but I got away and took a horse, came for help. We must be quick, for they mean to harm Miss Nussey!'

'Who?' Charlotte stood up at once. 'Who means to harm her?'

'Abner Lowood,' Emily said, slamming the book down on the table. 'And his cunning enslaver and puppet mistress, one Miss Rosalyn Tolliver.'

THIRTY-SEVEN

Charlotte

The poor, terrified young Benjamin had half relied on his horse's homing instincts to carry them across country back to Haworth, but he believed that he could take the party to the place where Ellen was being held, or at least where she'd been when he got away: a half-derelict cottage that stood forgotten in the thick woodland just above Stanbury.

'They will have realised I am gone by now,' he said, very worried. 'They might have moved on again.'

'Why didn't you release Miss Nussey at the same moment?' Charlotte asked desperately, as they ran out into the rain, looking for any cart that could carry them as quickly as possible towards the danger. Mr Reaper saw the brewer's cart unloading the last barrel into the cellar of the Black Bull and ran to the carter. Money changed hands and a swift agreement was made.

'I tried, miss,' the young man said. 'But the girl had made Miss Ellen sit right next to her in the hut – so they could talk, she said. I was tied up outside. I peered in at the window and Miss Nussey saw me, and nodded, like she meant me to come and get help. That is what she meant, isn't it? I didn't leave her to be killed, did I?'

'You did the right thing,' Emily said. 'There is no time to be lost.

'But Rosalyn?' Anne asked as they climbed into the cart. Mr Reaper took the helm, with Benjamin at his side; he drove the cart on at once, jolting them all left and right. The noise of the cart on the road, the roar of the wind, and the clatter of horses' hooves threw a shroud around them that meant if they kept their heads together, they could not be overhead as they talked. 'Sweet, poor, broken Rosalyn has somehow masterminded all this chaos and killing. How did you realise, Emily, and can you be entirely sure? For it seems impossible to me. The girl is hardly more than a child, and seemed firmly in Lowood's thrall.'

'Yes,' Emily said. 'And I have no doubt – for the vast majority of her association with Lowood – that was true. But then I believe, in fact I am certain, that there came a crucial time when something in Miss Tolliver broke. When she awoke from the trance of deluded devotion and realised what horror had been done to her. That she was headed for the same fate as Grace and Barbara. Then she took it upon herself to take another path. One that was signposted "Vengeance."'

'How so?' Charlotte asked, holding on tightly as the cart rattled on at a pace. Their voices shook in time with the rattle of the tack. 'How do you propose that dear, sweet Rosalyn masterminded all of this?'

'Through great intelligence and cunning that none of us considered for one moment,' Emily said grimly. 'And the use of mesmerism, which she must have learned from Lowood himself. As you know, mesmerism gives those skilled in its usage the power to exert unseen influence over the susceptible, using only certain phrases and gestures. Through repetition, deception and the gradual disintegration of truth, it can indoctrinate a gullible victim into believing and doing everything that you tell them. A mesmerist can even imbue an innocent word with a hidden command, which provokes violence in their victim whenever it is heard.' Emily shook her head in something like awe at the cleverness of it all.

'Could that be why Lowood attacked us so suddenly, and then just stopped after the lightning strike?' Anne wondered.

'I believe so,' Emily said. 'It is not effective with everyone; it obviously did not work on us – at least not entirely – as I'm sure they would both have tried to use it against us. I *knew* there was something crucial that we were not seeing, and that's the beauty of it. We ignored Rosalyn as anything more than a victimised girl. Just as the world looks at us and sees only three useless spinsters.'

'But how? What words and gestures?' Charlotte asked. 'Surely we would have seen them, and marked them as unusual or out of place?'

'They were meant to go unnoticed, but there were certain words and gestures that Rosalyn repeated often. I checked Ellen's notebooks, and her meticulous records confirmed it. Rosalyn has been seeking revenge on all who have wronged her.'

'Including us?' Charlotte asked, clinging on for dear life as the steady shire horse picked up pace in the narrow lanes, the sky gradually darkening with the threat of more rain.

'The first time she conversed with us,' Anne said, 'she cautioned us to leave her alone. She told us we would be sorry if we did not.'

'Quite. And if you read Ellen's notes, you will see the phrases she used again and again,' Emily said. '*Believe me, It's the truth. Do you see it? This is how it is. Imagine this.* And each time she used these terms she would touch one of us, on the shoulder or hand. Or clap her hands, or bang something. Somehow this reinforces the manipulation and makes it take hold. I'm not sure it was ergot in the grain store that poisoned us that night with Mrs Crowe. Lowood was a druggist. I am sure Rosalyn saw how he used poison to increase the effect of his evil, and that on the awful evening *she* dosed the food, similarly. I saw a vision, as did Papa. Anne, you and Charlotte were immune.'

'Because we did not eat,' Anne said, as all the pieces fell into place. 'Emily, I believe you are right.'

'Naturally,' Emily said. 'I always am, eventually.'

The cart came to a clattering stop at a narrow path that led down into the woodland, almost throwing them into the mud.

'Let me go first,' Mr Reaper whispered as Benjamin secured the horses. 'I know that if Carus sees me he will come to his senses, and help your friend.'

Charlotte was not prone to letting a gentleman take the lead in anything, but on this one occasion she relented. Lowood had loved his brother when he wrote the letter Emily had read out to them earlier. They could only hope that a trace of love remained all these years later; at least enough to turn Lowood to their advantage.

'You have done well, Benjamin, now take the cart towards Bradford,' Emily told the young man. 'With luck you will find Mr Nicholls returning with men of justice. You must bring them here at once with not a moment's delay, do you understand?'

'I understand, miss,' Benjamin said.

The path into the woodland was narrow and dark, wending into dense shadow within a few feet. Renewed thunder rumbled overheard.

'There's something else I must tell you,' Benjamin called out, as he made to drive the cart away. 'I feared it were too awful for ladies to hear. But you must know all if you are to attempt to save your friend.' He swallowed, tears filling his eyes. 'There were two there already dead. Hanging by their necks. The lady called them Mama and Papa.'

'Well then,' Charlotte said, repressing the swell of nausea that rose in her chest 'We know our true enemy at last. Now we rescue our truest friend.'

THIRTY-EIGHT

Anne

The cottage sat huddled in the trees, almost entirely hidden by the lush wet greenery that had benefited from a wet spring and warm summer. It was very small, the upper storey all but crumbled away and probably only two rooms remaining more or less intact, as far as Anne could tell from their vantage point in the undergrowth. It had probably once been a shelter for a shepherd or such, or a place of refuge for a weary traveller. Now it had become a dead house and a prison, with Ellen trapped inside. In the second room, Anne had caught sight of dark shapes swaying through the broken glass of the window. She did not look that way again.

'I will go in and appeal to my brother,' Mr Reaper said.

'No,' Emily shook her head. 'Rosalyn has used Lowood's old tricks against him. She has turned him into her attack dog. He responds only to her orders. I suspect she used the same tactic on Mrs Wilson to send her to murder her own husband, though I cannot fathom why. And she probably had Lowood dispatch her poor parents. They are both acutely dangerous, sir. You cannot assume that your brother will even know who you are.'

'He will,' Mr Reaper said. 'I have faith that he will.'

'What other choice do we have, Emily?' Anne asked her desperately. 'Rosalyn has lost her mind and taken Lowood's from him. If Ellen is still alive . . .'

'Ellen must still be alive,' Charlotte said, her face tight with fear.

'We do not have much time,' Anne said. 'I believe that Mr Reaper is our best hope.'

'Then I shall go with him,' Emily said. 'So that he is not tricked or overwhelmed.'

'Then we all go,' Anne said. 'Four of us may have a chance of overcoming them.'

'It is dangerous,' Emily told each of them. 'I do not believe that we have ever been so close to the chance of serious harm before. Are you ready?'

Each of the other three nodded grimly.

'Then we walk in, heads up, smiles on our faces as if we have come for afternoon tea,' Emily told them. 'Let us play them at their own games.'

'Why, Rosalyn,' Anne said, the second person to step through the broken doorway after Mr Reaper. 'Thank you so much for inviting us to tea. I see that Ellen has already arrived; I do hope we are not late.'

Rosalyn, who was sitting on a broken chair, next to a table covered in detritus, tilted her head towards them, a small smile playing on her pretty lips. Their arrival had surprised her, Anne thought, and she enjoyed it. The girl's sweet smile frightened her even more than the strange happenings at the master's house and Lowood chasing them with a knife put together.

Lowood, who had been standing in the corner, turned to look at them, his expression vacant. He must be drugged too, Anne surmised, for surely it could not be mesmerism alone that had brought the man under such control. He emitted a curious whimpering noise from somewhere deep inside his throat, like that of a dog who had been beaten almost to death.

'Why, Anne and your odd sisters,' Rosalyn said, with none of the deference or formality they had been used to. 'You are perfectly on time. Please do come in and take a seat.'

She gestured at the dirt-strewn floor, where a white-faced Ellen, tears streaking through the dirt and dust on her face, sat at her feet, her hands tied and a silk scarf knotted around her head acting as a gag. The sight of their friend hit Anne like a physical blow, and for a moment she was afraid that she might faint. Courage, she told herself. Rosalyn must see no trace of weakness and fear, Anne thought; the moment she did, the game would be up.

'No, thank you, we'll stand,' Charlotte said, politely. 'I hope you don't mind, we have brought a friend with us. You won't know Mr Reaper, but Abner does. It is his brother, you see.'

'Abner, step forward,' Rosalyn commanded. Lowood took two steps forward. His face was florid, there were flecks of spittle around his cracked lips. Anne found herself wondering when he had last taken a drink of water, or eaten. Perhaps not for hours if Rosalyn had not commanded it. 'Do you know this man?'

Stephen Reaper came forward, until the last of the watery afternoon light shone on one half of his face, throwing his distress into sharp relief.

'Carus, is it I, your little brother, Stephen. Let me take you home, I beg you. Whatever you have done, we will face it together, and I will be at your side. Let this torment end now, Carus. Give yourself over to me and we will make amends with God.'

Lowood leaned forward towards Mr Reaper, frowning deeply as he peered at him.

'Want to kill it?' he asked Rosalyn, causing Mr Reaper to recoil in distress.

Anne linked her arm through his and held it tightly. Looking up at him she did her best to convey that they must not let loose their emotion, and that he should hold on tight to his nerve. She felt the muscles in his arm tense as he steadied himself.

'No, Abner,' Rosalyn told him in a light voice. 'Not just yet. Now, ladies, why don't you tell me why you are here?'

She looked at each of them in turn, eyes narrowed, chin lifted in defiance. Anne very much had the sense of a snake readying itself to strike.

'We want to help you, Rosalyn,' Anne said gently. 'You've been very hurt, so very hurt, and so very badly used, and you are full of rage. We understand that rage. We know how you have suffered and it is natural that you should want others to suffer too. Let us help you, that is all we ask.'

'Oh, so many nice ladies queuing up to help me while they hide their disgust and horror,' Rosalyn said. 'You sit in your ivory towers all prim and proper and not one of you knows the first thing about what it is to truly be a woman in this world. I'm done with you all, but don't worry. Before I dispatch you, I'll show you how terribly cruel life can be.'

She drew a small blade from somewhere and held it to Ellen's throat.

Anne stifled the sharp scream that rose in her throat, preventing herself from lunging forward as she saw Ellen recoil in fear. She felt Emily's hand reach for hers, and hidden in the folds of her skirt they clasped one another, so tightly it hurt; but she did not scream.

'Abner, my dear friend,' Rosalyn said, getting up from her chair and crossing to the man. She laid her hand on his shoulder, patting him three times. 'I believe it is time to go to bed now. Time to go to sleep, dear friend Abner. Do you believe me?'

They watched, frozen by a strange, unnatural terror as Abner Lowood climbed the broken stone staircase that led to nothing but a gaping hole. At the top he reached for a thick rope that was knotted around one of the exposed beams. Anne gasped as she realised that it had a noose tied at one end. Lowood slipped the loop of thick rope over his head.

'Goodnight,' he said, stepping off.

'Carus, no!' Reaper cried in anguish. Rushing forward, he grabbed at his brother's legs. The moment the weight of Lowood's body drew the rope taut, there was the sound of rotting wood splintering, and the bulk of one man tumbled onto the other. In the confusion, Anne released Emily's fingers and ran forward, hurling herself at Rosalyn and gripping the wrist of the hand that held the knife, falling backwards with her onto the floor. For a moment she had the advantage, and was dimly aware that Charlotte had rushed to untie Ellen's hands, as Emily attempted to extract the knife which still flailed wickedly in the girl's hand. And then Rosalyn laughed as she brought her knee up sharply into Anne's stomach, knocking the air out of her lungs. Anne was gasping for breath and the young woman rolled her onto her back, and sat, legs astride her.

'Stay back,' she told the others as she lifted the blade up, ready to strike.

Still gagged, Ellen struck Rosalyn from behind with a broken brick, sending her reeling sideways and the knife skittering across the broken flagstones. Ellen threw herself onto the dazed woman, securing her arms, and Anne sat on her legs. All the while, Rosalyn smiled as if she was having the time of her life; given all she had endured, perhaps she was.

The sound of men shouting, and trees breaking, broke the tense silence.

'It seems the cavalry is here, and predictably making rather a fuss about it,' Emily said.

'Carus,' Mr Reaper sobbed as he rocked Lowood in his arms. 'My poor brother.'

'Is he dead?' Emily asked, bluntly.

'No, he will survive. He fell before the rope could tighten enough to strangle him.' Mr Reaper sobbed.

'Then you should be glad,' Emily said, returning her gaze to the window through which a group of men appeared.

'He lives only for another rope to do the job,' Mr Reaper said. 'I have found him only to lose him.'

'And yet, if he repents, you will be able to save his soul,' Anne said. 'I am sure of it.'

'She's fainted,' Ellen said through the gag, giving Rosalyn a smart slap around the face to make sure of it, and pulling the scarf free of her mouth. 'Goodness, that was rather unexpected.'

She rolled off the prone woman and into Charlotte's waiting arms.

'Ellen, forgive us,' Charlotte wept as she embraced her friend. 'I will never forgive myself for putting you in danger.'

'You are here,' Ellen said. 'You came for me, Charlotte. You all came for me. You are true sisters and dearest friends, and though I plan never to set foot outside again, I cannot forgive you for something you did not do. It was I who was determined to be involved in everything you did.'

The four women embraced one another and wept in relief as finally their rescue party entered the cottage.

'Never fear!' Arthur Bell Nicholls said as he appeared in the doorway. 'For you are saved!'

THIRTY-NINE

Emily

There was no trace of humanity to be found in the impos-
ing edifice that was York Prison, situated as it was behind
the ancient bailey of Clifford's Tower and the regal Georgian
buildings meant to disguise the horror that lay within from
the eyes of respectable townsfolk. Emily had regretted coming the moment that she arrived, standing outside gazing up
at the thick, looming walls. It was somewhere very close to
here that convicts were 'launched into eternity' or hung from
the prison gallows. The very same fate that awaited Abner
Lowood and Rosalyn Tolliver.

And yet Emily could not turn back, because Rosalyn
Tolliver had written to her in person, asking her to visit.
Not Anne, with whom Emily had thought Rosalyn had a
bond of trust, or Charlotte, whom the young woman had
seemed to respect the most, but her. Emily was conscious
that Miss Tolliver had particularly asked for the one among
the Brontës who had been most susceptible to her skills of
manipulation, and was now certain that the terrible vision
she had seen the night of Mrs Crowe's investigation was
a product of being dosed with ergot and falling under the
influence of mesmerism.

As soon as Lowood and Rosalyn were safely imprisoned,
the Brontë sisters had written to Mrs Crowe to tell her how

events had unfolded. A few days later, the good lady herself arrived.

'That I left you in such danger has haunted me,' Mrs Crowe told them. 'I cannot fathom why I didn't discern the truth of what that awful girl was up to.'

'None of us did, Catherine,' Charlotte had told her over tea. 'Her disguise was our disguise, or at least very near it. The mantle of womanhood is so often mistaken for nothing more than a vacuous shell. That we ourselves made the same assumptions is . . . unedifying.'

It was then that Anne confessed to seeing something that same night of Emily's vision. A fleeting shadow around Emily just before she fainted.

'Perhaps that was Rosalyn's influence too,' she said. 'And if I had eaten that night, it might have been as vivid and as terrible as Emily's experience. And yet, none of that explains the voice we heard or . . .'

It had taken some more moments to coax out of Anne the experience she had had in the master's house while she was looking for Rosalyn on the day of the storm. Emily had leaned in eagerly as her sister grew pale in the telling. 'But I believe it was the same . . . presence, that showed us the way to safety when we were in grave peril. In the house, what I heard was very frightening indeed. Yet in the field it shone, like a torch burning, even in the rain. Like an angel.'

'It would not be the first time you have seen an angel,' Charlotte told Anne fondly, 'though you barely remember it, you told us all with great certainty that you had seen such a being soon after we lost dear mama.'

'The dead are only rarely malicious,' Mrs Crowe had told them. 'Though their appearance might terrify us, usually all they want is to be seen and acknowledged. Often to prevent others meeting the same fate as they. In this case the spirit helped you, Anne. We can be grateful for that at least.'

The business with Mrs Wilson had been a little more difficult to resolve. There was no doubt that this was the poor woman who had turned the knife on her husband after all, and she had been removed to the very establishment that Emily stood before now. Fortunately, after months of derision and insults, Rosalyn wanted the whole world to know how cleverly she had manipulated Mrs Wilson. Gleefully she told the court of how she had visited Mrs Wilson once a week for several weeks before the murder of Mr Wilson, posing as a pedlar woman, always with an array of pretty things at cheap prices. Mrs Wilson was so unhappy, you see, she told everyone. A woman with a broken heart will always try to salve the pain with trinkets. With each visit, she had worked on bending Mrs Wilson to her will, just as she tricked and seduced Mr Wilson into believing he was to be reunited with Barbara again. When the Justice asked her why, she shook her head and laughed gaily.

'He loved Barbara, she loved him, that was reason enough.'

The courtroom had gasped in horror, but in the days that followed Mrs Wilson was acquitted of the murder and returned to her former life, and the love and dedication of her small friend, the kitchen girl who loved her so.

The havoc that Rosalyn had wreaked in her tumult of far-reaching revenge would have equally far-reaching consequences, Emily was certain of that. Yet perhaps there might be something Rosalyn wanted to say to her that would make sense of it all. That, and that alone, was the reason she had agreed to this visit.

Emily was on her guard as she was led to the small, dank cell where Rosalyn waited for her. On her guard, but also sick to her very stomach when she thought of the fate that awaited the girl who was barely more than a child. Even after all she had done, it seemed impossible to imagine her swinging on the end of a rope.

'You came, Miss Brontë,' Rosalyn said as Emily stood in the doorway of the cell. 'Come, take a seat on my bed. It is hard as stone, for it is stone, but you are welcome to it.'

'I will stay here, I think,' Emily said. Despite her impending fate, Rosalyn looked well, spritely even. Her eyes shone and her complexion was rosy. It was a peculiar sight, such beauty in such a dire setting. 'What do you want from me, Miss Tolliver?'

'You found me out,' Rosalyn said. 'I had thought you were the weakest; you played my game so beautifully, you see. Yet, it was only you who saw what I was about. You are a formidable adversary. I do hope that we will spar again one day.'

So, she was thoroughly insane, Emily thought, if she did not realise the seriousness of her situation. There would be no 'one day' for Rosalyn Tolliver.

'You confessed to the murder of Barbara Lowood,' Emily said. 'Why?'

'It was I that killed her, after all,' Rosalyn said with a shrug. 'Abner had me kill her for him. He dosed me, and cajoled me, and soon I was his, body, mind and soul. I do not know that I enjoyed one clear hour during the four years he entrapped me – not when he took me to his bed, not when he bade me poison his wife, not when he had me take the stand to draw all the attention away from him. I told the world what he wanted me to say. He threw me to the dogs to save his own skin. He thought he could use my shame as a cover while he weaselled his way out of the charge of murder, and still have me as his pet when he was free.'

'But he did not succeed,' Emily said, and she could not help the admiration that crept into her voice.

'He did not have sight of me for weeks,' Rosalyn said. 'No way to tell his pretty lies to me, or put a drop of his special tincture in my food. Your friend Mrs Crowe was half right, by the way, it does contain ergot, and a little henbane, and a small amount of a particular mushroom. Just enough to take control of a mind without sending it altogether mad.'

'Ingenious,' Emily said.

'I was on the stand, going into detail of what he'd have me and Barbara do when . . . I just woke up. I became myself for a second, and for a second it was wonderful and then everything came crashing down on me. All the hate that he deserved was mine, all the shame, all the fury of the public directed at me. That wasn't right, Miss Brontë. I was his victim. Just as Barbara was, just as so many others were before us. I was his victim, but I was being treated like a criminal.

'So, you tried to poison him,' Emily said.

'But he survived,' Rosalyn said. 'That's when I realised, that Abner explained it all to me. He thought me so foolish, so pathetic, that he could tell me how he went about the business of mesmerising and drugging, and I'd never think to use that against him. Well, he was wrong.'

'You could have told the law what he'd done to you,' Emily said.

'They wouldn't have cared,' Rosalyn said, probably correctly. 'I thought, if I couldn't kill him, I'd get my revenge another way. I'd do to him what he did to me, and make him my pet and my terror to use as I pleased.'

'Why did you make your parents and my papa see the revenant?' Emily asked.

'I wanted my parents to be ready to take me away from the workhouse, before I was discovered,' Rosalyn said. 'At least that was what I planned. But you see, they were not good parents, Emily. They did not protect me. They did not see what Lowood had done to me, did to me. Not for years. I thought at first I just wanted them to feel afraid. But then I realised, I wanted them to pay.'

Rosalyn laughed.

'And the Wilsons?' Emily asked. 'What had they done to you?'

'No one has ever loved me,' Rosalyn said. 'But I knew that Peter Wilson had loved Barbara; she often told me, weeping tears of bitter regret. I wanted to know what that was like, so I went to him and made him believe that I was Barbara. When I was done with him, I thought it only polite I let his wife dispatch the wretch. I would have written once I was safe away, to tell the judge she was not guilty.'

'How very thoughtful of you,' Emily said. 'For what it's worth, I am sorry, Rosalyn. You were a victim. You should not have been used and vilified in the way you were. I cannot help but mourn the loss of what you could have been, had your wit and intelligence been given an opportunity to flourish. It is not your fault alone that you have been brought to this place and must face the rope.'

'Oh, I will not be hanged,' Rosalyn laughed, delightedly. 'Old Jack Ketch won't claim me.'

'Rosalyn,' Emily said firmly. 'You must face the truth so that you can go to your judgement with a clear conscience. You have been convicted of two counts of murder and sentenced to hang.'

'Indeed,' Rosalyn giggled, her hand moving protectively over her abdomen. 'Except that I am with child, you see. The courts will not hang a pregnant woman. They will do as they always do when a criminal is with child and commute my sentence to life. One way or another, I will find my way out of here. Do you doubt me, Miss Brontë?'

With a rush of cold dread, Emily knew that Rosalyn was telling the truth and that she was more than capable of making her escape when the time was right.

'So, you see, Emily,' Rosalyn smiled sweetly. 'There is every chance that we will meet again one day. Now, isn't that lovely?'

CHAPTER

FORTY

Charlotte

Charlotte tied the knot in the string that secured the parcel in brown paper, and Anne cut it with a paper knife.

'Are you sure it is ready?' Anne asked Charlotte.

'I am sure,' Charlotte said. '*Jane Eyre* is more than ready, it is magnificent. If Mr George Smith doesn't publish it at once, then he is a fool.'

Anne and Emily smiled at her as she picked up the parcel. They had already agreed to walk to the post office together.

'May I accompany you?' Branwell asked, appearing in the hallway as they opened the front door. He was a wreck, a shadow. To Charlotte he looked like a corpse walking. How he hurt her and angered her, but now – as they came to what every person in the family knew was so very close to his end – they had each found a way to forgive him and, more importantly, love him again. 'I realise I have disappointed my sisters of late, hurt and frightened you. But if you would allow it, I would so enjoy some fresh air and good company for a step or two?'

'There will never come a day when you are not welcome in our company,' Charlotte assured him, blinking away the threat of tears and feeling that, if she could only hold on to him tightly enough, she might yet keep him in this earthly realm a while longer. 'You will always be one of us, brother. Our leader.'

329

'Our inspiration,' Anne added lightly, slipping her arm through his to support his faltering gait.

'Our very worst influence,' Emily added, brushing dust from his jacket. 'I regret to inform you that you will always have us at your side.'

Branwell nodded, too overcome with emotion to speak for a moment as his three sisters held him.

'Where are we going, anyway?' he said at length.

'We are going to post a very important document,' Anne said, steadying her frail brother as they walked down the front steps. Charlotte has finished her second novel, mine is almost complete . . .'

'And I'm going to write the most wonderful second novel the world has ever seen,' Emily said. 'About criminal over-lords, girl poisoners, lady murderers and vanished brides. It will be terrifyingly sensational.'

'Sounds dreadful,' Charlotte said.

'In any event, I expect the world to mistake it for a grand romance,' Anne said. 'They seem awfully fond of doing that.'

The sky was bright and the air was fresh, the scent of autumn just a promise, but one that Charlotte cleaved to. Strange how she always thought of the season of decay as a time for renewal. It made the timing of the dispatch of her manuscript seem all the more fitting. For in the packet that she carried under her arm was her manuscript of *Jane Eyre*. This was her truth. This was her *revenance*.

'It is fitting that you are with us, Branwell,' Charlotte said, 'for I believe it marks the end of a journey that we have all taken together.'

'Do you regret it?' Emily asked her siblings as they walked down past the church and turned left toward the post office.

'To see the end of our career as detectors, unravellers of mysteries extraordinaires?'

'I do not,' Charlotte said as she handed over the parcel and paid the postage. 'I truly do not. For I am certain, my beloved Branwell, Emily and Anne, that this is only the beginning.'

From George Smith, *A Memoir* (1902)

'After breakfast on Sunday morning I took the manuscript of *Jane Eyre* to the library and began to read it. The story quickly took me captive. At twelve o'clock my horse came to the door, but I could not put the book down. I scribbled two or three lines to my friend, saying I was very sorry circumstances had occurred to prevent my meeting him, sent the note off by my groom, and went on reading the manuscript. Presently the servant came to tell me that lunch was waiting; I asked him to bring me a sandwich and a glass of wine and still went on with *Jane Eyre*. Dinner came; for me the meal was a very hasty one, and before I went to bed that night I had finished the manuscript. My literary judgement was perfectly satisified.'

Author's Note

As I write this I can see the clear blue of the North Sea on a hot August day from my desk window. The ruin of Scarborough Castle stands proud against a faultless summer sky, and just below it, in a part of Scarborough named Paradise, stands St Mary's Church, where Charlotte Brontë buried her little sister Anne in May 1848, only a few short months after attending the funerals of her brother Branwell and beloved sister Emily.

Charlotte and her friend Ellen Nussey had come with Anne to Scarborough, a place she loved, in the last days of her life, and Charlotte made the difficult decision to hold her funeral in a place that meant so much to her, fearing that her father could not stand to bury another child. Anne's last words to Charlotte were, 'Take courage.'

Truly, a motto to live by.

When I began the Brontë Mysteries series five years ago my aim was both to bring new readers to the lives and works of the Brontës, and, perhaps more importantly, to give this extraordinary family a little more life than we already know of – if only in a fictional sense. I have always said that there is no evidence that the Brontë sisters were amateur detectives, but equally there is no evidence that they were not.

As a lifelong Brontë enthusiast these novels are a great joy to write, and I have been delighted by how warmly they have been greeted by Brontë experts, academics and fans alike, as well as readers who had never read a Brontë novel before.

A Gift of Poison opens just as Anne and Emily have had their first novels *Agnes Grey* and *Wuthering Heights* accepted for publication by Thomas Newby in July 1847 and published in December that same year. Charlotte's first novel *The Professor* was rejected by every publisher she sent it to, including Smith and Elder, who did at least send her an encouraging rejection. Elizabeth Gaskell later noted in her biography of Charlotte that the company 'declined . . . to publish that tale, for business reasons, but it discussed its merits and demerits so courteously, so considerately, in a spirit so rational, with a discrimination so enlightened, that this very refusal cheered the author better than a vulgarly-expressed acceptance would have done.'

It is a testament to Charlotte's great self-belief, enormous talent and resilience that she responded by writing one of the greatest novels ever published in the English language, *Jane Eyre*, in just a few weeks. The manuscript was accepted at once by George Smith of Smith and Elder and published the following October, and was an immediate success. Which is why, whenever I am struggling with work or life dilemmas, I ask myself, 'What would Charlotte Brontë do?'

Charlotte, Emily and Anne made good on their plan to write and publish novels as a means to support themselves, unaware that in the process they changed the literary world forever and inspired countless others in generations to come.

I chose to leave them here, for now, at the moment Charlotte is sending off the manuscript for *Jane Eyre* and before the great waves of tragedy that were to follow all too soon, because although their lives have often been defined by sorrow, I want to celebrate the amazing victories and achievements they carved out for themselves. They came from nowhere to fill the world with stories, and when they left this earthly plane their names were enshrined in legend.

The mystery in *A Gift of Poison* is inspired by the real case of the Haworth Poisoner John Sagar, although the death of his wife, subsequent sensational trial and his acquittal took place more than a decade later in 1857 and 1858 at Exley Head workhouse. There was no workhouse in Keighley in 1847, since the care of the poor was administered directly by the parish at that time, so I have brought forward its founding by ten years. It was alleged that the workhouse master John Sagar had poisoned his wife. Barbara, who had been 'fit and well' a week prior to her death, was certainly the victim of terrible, prolonged domestic violence, both physical and psychological, and had told friends that if anything happened to her it would be because her husband had killed her. Their nine children had all died before the age of four, and it was widely believed that Sagar, a former druggist, had killed them too, though it could not be proven.

As pressure to look more closely at the circumstances of her death grew, Mrs Sagar's body was examined by a surgeon in Leeds and found to contain more than enough arsenic to kill. It was decided that local magistrates would assess the evidence to decide if Sagar should be charged with murder. Before an enthralled public, witness after witness described how Sagar beat his wife with a poker, dragged her by her hair, banged her head against a chest of drawers and chained her to the bed in a crouching position for several hours. He also really did lock her in the dead house (the workhouse mortuary) for hours on end. Somehow, though he was described as 'dirty and repulsive', Sagar had a young mistress, a workhouse guardian's daughter, Ann Bland, who was twenty-five years his junior. She gave shocking testimony regarding her intimate relationship with both Sagar and his wife that was deemed 'too disgusting for publication' by the *Yorkshire Gazette*. Ann told the court that she had been coerced into sharing the Sagars' marital bed from the age of eighteen, and that she often helped Barbara procure other women and girls for him to abuse. At the end of the enquiry Sagar was charged with murder. However a series of unlikely and highly suspect events led to his acquittal. The judge declared that witness testimony about the long history of abuse against Barbara could not be included in evidence. And, crucially, the doctor who had treated Barbara before her death completely altered the statement he had given immediately after her death to rule out poison as a cause of death. Though the public believed him guilty, Sagar walked away from court a free man and returned to his former profession of druggist and house painter. He married again and lived to the age of seventy-one. Was there blackmail and foul play afoot during the trial? We will never know.

Ellen Nussey was staying with the Brontë family in July of 1847. Ellen was Charlotte's childhood friend from their time together at Roe Head School, her lifelong confidante and beloved by all the family. It is Ellen we have to thank for going against Mr Nicholls' express wishes and *not* burning the letters that Charlotte sent her.

Branwell Brontë did set fire to his bed at some point towards the end of his life when his addictions had begun to overcome him, though we don't know exactly when. After the fire he always slept with his papa.

So now it is time to bid a fond farewell to my dear fictional friends Charlotte, Emily, Anne and the recurring cast of the Brontë Mysteries. Until the next time, my friends. In the meantime, I will go on being continuously inspired by the very real lives and works of these three amazing women. Until we meet again.

As ever, dear readers, thank you for coming with me on this most delightful of journeys.

Scarborough
August 2022

Acknowledgements

Thanks so much to all the people that have helped me with your insight, knowledge, inspiration and practical advice along the way with *A Gift of Poison*. From the wonderful Brontë community as a whole, experts of twitter and especially the delightful people of the A Walk Around the Brontë Table group – special mention to Emmeline Burdett who came up with the name for Abner Lowood.

I am so grateful for the support of my dear friends, especially Julie Akhurst who has always helped me get these books into shape and is always there for me even when times are unbearably tough. My love and admiration for you knows no bounds. And to Kate Harrison, Julie Cohen and Angela Clarke without whom I would have gone quite mad long ago, as well as all the other writers out there in the creative community who share support and knowledge with such generosity.

Thank you everyone at Janklow, especially Ma'suma Amiri and Emily Randle who helped me knock this book into shape with some brilliant feedback, and of course my marvellous agent Hellie Ogden. And to my former editor Melissa Cox, my new editor, the remarkable Lily Cooper, and the team at Hodder.

Thank you to Diane Park at Wave of Nostalgia bookshop in Haworth for you unstinting support of this series and your life-sustaining enthusiasm for the beautiful bookshop you have made. And the everyone at the Brontë Parsonage Museum for the amazing work you do in continuing to build, preserve and protect the Brontë legacy, especially Ann Dinsdale. And to marvellous Leeds-based historical crime writer Christ Nickson, who has always been so helpful and generous with his deep knowledge of the region.

Thank you, niche experts and super specific nerds, you are my people. Thank you, local historians and Yorkshire folk who share their love and knowledge of God's own country, never yet met one of you who hasn't been unfailingly kind.

Huge thanks to my family who not only put up with me living in my head for at least 50% of the time but gamely supported my determination to move to Yorkshire, and have embraced our new life on the North Yorkshire coast within sight of Anne Brontë's grave, so now I can go and have a chat with her once a week. Yes, I know I am weird.

Thank you to Janis, Margaux and the amazing team at Bragelonne, my publishers in France, who not only gave me such a warm welcome when I visited them in 2022 but have done the most beautiful job in publishing The Brontë Mysteries.

I always put my whole heart into everything I do, so my biggest thanks goes to the readers everywhere, who pick up any of my books and especially those who let me know they enjoyed them. Thank you!

If you loved *A Gift of Poison*, read the rest of the series featuring the Brontë sisters, starting with…

Yorkshire, 1845. Dark rumours are spreading across the moors. Everything indicates that Mrs Elizabeth Chester has been brutally murdered in her home – but nobody can find her body.

The Brontë sisters are horrified. And before they know it, they're embroiled in a quest to find the vanished bride…

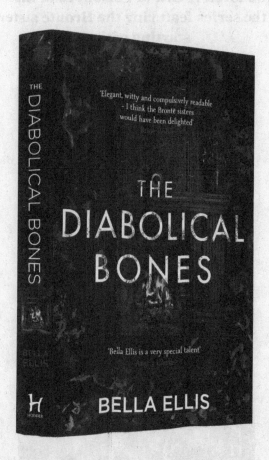

'Elegant, witty and compulsively readable
– I think the Brontë sisters
would have been delighted'

THE DIABOLICAL BONES

'Bella Ellis is a very special talent'

BELLA ELLIS

The bones of a child have been found interred
within the walls of a local house, home to the
scandalous and brutish Bradshaw family.

After another local boy goes missing,
Charlotte, Emily and Anne vow to find him
before it's too late... but in order to do so, they
must face their most despicable adversary yet.